A true believer in listening to one's passion, Patrick Greenwood began writing in early 2020 based on several trips he made while cycling in various countries. In this novel, *Sunrise in Saigon*, Patrick draws upon several non-fictional events that happened in Vietnam including the war with the US, the last days of Saigon falling, and the chaos at the US embassy. Having remembered these events as a young man, Patrick grew up wanting to travel to Vietnam someday and visit these places for himself.

In 2012, Patrick did make the first trip to Vietnam to find the lost US embassy and the catholic nuns that helped with 'Operation Babylift'. Patrick followed his passion for cycling by completing several bike tours in Ho Chi Minh City and the Mekong delta regions.

After military service, Patrick embarked on the 25-year career in the information technology field, working in various roles in sales, engineering, support, and design. Many of his inspirations for writing came via his business travels to places like Vietnam, China, Japan, Taiwan and Portugal.

Patrick holds a BS and MBA in Global Marketing from the University of Phoenix (online) along with completing several post-graduate certificate programs in information security, Internet of Things, and global management from MIT. Patrick is married and resides in Carlsbad, California.

Dedicated to the beautiful people of Vietnam for all the kindness and friendship during my travels to this wonderful country. Thank you to Ricky, Trang, Duong, Ms. Ly, Van, and the entire staff at the Renaissance hotel in Ho Chi Minh City for your hospitality and to my translator and my dear friend Phuong for taking every step in the journey to find the embassy.

To my loving wife, Jenny, for all your loving support in writing this wonderful novel. Without you, I could not have finished his book.

Patrick Greenwood

# SUNRISE IN SAIGON

AUSTIN MACAULEY PUBLISHERS™

LONDON * CAMBRIDGE * NEW YORK * SHARJAH

**Ordering Information**
Quantity sales: Special discounts are available on quantity purchases by corporations, associations, and others. For details, contact the publisher at the address below.

**Publisher's Cataloging-in-Publication data**
Greenwood, Patrick
Sunrise in Saigon

ISBN 9781649796905 (Paperback)
ISBN 9781638299998 (Hardback)
ISBN 9781649796912 (ePub e-book)
ISBN 9781638299981 (Audiobook)

Library of Congress Control Number: 2022914452

www.austinmacauley.com/us

First Published 2022
Austin Macauley Publishers LLC
40 Wall Street, 33rd Floor, Suite 3302
New York, NY 10005
USA

mail-usa@austinmacauley.com
+1 (646) 5125767

Thank you to my publisher, Austin Macauley, for your support and guidance in creating this novel. Thank you to my book cover designer, Arash Jahani, for a wonderful collaboration. Also, a huge thank you to all my beta readers for your valuable insight and feedback!

Proceeds from the sale of this novel will benefit the 'Helmets for Kids' program by Child Health Initiative's regional NGO partner, AIP Foundation, in Vietnam and Cambodia. In both countries, thousands of children receive subsidized helmets and road safety education through AIP Foundation's award winning schools-based 'Helmets for Kids' program.

**Press Release: July 30th, 2022. Carlsbad, California**

CyclewriterLLC Publishing and author Patrick Greenwood announced today that proceeds from the upcoming novel *Sunrise in Saigon* are due to release in late 2022 and proceeds from his coffee company, cyclewriter3espresso.com will be donated to the AIP Foundation's Helmets for kids in Vietnam program, a campaign benefiting children in Vietnam by providing cycling helmets and safety classes.

## About AIP Foundation

AIP Foundation is a non-profit organization dedicated to saving lives on the roads and increasing access to safe, equitable, and sustainable mobility for all. We envision a world with zero road injuries and fatalities. Beyond empowering the underserved road user communities, AIP Foundation tackles injustice related to youth engagement, workers' rights, gender equality, and environmental issues. As global citizens, we all deserve safe and equal access to education, work, transport, and above all, healthy and green cities and livable neighborhoods around the world

Proceeds from the book sale will help raise money and community awareness of road safety. Not only do these interventions ensure that students can get to school safely; but in the long-term, these healthy habits will serve to improve the entire road system in Vietnam.

Cyclewriter Publishing, cyclewriter3espresso.com, and Patrick Greenwood proudly support this noble cause.

For more information, please go to www.cyclewriterllc.com for more details.

# Foreword

Patrick Greenwood's debut novel, *Sunrise in Saigon*, sheds light on an important question we all ask ourselves in one way or another—What makes one's journey worthwhile? The author eloquently marries the question with one's pursuit of the truth surrounding the Vietnam war, inviting the reader to ponder upon the question both in personal and historical contexts.

The story spans from the fall of Saigon, which sparked eleven-year-old Jack's curiosity about the tragedy of the Vietnam war. Even though he knew the war led to millions of lost lives, thousands of orphans, and nationwide poverty, some of his questions remained unanswered. Decades later, Jack sets out for his trip to Vietnam looking for the answers to his childhood curiosity, hoping he could also find a way out of his troubling marriage and poor health.

In Vietnam, Jack constantly faces situations where he must make difficult decisions. In every single situation, Jack aligns his decision with what he is seeking: truth, happiness, and redemption. He pursues truth by following his incessant curiosity about the blurred parts of the Vietnam war, including Operation Babylift when Catholic nuns helped over a thousand orphans fly to America. He seeks happiness by confronting his family problems and pursuing a true passion, whether that is a precarious romance with a Vietnamese woman or cycling on triple espressos. In pursuit of truth and happiness, he strives for redemption by following the words of God and helping the ones who are most in need.

Throughout Jack's journey, Greenwood provides rich contexts behind the complex nature of Jack's circumstances and invites the reader to see the world through his lenses. Greenwood has the special ability to remove barriers between the characters and the reader, even when they are from different walks of life. His belief in owning up to one's decisions shines through the protagonist, who continues to move on despite heart-wrenching loss and disappointment.

As someone writing about mental health and cultural experiences, I had the pleasure of learning about the obscure parts of history and rethinking the values that make my journey worth pursuing. In the end, Jack may or may not have found everything he was looking for, but he stays true to the values close to his heart. Then, regardless of the outcomes, his decisions are well-made, and that makes his journey worthwhile.

Yujin Kim
Author – *A Place To Take Root*
December 27, 2021

# Prologue – 1975

On April 30, 1975, eleven-year-old Jack Kendall lay in his bed, listening to a radio program discussing recent events, which included President Nixon's departure from the White House the year prior, gas storages, and protests over the long-lasting Vietnam War. "This is WIEE 1310 AM radio—we have confirmed that Saigon has fallen. The Vietnam War has finally ended after ten years. Thank God!"

This newsflash caught Jack by complete surprise. Still, he had no idea how this event would shape the direction of his life, setting a lifelong journey in motion, driving a desire to understand what happened to the Vietnamese people before and after the war.

Jack began to dig into several media sources, including the Washington Post and NBC News. He studied images of people climbing over the US Embassy wall in Saigon. Many people tried to climb the fence to get a seat on the last helicopters leaving Vietnam. The pain and distress of the Vietnamese people only fueled Jack's doubts about the results of the war and the destruction of Vietnam as a country. Why was the US Government leaving so many supporters behind? NBC News also showed American servicemen pushing helicopters off the USS Midway, forgoing their promise to go back and get more people out of Saigon.

Along with several news stories about the helicopters being pushed over the end of the ship, Jack also read about how President Ford and the Roman Catholic Church in Vietnam helped organize 'Operation Babylift.' This operation was designed to land a series of C141 Military transport planes at Ton Shut Nhut Airport in Vietnam and transport several thousand orphans out of the country.

The Catholic nuns of Saigon helped to load the babies into boxes. The plane's crew assisted in carrying as many children as they could. However, only fifteen hundred children made it out.

After reading about this daring rescue attempt, Jack asked himself, *What happened to the rest of the children who couldn't be rescued? What happened to the nuns? Why did they not leave Vietnam?* He couldn't understand why those nuns risked their lives by staying behind, knowing that Saigon had fallen to the North Vietnamese Army. Coming from a Catholic family, Jack believed that God looks over all children.

The newspapers didn't provide any detail about the nuns. They only mentioned the fifteen hundred orphans who escaped on the planes. *Did all the children get out? What happened to the children who never made it out of the country?* This thought worried Jack. Shamefully, American soldiers had orphaned many of those children and now abandoned most of them after the city's fall. Would the nuns be punished for what they did? He could not get the image of these children and the people who tried to climb over the Embassy walls out of his head.

Jack, born in 1964, grew up following the start of the war. From the early age of four, he witnessed these events unfold on CBS. Most Americans, like Jack, did not understand why the United States became so involved in Vietnam. By 1968, most did not trust their government to tell them the truth about the war. In 1971, when Jack was seven, he remembered reading about the president ordering the bombing of Hanoi, the capital of North Vietnam, with the intention to force them to a peace agreement. At such a young age, Jack could not fully understand the reasoning behind this decision. Jack, along with many of his friends, had brothers, uncles, and fathers sent off to fight in Vietnam. Many of these men either did not return home from the war or came home with lifelong wounds that would never heal. The protests on American campuses continued along with riots at the airports that brought servicemen home.

By the time Jack heard the radio broadcast on April 30, 1975, he'd already witnessed many servicemen returning home from war and becoming outcasts in society. Seeing how many Americans turned their backs on these brave men and women, he began to wonder why the Vietnam War began in the first place.

After the end of the war, Jack entered junior high school in 1978, and he started to use his older brother's shortwave radio. The shortwave radio gave Jack the opportunity to listen to foreign stations like BBC London England, Radio Moscow, and Radio Havana Cuba. One evening, while Jack was listening to the BBC world service, the broadcast mentioned how several refugees from Vietnam had settled all over England. Jack was intrigued by this development. How had they ended up there?

After spending several hours in the school library researching, Jack found a set of newspaper articles showing photos of Vietnamese escaping their home country by boat. Many of these vessels were strung together by rope. With the boats well over-packed with people desperate to leave Vietnam, they risked their lives just to have a chance to be free from the communist government there. Many of the boats, as Jack continued to read, had been attacked by sea pirates. Staring at an empty bookshelf in the school library, Jack could not comprehend the amount of pain, suffering, and loss of life the Vietnamese had endured.

While spending the next few years listening to various overseas shortwave broadcasts, Jack came across one that forever stayed with him. "Radio Saigon, voice of Vietnam, signing off," said the broadcaster. Sitting in his room doing homework, prepping for his final exams prior to leaving high school, Jack quickly wrote down the time and frequency of this shortwave broadcast. For the next several months, Jack tried to catch the same broadcast but never heard it on the air again.

While finishing high school in 1982, Jack never lost his interest in Vietnam or its people. By 1983, many Vietnamese refugees had settled near Jack in Northern Virginia. Many of the Vietnamese students attending Jack's university rarely spoke to anyone outside of their group. One day, while in the library, Jack, struggling with his calculus homework, decided to close his books and give up. A young Vietnamese girl sitting at the next table walked over to him. "Don't. Keep trying," she said.

Jack looked up. "What?"

The polite young lady smiled back at him. "Open your book. I will help you." Jack, still frustrated by trying to learn calculus, pulled out his books. "Okay, look, the formula for the derivative is simple," she said. Jack watched in total amazement at how simple math was to this girl. After a few minutes of demonstrating, she said, "You try."

Several attempts later, Jack finally understood the formula and completed the assignment for class. "Thank you," he told her. "I am Jack Kendall."

The girl, shy, looked back at him. "I am Anh Vu Nguyen."

Jack had never heard that name before. "Where you are from?"

Smiling back at Jack, she said, "I am from Vietnam." Jack nodded and thanked Anh for her help.

In 1983, after dropping out of college, Jack joined the United States Marine Corps. After completing basic training at Paris Island, South Carolina, he was sent to Camp Pendleton, California, and his new unit. Soon after arriving, he was shipped off to Okinawa, Japan, to serve a two-year assignment as a military communications radio specialist. The top enlisted Marines in Jack's unit had served in the Marine Corps for twenty-one years, including four tours of duty in Vietnam. Still very much intrigued by the Vietnam War, Jack spent hours asking his Master Sargent, Kelly, several questions about the war "Master Sargent, were you stationed in Saigon?"

"Once," said Kelly.

"Where did you spend most of your time?" asked Jack.

"Well, I was the siege at Khe Sanh in 1968, the battle in Nha Trang Valley in 1970, and the battle of Hue city in 1975." Remembering his military history, Jack knew these battles were some of the worst fighting in the entire Vietnam War.

"Wow! What did you think of the Vietnamese people back then?"

Kelly looked away for a moment. "Corporal," he finally said, "we should have never been there." Knowing that his topic brought back terrible memories, Jack decided to not ask any more questions.

While stationed in Okinawa, Jack ran into several Japanese workers on the base. Many of these workers had worked on Camp Henson Okinawa since the 1970s. One, who cleaned Jack's uniforms every week, had worked on the base since he was born. "Mao Ahi," Jack asked, "were you here working during the Vietnam War?"

Mao spoke excellent English. "Yes, Corporal, I have been working here since 1963. I have seen many men through here. Many of them never come back." Jack nodded and walked back to his room.

Soon after he'd served two years in Japan, the Marine Corps transferred Jack back to California. Upon arriving on Camp Pendleton California Marine Base, Jack was assigned to the communications and training division. He spent most of his time training soldiers from foreign countries on how to use American military communications equipment. Several of these soldiers came from Panama, Japan, and Germany. Jack enjoyed learning about other people's cultures. He found that most soldiers from around the world were the same in many ways. They fought when told too. They drank lots of beer, and they'd experienced many ladies in their day. During the lunch break from classes, Jack would sit with the various soldiers from different countries and ask them if they had traveled anywhere. Most of the soldiers spent very little time traveling outside of their country.

By the time Jack departed the Marine Corps in 1988, the American news no longer mentioned much about Vietnam. China, along with Iran and Russia, dominated the broadcasts. Jack, though, still felt a deep sense of interest in the country. He needed to consider his future outside of military service. Having a technology background, Jack settled on becoming a system engineer for a telecommunications company in San Diego.

# Chapter 1
# 2010

By early 2010, Jack was working in the technology field, and he traveled over eighty percent of his time. The extended travel, eating the wrong foods, and not getting enough sleep caused several medical and personal issues for him. Jack eventually realized how much his health had deteriorated. Sitting outside of his doctor's office in San Diego, he knew something was wrong. He continued to become very dizzy when he bent down to tie his shoes, along with constant migraine headaches.

His health and overall life had fallen on hard times. Jack's weight was over two hundred and seventy-five pounds, his sugar level had increased to 210, and his AC1 was 7.8. At the age of forty-six, Jack knew his health needed to get better.

"Jack, come on in," said Dr. Chen. The doctor had been treating him for many years. Sadly, this time, she didn't have good news for him. "After reviewing blood tests and physical examination results, I have concluded that you will not live much longer."

Jack noticed his physician give him a sad look. Staring at her, Jack asked, "Dr. Chen, what's wrong?"

"Jack, do you want to die?"

Feeling a bit overwhelmed by the question, Jack answered the only way he could. "Absolutely not!"

After hearing the answer, Dr. Chen ordered Jack to lose weight. The doctor told him, "Stop eating junk food and drinking beer or you will die!"

He knew deep down that the doctor was right. Jack couldn't stand his own reflection in the mirror. After leaving the doctor's office, Jack decided to drive up north to Carlsbad and spend the day thinking about his health, his life, and what he could do to change.

During an afternoon walk in Downtown Carlsbad, Jack noticed two guys cycling on some real high-end road bikes. He stopped to ask them, "Hey, how are those bikes working for you?"

One of the cyclists replied, "I've lost fifty-six pounds in six months just by cycling." Jack thanked the men and decided to walk over to a bike store. Entering, he noticed several cycling jerseys hanging on the wall, including ones from Canada, Germany, France, and Japan. As he stopped to check out a few of the bikes, the shop owner walked over to greet Jack. "Hey, welcome to my shop. How can I help you?"

Jack smiled back at the nice man. "I am interested in getting into cycling to help lose weight—any suggestions on what kind of bike?"

The owner smiled back. "Son, let's go next door and have a coffee."

Jack accepted the invitation. The two men departed the cycle shop and entered the café next door. "Two triple espressos, please," ordered the shop owner.

The person behind the counter smiled. "Absolutely, boss!"

Jack gave the man a puzzled look. "I own both shops!" he explained.

The pair took a seat outside and waited for the coffees to arrive. "My name is Earl Henning," said the owner.

Jack, reaching over to shake the man's hand, introduced himself as well. "Jack Kendall."

Earl, smiling back at him, asked, "So, you think cycling will help you lose weight?"

Jack looked away in shame. "I guess."

Earl sighed. "Son, you are not well—look at you."

Jack, staring back at the man, asked, "It shows that much?"

The man nodded. "Jack, cycling is life—pedal constantly and stay in balance, as Albert Einstein used to say. Good health comes from what we feel from inside; cycling helps people feel good. The better you feel inside, the more you want to be better on the outside. Cycling helps with you feeling better and more accomplished and especially more challenged."

As the espressos arrived, Jack pondered what Earl had said. "So, you are saying that the goal of cycling is never stop pedaling and always look for better ways to finish the race?"

Earl took a deep breath. "Yes, in a sense, Jack, the race never ends."

Jack glanced back in the direction of the cycling shop. "I saw those jerseys on the wall—you have cycled in those countries?"

"Oh those, yes, that is just a small sample. I have cycled in fifteen countries around the world. I even traveled with my bike on the plane, along with my equipment," said Earl.

Jack, tasting his first triple espresso in his life, almost spat it out. "This is strong!"

Earl began to laugh. "Drinking that, Jack, is like climbing a hill on your cycle for the first time. Scary, painful, and you don't know what will happen, but once you have reached the top, you have challenged yourself to overcome the fear."

Jack smiled and took another sip as Earl continued, "I will recommend to you a bike—it is a starter model. Once you have mastered it, I will upgrade you to a faster model."

Jack appreciated the advice and the espresso. "Thank you, Earl."

Within moments after finishing their drinks, Jack and Earl returned to the bike shop and began to test various bikes. Earl, seeing how tall Jack was, set him up with a fifty-six-inch wheelbase Trek hybrid cycle. "This bike has six gears and two braking systems, a good starter for you."

Jack agreed. After trying on several helmets and gloves, he walked the bike out the street for a test ride. "Take the bike down Grand Avenue until you hit Jefferson. Then turn around and cycle back," said Earl.

Jack, after taking his first two steps with the bike, could not believe the feeling he was experiencing. Pedaling on a bike for the first time in twenty years, Jack could not believe the wonderful feeling inside of him. After making the turn on to Grand Avenue, Jack rode downhill and began to pick up speed. Using the braking system, the bike came to a smooth stop at the red light near State Street. As the light turned green, Jack pedaled faster until he reached Jefferson Street. Using proper hand signals, Jack turned around and headed back up the hill toward the bike shop.

Seeing the smile on Jack's face upon returning to the shop, Earl came over to his new friend. "Well?"

"I'll take it!"

Earl gave him a huge hug. "Don't stop pedaling, Jack," he said.

Jack continued to hear Earl's advice in his head for many weeks after the purchase of the cycle. Each day, he made a point of cycling around his neighborhood, and on weekends, Jack would cycle along the coast from Carlsbad to Del Mar. He enjoyed visiting Earl and hearing stories about cycling in other countries. With each ride, Jack felt better inside. These positive feelings started to change him in so many ways. Knowing that his work and his schedule were a source of pain, he began to consider working for another company that would require less travel.

Jack had become a world-renowned technology sales professional. Companies around the globe hired him to sell their technology and help firms market their products. After struggling for many years, Jack had started to make enough money to help support his wife, Silvia, and his children, William and Regina. He made enough that Silvia did not need to work.

While researching several new technology companies, Jack realized that most of them wanted him to travel even more than his current job entailed. Listening to Earl's words, "Keep pedaling," Jack realized that the business travel was not the core issue for his unhappiness—the deeper issue resided with his marriage to Silvia.

Jack thought about his life, daydreaming on what else would give him a greater sense of purpose, a more incredible feeling of accomplishment and overall health. What Jack needed more than anything else, he realized, was true love.

While cycling one day in Carlsbad, Jack felt a sharp pain coming from his chest. He'd felt this pain several times when thinking about his wife. Unhappily married to Silvia for a long twenty-five years, the relationship had brought him more pain and tragedy than anything else. Silvia, five years older than Jack, enjoyed her lifestyle of partying, drinking, and hanging out. After their two children were born, Jack wanted to stay home and raise them, while Silvia still wanted to go out constantly. The ongoing conflict led to many problems between Jack and Silvia and caused great pain in their relationship with their two children.

In their younger years, Jack and Silvia had loved to party together. They also used to enjoy traveling, like most couples do. But after Silvia became out of control several times after drinking too much wine, they stopped going out together. Now the children were teenagers, and she hadn't changed a bit.

Jack had decided to drink less, travel less, and spend more time with his children. Now, he continued to cycle each day. On weekends, Jack would stop off at Earl's shop and visit with his new friend. "Jack! Looking great, pal," said Earl.

"Thanks! Better from the inside." Since starting cycling, Jack had managed to lose ten pounds. Stopping drinking beer had helped as well. "I still have more to go, Earl, but I'm getting there."

Earl smiled. "Oh, Jack, you should be the first to know—I'm moving my bike store to Pasadena. If you're ever up there, stop in. I'd love to see you again."

Jack felt a bit lost that his friend was leaving Carlsbad. "I sure will, Earl. Pasadena is a great city." The two men shook hands, and then Jack continued cycling along the 101.

Outside of cycling, Jack enjoyed coaching Regina and William in sports and helping them with their homework. Due to his work and travel as a salesman, he relied on Silvia to help the children with their assignments, though he continued to help at home as much as he could. He loved aiding them on homework and sports activities.

As the children became older, Jack realized that Silvia spent more time watching television than focusing on their children's development. This reality became a source of pain and trouble between the two. These pain points only drove Jack to consider other options in his life. He, through the help of Earl and cycling, had developed a better sense of inner peace for the first time in many years. Jack continued to excel at his job as a professional sales professional. Deep down, though, he knew his life with Silvia was the cornerstone of his pain.

Jack took great pleasure in watching Regina and William grow up. He watched William excel in school and on the tennis courts, while Regina became the first female high school wrestler in her city. Both children made Jack very proud. Being a great parent brought Jack honor and fulfillment. Realizing someday his children would be on their own, he started to think about his own future. *What will I be like when the children are all grown?*

For many years, he had known his marriage to Silvia would not stand the test time. Knowing how destructive a divorce would be to William and Regina, Jack decided to focus on making his circumstances work, even though the entire situation tore him up from the inside. Jack knew that even with cycling, his overall health would continue to decline over time if he did not find complete inner peace he desperately wanted. Seeing Silvia self-destruct through her drinking and drug-taking, the whole situation became hard to bear for Jack. Watching his wife destroy herself, Jack felt a deep sense of responsibility for how she'd turned out. That inner also compelled Jack to stay in his marriage. Seeking someone else to fill his desire for love seemed far away and unreachable.

While attending a technology sales conference, Jack met up with several prospective new clients for his company. During the social hour, Jack walked around the room, looking to meet new companies. Several companies that attended were from Asia. One specifically, Da Nang Technology services, had made the news recently. The company, based in Da Nang, Vietnam, had become the first Microsoft and Google partner in Southeast Asia. Jack decided to walk over to their demonstration booth and meet them.

"Good evening. I am Jack Kendall, sales executive for Storage OpsIT."

An older lady working the booth rose up. "I am Chi Cho, VP of sales for Da Nang Technology Services—very nice to meet you, Mr. Kendall." Jack and Chi exchanged business cards using the traditional method—holding it in two fingers, with the business card facing the person you wish to present your card to, you wait until the person grabs the card with their own fingers. Clearly impressed by Jack knowing this, Chi reached for his card.

"Thank you, Mr. Kendall. How can I help you?"

Jack started by asking about how Chi's company could help American companies gain market share inside of Vietnam.

"Well, Mr. Kendall," she said, "we have a very detailed partnership onboarding process. I will email the specifics."

"Thank you, Ms. Cho. Do you know of any other companies in Vietnam that our storage and technology people should be speaking to?"

Chi smiled. "Well, Da Nang Technology is considered the best in Vietnam—why not start with us?"

Jack, appreciating Chi's sales and marketing skills, replied, "Good idea."

Before departing the booth, he asked, "Ms. Cho, how long are you here at the convention?"

"We actually leave tomorrow to go back to Da Nang. However, I am free in an hour. If you want to grab a green tea with me, we can discuss what's on your mind?"

Jack grinned. "Yes, I'd like that." He bowed and walked away. Looking back briefly, he noticed that Chi was smiling at him again as well.

Jack continued to walk around to meet other companies at the conference, including a few from Japan and Taiwan. After spending some time with each of these companies, Jack meandered back to see if Chi was ready to have tea. His phone rang.

"This is Jack."

"Jack, where are you?" asked Silvia. Her tone was angry.

"I am in Los Angeles at the moment, at a technology conference."

Silvia sounded like she had already finished three glasses of wine. "Look, you are always at some conference. I need you here, Jack—I have needs!"

Jack had heard similar words come from his wife before. "Okay, dear, what can I do to please you?"

Silvia always knew how to get what she wanted out of him. "My sister and I want to hit Vegas this weekend—do we have enough money and hotel points?"

Jack moved off the convention floor to keep the conversation private. "Silvia, we don't have the money now to pay for every trip or party."

Silvia was not satisfied with her husband's response. "Sell your bike, Jack!"

"No, I am not selling my bike."

She began to scream at him over the phone. He cringed, knowing his children were probably in the next room. He hated the thought that William and Regina could hear their mother screaming. "Silvia, we are not going to keep doing this every time you want to go out and party!"

Silvia just laughed at him. "Oh really? Well, if you want to make me happy, you need to do this."

Jack didn't want to fight anymore. "Fine, I will book you for three nights at the MGM—we have points."

Silvia was clearly enjoying another victory over him. "Well, that was easy!" She proceeded to hang up.

After taking a moment to drink some water, Jack headed over to meet Chi for some tea.

"Ah, Mr. Kendall—ready for that tea?" Jack nodded, and the pair headed over to the coffee and tea table outside the convention floor.

"Here, Jack—may I call you Jack?" asked Chi.

Jack nodded. Chi poured him a green tea with no sugar. Checking for available seating, Jack directed her to follow him to a pair of chairs. As Chi sat down, Jack could not help but notice how beautiful Chi was. Her beautiful, strong legs and lovely smile made her very attractive. Chi clearly noticed him checking her out and seemed embarrassed. "Ah, Jack—eyes front, please."

He felt embarrassed in return, but she quickly eased the tension.

"So, what is on your mind other than my legs?"

Jack smiled. "I have studied your country for many years. Even as a young man, I was deeply impressed with your country and the people there."

Chi, already impressed with Jack, decided to test his knowledge of Vietnamese history. "Okay, Jack, how long has Vietnam existed?"

He was a bit embarrassed by the question. "I don't know. Based on what I read, five thousand years?"

Chi began to frown. "That is what the Chinese want you to believe, Jack—Vietnam has been around for ten thousand years."

Jack stared down at his feet for a moment. "I'm sorry. I didn't know."

"Anything else you want to know?"

Jack took a moment to consider this next question. "Why are Vietnamese people so determined to be successful?"

She shook her head. "Jack, to be honest, many Vietnamese are not successful. We are very determined people. We have overcome centuries of war from foreigners. Our country has been many times wiped out from typhoons, and our people have died of diseases."

Jack realized that these questions were painful for Chi to answer. "I am sorry for asking this."

Chi nodded. "Jack, I wish you well in your business success. If you really want to know about my country, come visit sometime and decide for yourself." She got up, bowed to Jack, and then headed back to her booth.

After finishing his tea, Jack decided to head home to San Diego. While getting his car from the valet parking, Jack noticed Chi departing with three gentlemen. Observing Jack from a distance, she decided to give him a small wave. Jack smiled and waved back at her. Within minutes, the valet pulled up Jack's white jeep. He handed the parking attendant a five-dollar tip and then climbed in and headed off for his two-hour drive home.

After seeing the kids off to school, Jack headed off to the home office to check his emails. Also scanning over forty new messages, Jack noticed a few emails from Chi.

*Dear Jack, thank you again for stopping at our table. As per our conversation, enclosed is our partnership package. Please review and let me know if you have any questions. —Chi*

The second email she wrote seemed to be more personal in nature.

*Dear Jack, my deepest apologies for getting a bit testy in your questioning last night. I am very proud of my country and our people. As you know, the Vietnam War took a toll on everyone. We lost close to three million people in the war with America. I lost many of my family members. I did not mean to answer you in a rude way. I hope someday you make it to my country. If so, please come up to Da Nang and allow me to show you around.*

Jack decided to write back.

*Dear Chi, no apology needed. My questions were not professional in a business conference setting. I do look forward to someday come to your country. —Jack*

While finishing his emails, Jack began to book Silvia's trip to Las Vegas. With every keystroke on his computer, he became more resentful toward his wife. Jack used up all his hotel points just to make Silvia happy. After completing the hotel booking, along with the airline tickets, Jack also transferred $2,500 to Silvia's spending account.

With his coffee in his hand, Jack headed up to their room. "Love, all set. Your trip is booked."

Silvia was still in bed with a hangover. "How much money did I get?"

Jack stared back at her. "Twenty-five hundred dollars, dear. Enjoy."

Silvia began to laugh at him. "That's not enough. I guess you need to go earn more commission?" Jack turned around, walked out of the bedroom, and headed back to his office, feeling completely unappreciated.

When Jack reached his office, he slammed the door shut out of anger. Sitting at his desk, he tried to compose himself. Needing a distraction, he decided to check his personal emails. While doing so, for the first time, Jack noticed Yahoo personal ads. He'd never before ever searched the personal ads. Finishing his coffee, Jack decided to look at the ads. Out of curiosity, he earched for women in Vietnam.

He was always taken aback by the beautiful mix of Vietnamese and French loodlines. Many of the profiles that he saw on the screen were completely reathtaking. Jack could not believe how beautiful Vietnamese women were— ong hair, beautiful smiles, and lovely eyes. While reviewing the various rofiles, Jack received a poke from a young Vietnamese lady who was online. le reviewed her profile, becoming very interested in knowing more about her. xcited, Jack returned the poke, hoping she would soon communicate back. fter a few hours, Jack received a lovely message from her. Her name was .inh Ngo.

Linh had noticed that someone poked her back and that they did not have complete profile on Yahoo.com.

*Dear gentleman, please tell me about yourself. Your profile is incomplete,* he typed.

Jack, reading this chat, could not contain his excitement.

*Dear Linh, my name is Jack Kendall. I live here in Carlsbad, California.*

Linh read the return message from Jack. *Very nice to meet you, Jack.*

*I live in Bien Hoa, Vietnam,* she typed.

Jack pulled up Google and typed in the location.

*Population of 500,000 people. City known for industrial parks and egional education centers.*

Linh also brought up her yahoo.VN browser and typed in: *Carlsbad California.* She read about Jack's hometown. Linh dreamed someday of going o America.

*Jack, you have a beautiful city. What do you do?* she typed.

Jack continued to read more about Linh's hometown as he responded, *I am technology sales professional.*

Linh was very impressed with Jack's occupation. *How old are you, Jack?*

He'd known this question would come up at some point.

*I am forty-six years old, and you?*

Linh, seeing how old Jack was, said out loud, "Oh my." She was hesitant o answer. "He is forty-six? I bet he's married," whispered Linh.

*Jack, I am twenty-four.*

Jack, looking at Linh's profile picture, could not believe she was even that old.

*Your profile picture makes you look like you're nineteen.*

Linh was flattered by Jack's comment.

*Oh, thank you. Do you have a picture?*

Jack started to look through his laptop's picture folder for one to send to Linh. He soon found one.

When she opened the file, Linh had to take a deep breath.

*Jack, you are very handsome.*

He smiled at her words: *You are very beautiful.*

Jack noticed he had a business meeting about to start.

*Ah, I need to go. Can we chat again?*

Linh, already in bed in her home in Vietnam, wrote:

*Of course.*

Jack and Linh began to chat on a daily basis. Managing through the time-zone differences, Jack would send a message to her in the morning. While getting ready for bed, Linh would launch her browser and read Jack's messages. The new friends started chatting each day, and soon afterward, they began to chat more than once a day.

Jack enjoyed learning more about his new friend in Vietnam. He discovered that Linh had grown up on a coffee farm owned by her parents. To his surprise, he found Linh to be an amicable and enjoyable person to chat with.

Linh, in turn, enjoyed meeting an older American man, someone to ask questions and learn from. Over the next few weeks, Jack and Linh began to ask more personal questions from each other. Linh became interested in Jack's married life and life with his children. Jack became intrigued by Linh's personal life growing up in Vietnam.

On one occasion, he asked her, *Do you go to school?*

Linh replied, *Yes, I attend night school in Saigon, why?*

*Linh, how can I help you? I don't have much to offer you, but if you need anything, I will do my best to help you.*

*Yes, Jack, I could use some money for food, please.*

*Absolutely, let me figure out a way to send you money.*

Linh wanted to be closer to Jack as well. *How can I help you, Jack?*

After giving some thought to her question, he replied, *Just be here chatting with me, please. I love our chats and our friendship. I need that very much in my life.*

Linh began to be teary-eyed. *Absolutely, Jack, I am here for you as well.*

Over the next few weeks, Jack sent her money through Western Union. He managed to send fifty dollars at a time. Jack messaged his friend. *Linh, is the money helping you? Do you have food and a place to live?*

*Yes!* replied a very thankful Linh. *I have food now, and a place to live. Thank you, Jack!*

Jack felt good after helping her; he sensed that she was a good woman who really needed a hand. Within a few weeks, he asked Linh about her life, trying to better understand why she lived alone and not at home with her parents.

*Linh, may I ask please why you don't live at your parents' home?*

*Jack, I am living alone for now.*

He realized that Linh wasn't telling him everything.

Jack also began to have his own problems and started to chat less with Linh. In the past weeks, his home finances had become an issue. His technology company had begun to lose many clients due to competitors, and Jack had to start using his savings to help pay his bills.

Jack's children, William and Regina, needed more clothes and sports equipment to continue playing for the school teams. Realizing his financial problems, Jack stopped sending money to Linh.

In a state of desperation, Linh reached out to Jack via chat, but he stopped replying to her messages. He started to feel ashamed at placing the financial wellbeing of an unknown woman before his own family. This emotion brought another level of shame. Regardless of the pain he felt about Silvia, Jack felt wrong for sending money to Linh, even though this act of kindness initially had brought him happiness. Unable to face the shame, Jack decided not to communicate with Linh anymore. This decision completely tore Jack up inside. For a moment, he'd begun to feel a sense of appreciation and love from someone, only to realize the pain this decision brought upon him and his family.

Over the next several weeks, Linh left several pokes online, but Jack didn't respond. After a few weeks, he decided to reply to Linh's messages. *I am sorry, Linh. My life here isn't well, and I don't have any money to send you.*

Linh, understanding Jack's position, replied, *Okay, I will be fine. Please keep with chatting me, my Jack.*

Jack noticed something different on Linh's profile. *Linh, are you now a mother?*

*Yes, that is my daughter, Ngoc, and my husband, Vo.*

She wrote more a moment later.

*My parents didn't agree on our marriage, which forced us to leave their home.* Linh told him the story in painful detail. *Jack, I am married, and I am now living with my husband's mother.*

Jack realized that his kindness toward Linh did help out. *Did my money help you, your baby, and your husband?*

Linh, wanting to tell the truth about how she felt about him, decided instead to keep her feelings a secret. *Yes, Jack, you helped greatly—we have food now, a place to live, and my baby has the needed medicine. I will forever be thankful to you.*

Jack got emotional while reading the message from Linh. *I also will never forget you.*

# Chapter 2
## 2012

Jack hadn't contacted Linh for two years. He received emails and pokes from her new profile on Skype, but he chose not to reply. Finally, Jack messaged Linh just to ask if she was doing well. Meanwhile, his health continued to decline, even after the doctors warned him about his eating and drinking habits. Deep down, Jack missed the chats and video calls with Linh. Her beautiful smile and loving words had always warmed his heart.

Linh also missed her chats with Jack. Not having a father figure around, she sought Jack's advice on being a good parent with her daughter, Ngoc.

Linh, who was now twenty-six, had become a successful shipping agent. She even offered to pay back the money to Jack. He told her, *I don't need the money; everything is fine now.* While waiting for Silvia to pass out from drinking or fall asleep watching TV, he continued his chats with Linh.

During one of their nighttime chat sessions on Skype, Linh asked Jack a question. *Do you miss me, Jack?*

He wasn't sure if he could honestly answer this question. In the end, he decided to. *Yes, I do miss you, Linh.*

Linh also missed Jack. She loved his soothing voice, his gentle words of encouragement, and his masculine look. She often dreamed of what life would be if they could be together as a couple. Similar to Jack's situation, Linh's marriage was loveless and painful. She decided to ask him a question to see how he really felt. *Jack, promise me that someday we will meet. Can you do that for me?*

Jack thought about the best way to answer that question. Deep down, he knew pursuing a relationship with Linh would be very detrimental to his marriage to Silvia. During the two years of not chatting with Linh, Jack had longed for her voice, the look from her eyes, and her calming words. He knew that his family life was also continuing to fall apart.

William and Regina both struggled with their parents' problems. In many cases, the children turned to their grandparents for help. Jack, still trying to find a way to fix his marriage to Silvia, offered to attend counseling. After a few sessions, the counselor continued to place the blame on Jack instead of holding both partners responsible. Completely discouraged by his life, Jack needed to consider what more damage he could cause by considering a relationship outside of his marriage. Silvia seemed to enjoy her lifestyle and paid very little attention to Jack's work and medical problems. She only wanted her money to spend. Realizing the position he was in, Jack knew he needed to stay in the marriage in order to ensure William and Regina would have a stable family environment until they were old enough to be on their own. Jack knew that time would be many years in the future.

Jack asked himself often, *Am I in a place to decide it's time to have a relationship outside of marriage? How could an extramarital affair impact my life?*

After thoughtful consideration, he sent a message: *Linh, I promise you; someday, I will come to Vietnam.*

*Thank you, Jack; I can't wait for our time together,* Linh wrote back.

Jack knew that traveling to Vietnam to meet a married woman was against the law and also realized this trip would place a financial burden on his family expenses. Yet, even with all those risks, he needed to know if his feelings for Linh were real.

Linh understood that meeting Jack, a man twenty-two years older, could impact her job and her daughter's future. If she got arrested for spending time with a foreign man in a hotel, her husband would sue her in court, and she would lose Ngoc. Was this relationship worth all the risks?

Jack also had so much to think about. Silvia would most certainly file for divorce, and the children wouldn't speak to him again. Financially, he would lose his house and most of his money—he would have to pay alimony to Silvia for years. Considering all the risks, the lovers decided the journey was still worth the effort and committed to meet each other in Saigon.

The journey to Vietnam took almost six months to plan, schedule, and obtain a visa for. Jack also had to arrange to take a vacation from his work. There were many reasons he wanted to travel to Vietnam. Jack loved cycling.

Cycling helped with his health issues, assisting him as well in his mental fitness. He remembered early in life the fixation he'd had for Vietnam when he was eleven years old. He remembered seeing the chaos at the US Embassy and the pain and suffering of so many people trying to escape. These memories continued to drive his desire to find the lost embassy and locate the surviving nuns from Operation Babylift.

To make his plan work to meet Linh in Saigon, he had to think of a reason to travel so Silvia wouldn't be suspicious about his true intentions. He discussed with her about leaving for a bike tour in Vietnam. This trip would also give them a chance to take a break, for deep down, Silvia also sought a break away from Jack.

After explaining his cycling tour plan to Silvia, Jack needed to assess where his finances were. Three years before, in 2009, after the stock and real estate market crashed, Jack and Silvia struggled to pay their bills. At the time, only Jack worked, while Silvia stayed home taking care of the children. By 2012, Jack had changed jobs and started to make a lot more money. Being a technology sales professional for the last twenty-four years, Jack understood the need to win deals and provide better technology for his clients. He logged thousands of miles flying to clients and staying in hotels globally for most of the year. Those business trips wore on Jack's family life. Also, the food and entertainment lifestyle added to Jack's poor health. *Yes, this is on me to make this right.*

He also learned to save money better. He started by reducing the funds he gave to Silvia. She didn't work anymore, but she managed Jack's paychecks and family bills. She was also sending money to a secret bank account. Silvia had created this secret bank account in case one day Jack decided to leave her. Already suspicious of her husband's faithfulness, she agreed with his plans. "Absolutely, I agree with you. I would like to do something too!" She didn't want to spend time with him either. She was grateful for Jack's support of her lifestyle. However, she preferred to enjoy her life away from him.

After 2011, Jack's sales and cash flow significantly improved. Silvia wanted to enjoy more of life the way she wanted to. Most of the times, her choices didn't align with Jack's. She also came around to the reality that the reason for Jack's trip was because there was another woman in his life. She knew that Jack yearned for a loving and passionate relationship, something long gone in their marriage. With Silvia's approval, Jack planned his trip to Vietnam.

Overall joyed with the opportunity after so many years, Jack was finally going to Vietnam. His first step was to contact a cycle tour company to arrange a bike adventure. As the next step, Jack used his platinum status at the Renaissance Hotel in Saigon and booked a suite on the executive floor along with setting a date and time when he would be arriving.

He saved his airline points and hotel rewards, along with his savings funds, to make this trip possible. During one evening's chat with Linh, Jack broke the wonderful news to her. *Linh, I am ready to come to see you for the first time!*

Linh, startled by the news, wrote, *Is this true? I am so happy!*

Jack scheduled his vacation with his company and counted the days before departing to Saigon. He planned to arrive on 12/12/2012 to finally meet Linh. The chosen date was very symbolic; 12/12/12 only happened once every thousand years. Spending it with Linh made their meeting together even more special.

Linh and Jack's meeting for the first time became a dream come true. Both lovers wanted something else in their lives. They needed someone who made them feel loved more deeply than they had ever experienced, someone they could share their thoughts and dreams with without any pessimistic judgment.

Jack couldn't wait to meet Linh for the first time. After years of online chats, emails, and video calls, he wanted to meet his online lover in person. Linh, filled with so much happiness, could not wait for Jack's arrival. With over twenty-two years separating them in age, Jack and Linh were open to exploring what a possible relationship would be like, even with their respective marriages.

Jack boarded the plane from Los Angeles with nothing more than his vision of seeing Linh for the first time. His only view of her had been through a computer screen. Jack had no idea what Linh was like in real life. Jack knew he was risking everything to make that trip to Vietnam to see her. He was aware Silvia also knew in her heart that her husband sought another woman in his life, and chose to let him go, clearly considering moving on in her life as well. Yet, Jack knew that his future could not be with Linh. Choosing to live in the present only made Jack consider the darker side of this relationship. He hoped that something good could come from meeting Linh.

Knowing all that, Jack still chose to see this journey out. Seeing Vietnam meant a great deal to Jack. Remembering his younger days and the news footage from the end of the war, he felt compelled to visit in person, regardless of Linh.

Linh, twenty-six hours away, was in her home in Bien Hoa, lying in bed next to her husband, Vo. She also knew she took a huge risk in her life by agreeing to meet Jack. Linh thought over the first chat she had with Jack, three years before on Yahoo. Hearing his voice, reading his words, and seeing his handsome face, Linh had been immediately attracted to him.

Turning in her bed to look at her husband, Linh began to look back at her short married life, trying to understand where it went wrong. *Why don't I love this man?* Becoming teary-eyed, Linh rose from her bed and went next door to check on her daughter, Ngoc. Seeing her lovely girl asleep, Linh stroked her hair. "I want so much for you, my dove," whispered Linh. Then, wiping away her tears, she went back to bed with her husband. As she lay down, Linh could not take her eyes off Vo. "Forgive me someday for doing this," she whispered again.

Linh needed a way to leave her home for the night in Bien Hoa, so she told her husband that she had to take a night class in Saigon to learn about advanced shipping management. Vo responded, "I need to head up to Hue city for work. Mother will take care of Ngoc."

Linh was intrigued by her husband's sudden travel plans. "Oh, when will you return?"

Vo looked down at his feet. "When I want to."

"When you want to come home?" she asked, confused.

Vo looked back up at her. "I am the man of this house. I can come and go as I please!"

Linh nodded slowly. "My husband, this is your choice."

Vo smiled. "Yes, wife, I want you to be home after you're done with school."

She nodded again and looked away.

# Chapter 3
## Arrival

Arriving in Vietnam on December 11, at 8:00 p.m. local time, Jack walked off the plane and immediately felt the humidity that made Vietnam famous. "Even in December," he whispered.

While heading into customs at Tan Son Nhut Airport in Saigon, Jack noticed several foreigners also arriving, speaking a variety of different languages. Walking up to passport control, he handed over his visa and papers. After reviewing the documents, the officer asked Jack, "Work or pleasure?"

Jack thought about the correct answer. "I'm planning to enjoy the cycling here."

The customs officer checked the visa and stamped his passport book. "Welcome to Vietnam."

After collecting his luggage, Jack headed to customs control. Traditionally, many Vietnamese who returned home from abroad placed Vietnamese dollars inside their passports. The customs officials would take the funds and allow the luggage to pass. Jack also remembered reading that if a foreign attempted this bribe, it would be considered an insult, so he didn't. After placing his luggage inside the x-ray machine, Jack picked up his luggage and headed to the international gallery.

The international gallery was normally filled with family members waiting for their loved ones to clear customs. As Jack entered the galley, several hundred people crowded the area, yelling for their loved ones. Several people, cab drivers it seemed, began to scream at him, "Cab? Marriott, Hilton?" Along with the drivers clamoring for attention, several local cameramen also were shouting for a picture with Jack. He started at the spectacle and kept walking toward the taxi to get a ride to the hotel. Jack kept his hands on his pockets; as in many other cities, pickpockets were common here.

Arriving at the taxi line, Jack handed a driver a document showing the address of the Renaissance Hotel in District 1 near the center of Saigon. The taxi coordinator waved off a new white taxi and helped him to get inside the vehicle. Jack placed his bag next to him in the cab, keeping an arm around it in case someone tried to steal it.

Jack enjoyed every moment of the ride to the hotel. Seeing Vietnam firsthand, Jack started to think about the news films, newspaper clippings, and books that had shown him the city. Now, he was actually here.

When they arrived at the hotel, several bellmen came out to welcome Jack. "Mr. Kendall, welcome sir," said one.

Jack was shocked that the bellman knew his name. "Thank you," he replied. As he approached the main desk, a very lovely lady stepped up to assist him.

"Mr. Kendall, I am Ms. Bui. Welcome to Saigon. We have you booked on the club level in the executive lounge. If you need anything, here is my card." Jack accepted the woman's card and thanked her for the hospitality.

Upon entering his room, Jack could not believe the sight in front of him. "Oh, that must be the Saigon River," he said aloud to himself. He looked down from the eighteenth-floor suite and noticed several boats hosting dinner cruises on the water. Feeling very tired from the twenty-six-hour trip to Vietnam, Jack opened the minibar and took out a tiger beer, a local brew made in Vietnam. Jack took a long drink and decided to crash on his bed. Soon after, he fell sound asleep.

The next morning, while sitting at the hotel restaurant, Jack found himself wondering what Linh looked like in real life. His only view of Linh was through video chats and the pictures that she sent him. Jack felt very nervous about meeting her. He also kept looking at the hotel security as a precaution in case his meeting with Linh broke local laws and the police were notified.

Jack considered that he, outside of meeting Chi Cho and the student in college who'd helped him with math, had not met many Vietnamese women before. *Is she tall? Or short as most Vietnamese women are? And what will she think of me?*

Jack had several emails from work and from his children that needed replies. After a few minutes of working through them, a white taxi pulled up to the hotel lobby. For the first time in a long time, Jack felt nervous and excited—he was about to meet someone he could potentially fall in love with.

As he rose from the chair, a beautiful Vietnamese woman got out of the taxi and entered the grand hotel.

Linh Ngo was even more gorgeous than Jack had imagined. As the morning light entered the hotel lobby, Jack saw the beautiful light touching her body.

She looked stunning as she glanced around to find Jack, with her long brown hair and lovely burgundy dress. After a moment, Linh spotted him sitting in the hotel restaurant. The gentle glaze in her eyes and her soft smile embraced Jack with a loving feeling, the kind he had been dreaming of for ages. Now, after waiting for nearly three years, Jack finally got to meet his Linh.

Linh composed herself and walked across the lobby, extending her ever-so-gentle hand. "I am Linh. Jack, it is very nice to finally meet you." Both paused for a moment, staring into each other's eyes. Then they walked back toward the table to share a morning tea. The hotel lobby was busy with other guests and businesspeople; no one noticed the two lovers as they met for the first time. As Jack gazed deeply into Linh's eyes, he could not get the thought out of his head how beautiful she was. Her soft eyes and her silk voice held Jack at bay, causing him to freeze in his steps.

"Please join me?" Jack requested. Linh, bowing gracefully, followed him to the table next to the window.

Before opening his mouth, Jack started to feel a sense of panic. He knew this meeting could get both of them into trouble. By law, Vietnam didn't permit married people to have an affair, nor would the hotel allow any guest inside a foreigner's room.

"Very nice to meet you, Linh," he eventually said. "Thank you for coming to meet me. I wanted to travel to Vietnam, and I am glad I did."

Linh was still catching up with the moment. "Jack, thank you for coming all this way to meet me." As the two gazed gently at each other, Jack brought up how the two would get up to his room.

"Linh, please see below my tablet; this is your key. Please take it and turn around. Make a left and go to the elevator—eighteenth floor, two left, second door on the right."

As Linh listened, she flashed a very seductive smile and a smooth 'oh' came from her lips. She opened her notebook, writing a brief message to Jack: *I want to eat you!* Jack could only smile. He hadn't felt this excited in several years. With Linh, he felt a strong and passionate connection. They both looked forward to making love for the first time.

As Linh departed for the room, Jack paused for a moment, watching the hotel security guards. He couldn't believe he'd flown twenty-six hours to Saigon to meet a Vietnamese woman. Though journey would hopefully help Jack answer several questions that dated back to his youth as well.

After paying the breakfast bill, Jack proceeded to the elevator to join Linh. Watching for any security guards, Jack pressed the button for the eighteenth floor.

Upon arriving at the room, he couldn't believe the sight of Linh standing by the window, overlooking the Saigon River. Her soft, gentle hair and smooth body clung to her dress. He could only stop and admire the unbelievable woman before him. As he approached, she slowly moved to Jack and placed her fingers on his face, extending her lips for their first kiss. Being much taller than Linh, Jack reached down, pulling her body closer as the two lovers exchanged a soft yet passionate embrace. Jack's heart pounded stronger than it ever had. He found himself breathing harder with every soft touch from Linh and began to gently caress her hair with each kiss and touch.

Linh kissed Jack's neck, starting to unbutton his shirt. Letting her dress drop to the floor, Jack began to kiss Linh's neck as well while slowly caressing her body with his fingers. Linh enjoyed the passionate touch of an older man and moaned softly in Jack's ear. "I am glad you came to me, my Jack." He felt his heartbeat skip with excitement listening to Linh's soft words.

As he removed her undergarments, Linh slowly undid Jack's belt and zipper. Feeling his member for the first time, she smiled. "Please be gentle, my love."

Jack smiled back. "Of course."

He lifted her onto the bed and then began to slowly run this tongue along her beautiful breasts. Linh guided her fingers through Jack's hair and began to moan louder. Jack, feeling her wetness, inserted himself very slowly so as not to hurt his new lover. "Linh, you are so beautiful," said Jack.

"You are wonderful," she said in response. Soon after the lovers pressed their bodies together, the couple climaxed together for the first time.

They lay in the bed afterwards, each reflecting on the passionate lovemaking. As nighttime fell, they made love again, taking time for some food and water. Linh hadn't felt this passionate for a man for several years.

Even for giving birth to her daughter, the romance in her marriage had never reached this level.

While they were lying together, stroking each other, Jack noticed Saigon's night lights and how beautiful the city was in the dark. Linh followed his gaze and said, "Oh, you should see the sunrise with me." They drifted off as night turned to morning.

Still jetlagged, Jack opened his eyes a short time later for the first time in Saigon to see the most incredible sunrise he had ever witnessed. The sun just peeking over the horizon cast a light on the Saigon River below. As Jack leaned over to kiss Linh, a glaze of light hit her light brown skin, and her hair caused him to pause. The radiant glow that touched Linh's body could only be described as breathtaking. Jack had never seen such a beautiful blend of light against a woman before in all of his years. In his eyes, Linh was a masterpiece of beauty. Their emotional and physical connection had been clear from the first moment in the lobby and had only intensified with each minute they were together since. With every touch of Linh's soft fingers, Jack would lean over and touch her body in return. Her beauty, her grace, and her loving passion made him feel that he was genuinely a wanted man in her arms.

Linh, feeling Jack's strong arms around her, didn't want to let go.

# Chapter 4
# Passion

While the sun continued to rise over Saigon, Jack and Linh smiled, their faces full of love. Allowing themselves more pleasure, they held each other continuously after each session of lovemaking. Both lovers cherished the moments together. In their separate lives, Jack and Linh did not have the burning love and passion their hearts desired. With every touch from Jack, Linh's heart raced faster than ever before in her life. With every touch from Linh, Jack knew what being desired by a woman really felt like. With each kiss, the lovers never wanted their lips to part. Every time they locked eyes, Jack and Linh never wanted to look away.

Afterward, they sat in the executive lounge, enjoying breakfast. "My love, what do you have planned today?" Linh asked.

Smiling back, Jack whispered, "We need to find a certain building."

"Oh, that should be fun. Does the building have a name?"

Jack was focused on the scenic view of the Saigon River below. "Yes, it was the US Embassy during the Vietnam War." He told her the story of the event that had impacted him early in his life. The visions of the helicopters leaving the embassy in 1975 continued to be fresh in his mind. As Jack began to tell the story, Linh's face showed a sense of confusion about her lover's words.

"I don't remember this in our history. April 30, 1975, that is Vietnamese Independence Day. I don't know this place, but I know where we can start to look."

"Thank you, Linh."

As they finished breakfast, Linh rose up and whispered into Jack's ear, "I need to go first; we have rules here."

Jack understood the local law, not allowing any form of affection in public view. To the public, Linh was serving as his translator. He realized they not only had a twenty-two-year age difference between them but their experiences of history would be entirely distinct as well. Linh was born in 1988, long after the Vietnam War, and she might not have any reference to the time Jack described to her.

They walked through the lobby, heading outside to get a taxi.

"Jack, let's head over to the old post office building and start there," said Linh. Jack wanted to place his hand on Linh's beautiful legs, but he knew this wasn't allowed.

When the couple exited the taxi, Jack searched for the map app on his phone and typed: *American embassy 1975, Saigon.* As expected, the search result came back blank. The internet in Vietnam was censored. Similar to China's famous 'great firewall,' many historical events in Vietnam were blocked by the government, including details about the war with the US. "Let's go somewhere I know. Maybe it will be a good place to start," said Linh. As the two walked, Jack tried to reach for her hand, only to have his loving request rejected. "Please, my Jack, not here."

Together, they walked the historic streets of Saigon. The boulevards architected by the French led to a point of origin. There, the Notre Dame Cathedral served as the central point of Saigon, along with the unification park and the renowned Presidential Palace, where the military tanks crashed through the gates on April 30, 1975. The same armored tanks still rested on the palace grounds as a reminder of that famous day. Several of the members of the army units from that day visited this historic site every day.

"I have an idea," Linh proposed. "Let's try down the street."

Jack, filled with so much emotion remembering his childhood visions of the embassy event, responded, "Absolutely, I will follow you anywhere." He could not have thanked her enough. "My Linh, I will always remember this day."

She turned to face him with a loving smile. "It's 12/12/2012, Jack—let's remember this day for the next thousand years."

Over the next two hours, Jack noticed something about Linh. She wasn't only beautiful, but she also could walk for long periods, seemingly without effort. "Linh, I just noticed something; you are walking in heels. Are you okay?"

"Yes, though my feet are killing me!"

"I am so sorry. I'm asking too much from you."

Without missing a beat, Linh replied, "Don't worry, Jack. This is so worth the walk."

Jack decided to invite her for dinner before she headed home to Ngoc and her husband.

"Yes," she accepted, "dinner would be wonderful, though I do need to go back to my daughter soon."

Jack understood. Linh motioned for him to follow her to the next street over from the park, where she knew a wonderful Pho restaurant. "This is a Pho soup restaurant, one of the best in Saigon."

He'd never had Pho before. "This will be a first!" he proclaimed.

The waiter seated Linh and Jack outside with a view of the Presidential Palace.

"So, Jack, what do you think of my city?"

Jack smiled across the table. "I am glad I made the trip."

Linh grinned and began to order dinner for the both of them.

When it arrived, Jack spoke up about something that had been bothering him. "Linh, I want to ask—am I taking you away from your family too much this week?"

Linh, already enjoying her noodle soup, replied, "Jack, my husband has another woman in Hue. There is no place more important to me than being here with you and at home with Ngoc." Jack smiled back, feeling the same way.

Linh had so many questions she wanted to ask him but decided to only pose a few. "Jack, does Silvia know you are here to meet another woman?"

Jack had known this question would come up. "I believe, deep down, yes."

Linh remembered how painful it had felt when she found about her husband's other relationships. Even knowing his pain, Linh felt at ease with the choice to spend time with Jack, knowing that within a week, he would return to America.

"Love, is something wrong?" he asked.

Linh took a deep breath. "No, love, everything is fine. Let's finish this wonderful dinner."

Her departure that evening served as a bittersweet and painful moment for Jack. As she departed in a taxi, he felt a sense of emptiness, and began to walk back to the hotel through unification park. When he entered the hotel lobby, Tien, the food and beverage manager, stopped him. "Mr. Jack, welcome to our hotel. Can I get you anything?"

Jack felt grateful at the offer. "Tien, a nice Tiger beer with you would be great!"

As the gentlemen entered the elevator, Tien commented to his American guest, "Mr. Jack, we have rules here in Vietnam. Please be careful."

Jack was astonished by the comment. "Absolutely, I will remember. Did I break a rule?"

As the elevator arrived at the fifth-floor bar, the men departed to enjoy a nice cold Vietnamese beer. Jack couldn't help but ask, "Tien, are you referring to my friend Linh?"

Tien, in a very smooth and quick return, commented, "Mr. Jack, we spotted you both on camera in the hotel. Here in Vietnam, we are all being watched."

Jack was taken aback at the man's directness. "Okay. How should I proceed then?"

"Buy me a beer, and I will tell you!"

Tien, well-educated and very professional, was a true reflection of the Vietnamese people's spirit and hospitality. "Here's what I would recommend. Please do not enter the elevator with the lady, and have her leave the hotel before you."

"Thank you, Tien."

Tien, filled with great passion for his country, began to describe his childhood to Jack over a couple of beers. "I was born in the Mekong delta, Mr. Jack. My brother and I moved here when we were seventeen years old. I've been working at the hotel ever since. What do you do?"

Jack replied, "I sell technology globally."

Tien didn't quite understand what that meant but simply asked, "Are you happy?"

Jack took longer to respond than he would've liked. "I think so."

After a few beers, the man started to help Jack better understand Vietnamese culture and laws. "Look, Mr. Jack, Vietnamese people have been very protective of one another dating back thousands of years. When the Japanese invaded in the 1940s, many Vietnamese women were raped and taken away from our country. In the 1950s, the French came, and many women married and moved to France, seeking a better life. In the sixties, many

American soldiers impregnated Vietnamese women and left them behind with their children. Those half-American half-Vietnamese children became outcasts and orphans. Our society has laws to stop this behavior from happening again."

"I understand, Tien. I heard about this in America while growing up."

Tien nodded. "So, Mr. Jack, while you are here in my country, please follow our laws."

Jack nodded back at his new friend.

Afterward, he returned to his room, holding the beautiful Linh in his mind. As he made his way to the breathtaking view of the Saigon River, he became short of breath and couldn't stay up. Overwhelmed with a sense of guilt and emptiness, he phoned Silvia, seeking to reach out to his wife for comfort, hoping that she missed him. Even though Jack knew that his marriage was broken and would not be healed, he couldn't help himself.

The phone rang back in California, and Silvia answered. "How is Vietnam, Jack? Did you find what you were looking for?"

Jack detected the same negative attitude from his wife but tried to respond favorably, "Oh yes, Silvia. I saw the embassy today, and tomorrow I will begin the cycling tour. How are the children doing?"

Silvia didn't care to hear from him. "Look, you told me you were not going to call anymore while you are in Vietnam, so don't call!" she shouted.

Driven by the reality of their circumstance, he remembered why he'd stopped loving Silvia so many years ago. The love, respect, and overall togetherness between them had been missing for several years. A deep sense of helplessness overwhelmed Jack. After hanging up the phone, he cried, sitting on his bed, overlooking the Saigon River. Jack continued to deal with issues of depression, which he had suffered for several years of the loveless marriage.

The impossible hope of healing or seeing a better future brought on these depressive mood swings. Even with everything he could long for in his life—the great career in technology sales, beautiful kids, lots of money, and great friends—the depression that crept into Jack left him breathless and in pain for hours on end. As he lay down on this bed, his vision of Linh provided the only peace in his heart.

Early the next morning, Jack woke up to the sunrise over the river. He checked his phone and noticed several calls from William and Regina. Jack dialed his son first to see what was happening at home. William was a senior in high school and captain of the tennis team, a quiet yet strong-minded boy. Very close to his mother, William continued to defend her no matter the condition he sometimes found her in. After drinking too much, Silvia would try to fight with Jack; William stood by her, helping her with everything she needed when Jack wasn't home. Regina, compared to William, resided often with her father and had huge problems with her mother's drinking episodes.

"William, it's Dad. How are you, son?"

William adjusted his phone. "Yeah, Dad, all is good here. How's Vietnam?"

"Beautiful country and wonderful people. How are you, son?"

William pondered his next comment to his father. "Dad, I got accepted to Arizona State University, and I would like to study there."

Jack, happy for his son, replied, "Great work. I know you hoped to get accepted there. What do you plan to study?"

William, taking advantage of the moment, answered, "Anything! I just want to get out of here."

Jack was taken aback by his son's comment, but he'd known this day would come. Over the last few years, William and his sister had struggled with their father's willingness to help and be so involved in their lives. The children had felt for years that their father was too involved in their lives. Jack often coached his children in sports and attended many high school events. Regina generally welcomed her father, but William grew tired of seeing him around too much. Jack believed that Silvia for years had encouraged the children to think badly of him because he was rarely home. Jack had explained to his children often that he worked hard so they would have what they needed, including money, clothes, food, and tuition for school. Yet, Silvia continued to say terrible things about Jack, trying to make him look like a bad father.

The children didn't like that he was on the school board or made donations to the tennis team. Jack thought that he was helping his children and only slowly realized how they were uncomfortable with what he was doing. The children felt embarrassed around their friends because of their father's public donations and board-of-director position. Jack suspected Silvia was filling the children's head with endless opposing ideas, and it had finally caught up with him.

In many family situations, the children feel closer to one parent than another. William had always felt closer to his mother and chose not to listen to his father. Regina loved her mother very much, yet knew that her father suffered deeply for being married to her. She also loved her father because she knew the sacrifices he made for the family. Instead of taking jobs in different cities, Jack chose to have his family stay in one home while traveling out for work. This helped Regina and William to have a more stable life outside their home, growing up with the same friends. And Silvia loved living in the same house because the location was close to her family.

"Son, let's discuss this when I get home next week; I would love to understand how you are feeling and why you want to leave so badly."

William took a moment before replying. "Yeah, Dad, let's talk when you are back."

"William, can I speak to Regina? Is she around?"

"Yeah, hold on."

Regina picked up the phone. "Dad? How are you? How's Vietnam?"

Overcome with joy, Jack replied, "Young lady, I am doing great. Missing you, though. How is school?"

Regina knew that her father was disappointed in her for not doing well in school, and she considered lying but decided against it. "Dad, not well—I will need your help when you come home."

"Reg, I will be home next week, and I'd love to help."

Jack had hoped that a good night's rest would remove the painful element of depression but only felt the emotion coming back in greater strength. Being nine thousand miles from home added to the damaged family life. The depression became so overwhelming that he said goodbye to his daughter and cried again on his bed.

*Why am I here?* In the last decade or so, he had been a reliable provider to his wife, children, and family members.

"Mr. Jack?" A knock came at the door.

"Yes?"

"This is Tien. How about a coffee?"

Feeling the need to be around people, Jack jumped at the chance. "Lobby in five?"

"Come to the front; my scooter is ready."

"Scooter?" Jack replied, curious. "But when in Rome, as they say!"

Jack departed the hotel lobby and found his smiling friend sitting on a scooter built for two and holding a helmet. "Come on, Mr. Jack. Coffee is awaiting!" He strapped on the helmet as Tien sped off. Vietnam, known as the number-two coffee producer globally, had some of the world's richest and most original coffee houses. Like in the cafés in Paris, all the seats faced the street. As Jack and Tien arrived, he noticed how simple yet pleasing these French-style cafés were to his eyes. Tien pointed to a table to their right and dropped inside to grab two coffees. Jack immediately noticed what the coffee place was all about—beautiful Vietnamese ladies walking by wearing Vu Dai dresses. The garments, most made of silk with beautiful patterns and colors, clung to the women's bodies like wrapping, showing their curves and figure.

When Tien returned with their drinks, Jack asked him, "Tien, why do Vietnamese ladies wear those dresses? They are so beautiful."

"Vu Dai dresses cover the ladies, but the dress hides nothing," replied Tien. Jack nodded and grinned. "Mr. Jack," the man continued, "similar to our Vu Dai, you seem like you are a well-mannered gentleman on the outside. Yet, why are you here in Vietnam? I mean, on the surface, you seem like you are a tourist. Yet, you spend most of your days with that young lady."

Jack noticed several Vietnamese men staring at him while he drank his coffee with Tien. He knew that many Vietnamese men hated westerners who came into the country. Dating back to the French colonization of the 1950s, the Vietnamese were very guarded, thinking that foreign men only came to the country to take their women away. Jack felt ashamed for a moment for coming here to meet Linh. "Yes, on the surface, I am a tourist, but deep down, I came to see her. I guess I felt like I was a Vu Dai; I was trying to hide something as well."

Tien thought about how to respond. "Mr. Jack, I believe you're married. Yet, you come here to meet someone else?"

Again, Jack was taken aback by his friend's questioning. "Yes, I came to Vietnam for various reasons that all seem to interlink with one another. I came here to find the lost embassy, to locate the catholic nuns, and to find a girl I have been chatting with for the last three years."

Tien was surprised by Jack's reasoning. "My friend, you still haven't answered my question."

Still feeling the effects of the depression, Jack paused. "Do you mind if we talk about something else?"

Tien, feeling disappointed, pressed his American friend again. Jack felt a bit overwhelmed. "I am here for my reasons."

"Mr. Jack, that is why your country came here when I was a child! Your soldiers and your own people didn't understand why they were here in my country!" said Tien.

Jack was startled by the sudden reality of the conversation. Tien was absolutely right; he didn't understand why he was in Saigon. Feeling exhausted, he asked where the bathroom was. Tien reluctantly pointed to a door. Jack headed there, only to find a small basic toilet requiring him to squat down to relieve himself. Feeling a fresh wave of depression from his conversation with Tien, Jack threw up on the floor. He felt that coming to Vietnam was turning out to be a terrible idea.

Once his nausea passed, Jack returned to the table. His friend was waiting outside, finishing his coffee. "Mr. Jack, I think you should walk from here."

Jack still felt sick inside. "Why?"

Tien finished his coffee. "You are a terrible man, Jack. You come to my country and have an affair with a Vietnamese woman who is married. You broke the law; be thankful I don't turn you in to the national police!"

Jack knew Tien was right.

"I hope you someday realize what you are doing." Tien got up from the table and headed to his scooter. Jack stayed at the table and didn't watch as his friend rode away.

After sitting for a while, Jack began the walk back to the hotel.

# Chapter 5
# Fulfillment

Jack began the trepid journey back to the hotel, considering all that had happened in the last twenty-four hours—traveling across the globe to meet Linh for the first time, fulfilling his desire and passion within his heart, listening to Silvia's tone and troubling words from William and Regina, which only compounded the pain and anxiety he had been harboring for several years, and dealing with a depression attack while remembering why he made this journey which continued to drive a deep sense of guilt and pain.

Walking back to the hotel, he enjoyed the street views and people passing by. Though he was still coping with deep and depressive thoughts, he realized how incredible Saigon and its people were.

The scent of pho put a smile on Jack's face. No other dish in the world smelled as wonderful as that traditional soup. The city lights came up while people were still bustling around. He stopped for an espresso, absorbing the energy from the people around him. Jack noticed several Vietnamese mothers and daughters working hard inside the open markets. They were using their calculators as they negotiated with customers about prices. In constant high-pitched voices, they sold their products at the optimal price. Jack smiled, remembering his college days where Vietnamese ladies would help him with calculus homework.

As nighttime fell upon Saigon, Jack realized how lost he really was. On a typical day, he could find his way regardless of the time. Saigon's buildings were very similar to Paris; both cities shared a love for food, wine, and narrow one-way streets. Each street led to an alley; the alley led to a corner with four other passages. Without a map or GPS, he used his intuition to choose the right path. With each choice, he was determined that there wasn't a right or wrong decision. Each alley had the same French design with a touch of Vietnamese flavor, the smell of coffee or spring rolls, children playing, and men playing checkers.

After a few hours, close to midnight, Jack realized that he was approaching the Saigon River near the Renaissance Hotel. At last, he was close to his destination. While feeling drained, he headed into the hotel only to find Tien sitting in the lobby waiting for him, "Mr. Jack, impressive. You made it back alive!"

Jack, never missing a smart comment, replied, "Tien, when you come to America, I will show you the hood!"

Tien looked a bit puzzled. "The hood? Is that near Disneyland?"

Jack changed the subject. "I have some cycling to do in the morning."

"Cycling?"

"Yes, I've been cycling for a few years now. I cycled all over California, Oregon, and Washington. Deep down, I always wanted to cycle overseas and knew Vietnam would be an excellent place to start."

Tien looked at him with a sense of appreciation. "Well, my country is excellent for cycling—just watch out for those motorbikes; they are crazy!"

Jack smiled and thanked Tien for this advice.

He reflected on his past visions and experiences while studying Vietnam, which only fueled his desire to make this first step in his global voyage happen. Thanks in part to the internet, he had signed up with a local cycling tour in Saigon. Cycling had already been part of the Vietnamese culture. The touring company offered tours from Saigon to the Cambodia border and trips north to Da Nang. Being a seasoned cyclist with four years' experience, Jack asked for a tour around Saigon's streets. The tour owner, through email, called Jack 'the bravest western cyclist he ever met.' Many cyclists in Saigon chose to stay off the streets due to the number of motor scooters and cars.

Heading back to his room, Jack couldn't believe he'd accomplished so much in so short a time in Vietnam—his deep emotional need to be with someone who wanted him as a man as much as he wanted her as a woman. Linh, so graceful and beautiful, never left Jack's thoughts. Remembering the passionate moments with her, he longed to be with her again.

After he reached his room, he took a moment to sit on the couch and look out at the river at night. "I made it here after all this time," whispered Jack. In his heart, he knew he had more adventures in Vietnam yet to be accomplished.

# Chapter 6
## Verve

Jack began his day as he did each day—with prayer. Being a very religious man, he prayed for his family, friends, and other people who needed their prayers answered the most. And for the first time in a very long time, Jack prayed for himself.

"Lord, please pray for my family, friends, and please look after me in finding my way and grant me the guidance on the journey ahead." Jack knew he wasn't a perfect Catholic, but he prayed anyway.

While enjoying another splendid Vietnamese breakfast in the executive lounge, he received a call from Silvia. "Jack, do I need to remind you again and again? Send money. I have needs, and so do the children!"

"I will. This afternoon." Before he could say anything else, the phone went dead.

After collecting his cycling helmet and backpack from his room, he headed for the tour to join his first cycling event in Vietnam. Cycling in the country, especially on the roads in Saigon, was dangerous. The streets were filled with potholes and over two million scooters. Especially with the increase in personal autos, the roads in Saigon weren't built for street cycling.

Jack met Tuan, the owner of the cycling touring company. "Welcome! Are you ready?"

"Let's do this!" They mounted their bikes. "Let's hit all thirteen districts." Tuan looked a bit confused, but he immediately understood that this American man was different from the rest of the tourists he'd met.

At each stopping point during the cycling tour, the local people came up to Jack and asked for a photo, thinking he was a movie star from America. Jack's tall features and body size weren't standard in Vietnam. Being ever the gentleman, he went along with all the requests. Jack and Tuan stopped cycling after several hours and many close calls with the scooters and cars. Tuan found his favorite coffee bar and asked Jack to join him. As the men settled in their chairs facing the street, Tuan, without missing a beat, asked, "Why are you here, Jack?"

Jack, feeling happier than the previous day, answered with a smile, "To enjoy exactly what we are doing now—cycling and some coffee!"

Tuan smiled at his new friend. "Jack, where would you like to cycle? What else would you like to see?"

Jack thought about all his research. "Can we cycle to the Cu Chi tunnels?"

The tunnels, made famous during the Vietnam War, were built to protect soldiers and their families from American bombing raids. Considered a small underground city, Cu Chi became a secret hiding place for Vietcong and North Vietnamese armies to store weapons. Many children were born inside the tunnels, rarely leaving until the war ended in 1975. With an incredible sense of joy, Tuan explained, "Oh my, I was born near those tunnels!"

Jack felt a sense of ease with his tour guide. "I didn't know that. Can we cycle there?"

With only a few hours to spare, Jack and Tuan headed off to the tunnel. Jack realized that he was living what he'd dreamed of for so many years— being in Vietnam, cycling, walking, drinking coffee, and meeting new friends.

Tuan, reaching for his cellphone, asked Jack to pull over for a moment. "I need to take this."

Recognizing the tone in the man's voice, Jack pulled off the road; something must have happened. After Tuan finished his conversation, he walked over to his American friend. "Jack, we need to stop somewhere; it is an emergency."

"Absolutely, Tuan, let's go."

After cycling at high speed through Saigon's streets, the two men arrived outside a warehouse in District Thirteen. Tuan quickly dismounted his bike and ran inside the warehouse. Jack, close behind, walked into the building and saw something he didn't expect. It was a water bottling plant.

Several of the workers greeted Jack with questions. "Who are you? Why are you here?"

Before Jack could reply, Tuan snapped at the workers and told them to go back to work. Sensing extreme tension, Juan asked, "Tuan, what is happening here?"

"Back up, please. I need the room to think!"

Jack instantly retreated, moving away from all the commotion. As he walked around the factory, he noticed several leaks in the pipes, faulty electricity, and a foul smell within the air. Whatever was going wrong now, it had been going on for quite some time. When things seemed like they couldn't get worse, two local policemen walked into the factory. They demanded to see the water license and working papers. Feeling flustered, Tuan walked over to the visiting officers, handing them a series of Vietnamese dollars. Once the officers had collected, they departed the factory without a single word. *I guess that's how things roll here*, thought Jack.

After almost an hour, Tuan walked back over. "Mr. Jack, I am sorry, but my factory is falling apart, and I don't have time to finish the tour."

Jack completely understood the situation. "Tuan, if you don't mind, please tell me what is wrong; I may be able to help." Always willing to help others without being asked, Jack offered his cycling friend a hand.

Tuan, being a proud father of three and a local businessman, hesitated at first before accepting. "Okay, let me show you what is wrong."

Over the next three hours, Tuan walked Jack through the water flow process, including bottling and delivering. Jack noticed several technology and engineering issues, including the system computer rebooting and several leaks leading into reverse osmosis tanks. "Tuan, let me make a few corrections for you, please."

Tuan was stunned. "What can you do?"

Jack smiled. "I grew up building things with LEGOs." Both men laughed, though Tuan didn't understand how Jack could help him. The water factory was completely falling apart, but out of desperation, Tuan agreed to let him help out any way he could.

Over the next few hours, Jack cleared all the flow pipes with new tubes, began to re-tape all the connection lines to and from the tank, and restarted the electric pump system. The computer, Jack noticed, was several years old, with no chance to upgrade without internet access. Thinking about what options were available, Jack stepped out of the factory to make a call.

"Tien, this is Jack in 18125; I need a favor."

Back at the Renaissance Hotel, Tien was shocked to hear from him. "Oh, you need a favor. What can I do for you, sir?"

Jack sensed a bit of sarcasm in Tien's voice. "I need a new computer, ACER running 256 GB of RAM. One terabyte of storage, Wi-Fi, and Windows 7 with four USB ports."

Tien always loved to press his hotel guests' buttons. "Oh sure, would also like a sports car with that?"

"Come on, Tien, I am at some water plant in District Thirteen, helping a friend here; anything you can do for a platinum hotel member?"

Being a premier member of the hotel allowed Jack to pull a bit of rank. As Tien was about to tell him a flat no, he realized something startling. "Wait," said Tien, "where are you again?"

Jack told Tien about the cycling tour.

"Wait a minute. Is Tuan there?"

Jack handed the phone to Tuan. As the two men yelled at each other in Vietnamese, Jack realized that they must have already known each other in some way.

Tuan threw the phone back to Jack. "He will be here in twenty minutes with a new computer."

Observing Jack make the needed repairs on the factory, Tuan still did not trust Americans. He didn't understand why this man wanted to help him. As a child, he hadn't liked American soldiers for what they did to his country. Jack recognized that Tuan did not trust him but hoped he would be able to work through that.

Tien arrived with a brand-new laptop under his arm, walking past Jack and going straight to Tuan. "Here you are—you owe me, worm!" Tuan was about to get into Tien's face but decided not to show any emotion while Jack was present.

Tuan extended the laptop to Jack. "Here, please see what you can do."

Jack gave the two men a nod and booted up the new computer. He'd been a system engineer before becoming a sales professional and used the Wi-Fi from the tea shop across the street to access the same software used to power up the water plant. The current version was years old. Having downloaded the new software on the computer Tien brought, Jack started to make the needed configuration changes to control the water and reverse osmosis systems. Thankfully, the new computer had enough USB ports and memory to collect and control the water systems. Within a matter of an hour, Jack reset the entire system with new software and connectors. After the new computer activated the control layers, the whole water flow system produced clean water.

After a few pH tests, Tuan and Tien laughed and joked around with workers. Jack recognized that he didn't come to Vietnam to fix a water plant and realized a new purpose in life was in front of him. As Jack remembered, *God, please pray for those that need the most help.* Tien and Tuan's prayers had been answered.

Jack stayed at the water plant for the next two hours to clean up and create more bottles for the next day's production run. Soon, the plant was back in business, and all the next day's production run was completed on time and up to correct levels. Feeling a bit tired from the adventure, Jack asked Tuan if they could cycle back to the hotel. Tuan shot back, "Mr. Jack, absolutely not. We need to celebrate," Jack, never one to pass on beer and food, accepted the invitation. He was led by the workers and Tien down the street in the district to a converted patio restaurant specializing in Vietnamese hotpot and cold beers. The local people put ice in the beers because of the lack of refrigerators outside of District Seven.

Even while he enjoyed the moment with the water company team, his heart still yearned for Linh. Jack thought about what her home life must be like with a husband like Vo. Allowing himself a moment to speculate, Jack started to feel a deep sense of pain and guilt. He, in a sense, had committed similar actions in his marriage as Vo had. Jack tried to shake the feeling inside.

He realized that today might have given him the needed boost as to why he was in Vietnam. Jack always extended a helping hand to anyone who needed it. He now realized that his willingness to help anyone extended regardless of what country he was in.

Tien, ever the smart ass, said to Jack, "Hey, Mr. Jack, why are you here again?"

With a warm smile on his face, Jack replied, "To see your ugly face again!"

The entire table laughed. Tien, still dressed in his business suit from the hotel, cursed in Vietnamese. Jack smiled for the first time in two days. Tuan, noticing his new friend enjoying himself and striking up a conversation, said, "Mr. Jack, thank you for your help today; how can I pay you back?"

"No need, Tuan. Thank you for a great day!"

With the food running out and the beers gone, Jack thanked everyone for the fantastic dinner and paid the bill. The entire team thanked their new friend for dinner. Getting late into the evening, he cycled the twenty kilometers back to the hotel, catching some rest before Linh returned in the morning. Still coping with health problems, including diabetes and weight, Jack paced himself to not collapse. Once he started to cycle, Jack noticed several other cyclists following him. Not sure what to make of this, Jack rode slower to see who they were. As the group pulled alongside Jack, he realized that it was Tuan and the workers. "Hey, we will show you the way!" Thankful to the group, Jack cycled with his new team back to the hotel. With every turn, he felt a new sense of happiness and joy. Jack had come to Vietnam to cycle, meet people, and help answer his childhood questions. Now, close to 11 p.m., he was cycling with this new team, feeling that his life was becoming balanced.

After an exhausting yet fulfilling session of cycling in the dark, Jack arrived back at the Renaissance Hotel. Feeling fantastic, he invited the team members into the hotel for another beer. Tuan answered this time, "Thank you. But we need to get home. See you again, my friend." Jack watched the team cycling away, back to District Thirteen. Jack could only wonder what life was like for them at home. Being in Vietnam, Jack had noticed that people outside of the wealthy districts mostly lived very poor, including many from the water plant. While that factory created fresh water, the plant also was home to the workers.

"That plant is all they have," whispered Jack. Remembering his house in California, his 401k, and his cars, Jack felt ashamed for a moment for having more in life than most of them combined. After he reflected on his thoughts about the wonderful crew from the water plant, he made his way to the elevator and proceeded to go to his room for a well-needed rest. Jack expected Linh to arrive in the morning as planned. He wasn't sure what time she planned to come. But he knew they both yearned for the fire and passion they'd experienced the day before.

After a long, hot shower, Jack turned off all the lights and opened the curtains in his room. He wanted to see the Saigon River at night. The view to Jack was never the same. Each night, new boats floated there, with new reflections from the various buildings along the river. Some of the buildings lit up at night. Some didn't. Jack watched the traffic below on the various streets in District Seven, changing his view through the different windows.

Jack finished the night with his prayer and thanked God for everything i his life. He drifted asleep with thoughts of Linh and how she would look whe the sun came up again.

# Chapter 7
# Adoration

Morning came early in Saigon. Heavy rain on the windows served as Jack's alarm clock. Heading to the shower, he wanted to refresh and clean before Linh arrived. Before he could comprehend the moment, though, the door opened, showing the most beautiful woman entering the room. Linh was dressed in a traditional white Ao Dai dress and heels. Jack was awestruck.

Linh saw him still naked, coming out of the shower. She walked over to him and, after a very gentle kiss, said, "Ah, I see you were expecting me!" Without thinking for a single moment, Jack kissed Linh passionately while drifting his hands down her beautiful dress. Linh, feeling her lover's desire, kissed his neck while stroking her fingers down his body. Jack gracefully unzipped Linh's beautiful dress and let the garment fall gently onto the floor. Linh undid Jack's towel and gently caressed his member with soft hands. "Allow me," she said. Starting with Jack's neck, Linh ran her wet and soft tongue down Jack's chest and slowly kneeled in front of her lover, stroking Jack with a smooth motion. He looked down at his lover's eyes.

"My Linh, how beautiful you are."

Linh felt so much love for Jack, but she also had a life outside of this with her daughter, Ngoc, and her husband, Vo. While the two lovers held each other, Linh sat up in the bed and reached for a cup of tea, asking Jack if he'd like some. "My love, would you like some tea?"

"No thanks, my paramour."

She looked at Jack as her lover and her much-needed friend. Jack, twenty-two years senior to her, had more experience in life. Linh wanted him to help her figure out the direction to take with her husband. "Jack, I loved being married, but my husband wants to divorce so he can be with his lover. However, I want to stay married. What do you think I should do?" Linh wanted the security of being married in Vietnam. Single mothers were looked down upon by the older generation. Younger Vietnamese men looked at them as easy targets for abuse. Jack realized that depending on how he answered this question, it would either help his lover or hurt her. Jack and Linh knew they had begun a beautiful and loving relationship, but this only could go so far in their lives.

Each day, while Jack was in Vietnam, the two lovers woke up together, watching the sunrise over the river. While the beauty was breathtaking, the reality was that there always would be a river between Jack and Linh. They both knew that they would never end up on the same side of the river again. Jack gave his lover some advice. "Linh, if you feel you want to stay married without having love in your heart, what kind of marriage are you hoping for?" He knew firsthand what a loveless marriage felt like. Jack wanted to share with Linh his pain with depression and the effects this had on his life. Trying to make his marriage work and knowing that his partner wasn't going to give the effort emotionally impacted him. Linh, sitting quietly on the bed, looked away and sobbed. Jack felt that he hadn't provided the needed comfort. "I am sorry, my love."

"No, Jack, thank you. That is a question I need to answer within my heart."

Jack felt a sense of relief. "If you plan to stay to provide for Ngoc, then yes, you will have a marriage similar to mine."

Surprised by this statement, she asked him, "Jack, what kind of marriage do you have?"

Jack, still ashamed about how his marriage turned out, told Linh more about Silvia. In prior conversations, they'd rarely talked about their respective spouses. They'd both maintained a level of privacy even after they met for the first time. Jack started by describing the early years with his wife. "When our children were born, we were delighted. When we dated, we loved each other. After the children started to go to school, we sometimes stayed home and made love."

Linh, sitting on the bed with her tea, listened with a warm and supportive smile. He went into some detail about all the challenges, including the impact of Silvia's drinking. Jack explained how he felt like he was the only parent in the house. Linh appreciated that comment, knowing how special her daughter Ngoc was to her. After he completed his inspirational words, she reached over and kissed him on his lips, thanking him for sharing his life with her. After a few moments of kissing, the lovers went to the shower together, never taking their eyes off each other.

Linh loved the gentle touches of Jack's fingers through her hair. His sweet words of love, passion, and sexual voice made Linh feel deeply excited. She in turn began to wash Jack's body. She began to sing softly while spreading soap across his tall body. Linh gently guided her hands, bringing him to climax once more. Seeing the pleasurable look on Jack's face also made Linh feel satisfied as a woman.

"My love, just relax." He began to spread soap over Linh's body, listening to her moaning with great pleasures.

As Jack started to rise off his lover, Linh came to lick Jack's chest. With a slow yet strong motion, her lover came. Linh felt Jack's body becoming weak from the pleasure and then rose up, giving him a loving hug. "My Jack, I love you."

Jack smiled back. "Linh, I love you too." The two lovers, exhausted, lay down in the shower as they let the warm water hit their bodies.

While Linh was getting dressed after the romantic shower, Jack received a call from Silvia. "Where is the money, Jack?"

Jack remembered Silvia's previous call and realized he'd never sent the money to her. "Silvia, I will send it. Sorry, lost track of time here."

"Now, Jack!"

After the phone went silent, Jack sat down on a chair, staring out the window of the hotel. Linh, sensing the pain her lover was in, walked over to him to hug him gently. Attempting to lighten the mood, she asked, "That must have been the stick? Yes?"

Jack often thought of Silvia as a dead piece of wood with no feeling and had said as much to Linh.

He laughed. Now there was a name for Silvia that only he and Linh would understand. Jack thanked her for the love and support. "Love, I need to send some money. Be back soon." He went into the living room and accessed his bank account to send money to his wife. After completing the transaction, Jack returned to the main bedroom to find Linh on the phone, speaking to her husband. Unable to understand Vietnamese, he sat in the other room to give her the needed space. After an hour, Linh emerged from the room with tears in her eyes. Jack, wanting to comfort his lover, walked over to her and gave her a hug. "Linh, are you okay?"

"That was my stick." Linh wiped away her tears and finished getting dressed. "My husband wants me to move out now and leave my daughter."

Jack was stunned. "Linh, what can we do?"

She thought for a moment. "My love, I will be fine. Just please love me as you do." Jack came over and gave Linh another deep hug.

Within a few minutes, they proceeded to the elevator to head down to the lobby. As they entered the hall, Tien was standing near the bar with a stern look on this face.

"Yes?" asked Jack.

"Come with me, please." Worried, Linh reached for Jack's hand, knowing this action was against the law. They followed Tien to the back office, where a series of computer monitors showed the hotel entrance. Tien, not one to waste time with pleasantries, said, "Ms. Linh, if you plan to come to visit, please use the elevator southeast by my office."

A very shocked Jack looked at his friend. "Ah, thank you, Tien!"

"Jack," replied Tien, "I asked you not to break our laws. Ms. Linh, please leave after 11 a.m. through the north elevators."

Neither of them could believe what Tien had done for them.

"You choose to do this—if you are caught, you are responsible for what happens to you and Linh."

Jack looked back at Tien. "Why help me then?"

"Tuan is my only brother, and I want to thank you for fixing the water plant."

*Brothers.* It suddenly made sense. Jack felt a sense of happiness about discovering this. As he was thanking Tien again, Linh called a taxi.

They jumped in, and she asked, "Where are we going today? I'm hungry." Jack also felt hungry; they couldn't wait for lunch ahead. Saigon was famous for several Michelin two and three-star restaurants. Linh knew the best places for food, and she wanted Jack to experience a fresh bowl of pho. She asked the taxi driver in Vietnamese to take them to Ben Thanh Market, in the center of the city. Next to this world-famous marketplace, the famed restaurant pho 2000 was located.

"Jack, this restaurant has played host to several celebrities, including President Bill Clinton," said Linh. Linh knew most locals ate elsewhere, but Jack wouldn't have a strong stomach to cope with the various oils used in some of the restaurants.

While the taxi navigated through the narrow streets of Saigon, Jack can't help noticing Linh's beautiful legs and lovely smile. With each look, he blushed as Linh caught him glancing at her. Being a proper Vietnamese lady, she covered her legs and gave Jack a friendly wink back, reminding him of the rules while in public in Vietnam. After a few close calls with people spotting them kissing in the taxi, the driver stopped at the famous market.

Inside the restaurant, in an exquisite Vietnamese dialect, Linh asked the waiter for a top side table for two overlooking the street. The waiter seemed very impressed with Linh's Vietnamese dialect and rapidly moved through the crowded restaurant to show the two lovers to the table near the window.

"Jack, please let me order for you." With a playful smile, Linh ordered two bowls of pho with well-cooked meat and two tiger beers.

Linh loved showing Jack her country and everything it had to offer. "How was cycling in my city yesterday?"

Jack could not contain his excitement. "It was incredible!" He shared how they cycled through the thirteen districts, the close calls with cars and scooters, and then stopping at the plant.

"Jack, you really got to experience my city. I am happy for you." She looked concerned, though, about the plant. "Please remember this is still Vietnam; things run here, even if they are held together with a string and tape." Jack knew some of that. Telecommunications wires rolled up in the hundreds on top of phone poles, electric transformers smoking, and water pipes breaking. Yet, people still made phone calls, took baths, and powered their homes.

"In America," said Jack, "with all the regulations, these services would be shut down."

Linh agreed. "Jack, please remember you are only here for a few days. Please make the most of this."

Jack, seeing the concern in Linh's eyes, understood her more. Linh knew that this place was years away from being at western standards and wasn't safe for Ngoc. Her exquisite five-year-old girl was almost kidnapped by human smugglers when she was only three. While playing outside of Linh's mother-in-law's house in Bien Hoa, Ngoc was nearly grabbed by two men looking to steal little girls and sell them to foreigners and traders. Ngoc, seeing a man she didn't know, began to scream loud enough to scare them away. Linh was a driven businesswoman and a mother who wanted a better life and future for her daughter. Leaving Vietnam someday was a life goal she strove for each day.

They didn't speak much during lunch. Both simply enjoyed the fresh bowls of pho, the tiger beers, and the spring rolls. Feeling completely satisfied, Jack asked Linh for a favor. "Could we order a second bowl?"

Linh put her chopsticks and spoon down and replied, "My Jack, save your stomach for more later!"

Jack, feeling a bit embarrassed, apologized to Linh for the request. She returned his look with a very playful wink. Jack asked the waiter for the check, and Linh reached over and paid the bill. "My treat, my love." Linh, being a very classy lady, took Jack's hand, kissing it gently. They walked out of the restaurant. Saigon's weather was typical by most standards—hot, muggy, and very humid.

"Where should we go?" asked Jack.

Linh thought about all the places to go. "I know. Let's go to a great place for coffee and tea!" Jack, always up for Vietnamese coffee and green tea with lime, followed Linh to a taxi.

Once again, the driver seemed more like a race-car pilot than a taxi driver. Moments later, the taxi pulled up to a tea house next to Independence Palace. Also known as Reunification Palace, it was the site where army tanks rammed through the gate on April 30, 1975. Jack remembered the radio broadcast—*Saigon has fallen.*

Strolling to the palace gates, Linh asked him, "My love, where are you going?"

"Linh, do you know this place?"

She had grown up on a coffee farm one hundred and fifty kilometers from Saigon and never visited the palace, so she seemed just as curious as Jack. "I only read about it. I have never been here in person before."

He cried quietly, recognizing the significance of this moment. "This is where it happened—this is where the tanks actually crashed through the gates on April 30, 1975."

Linh glazed over. "Yes. This is where our independence started."

Ever the historian, Jack asked Linh if they could enter the palace grounds and walk around.

"Absolutely!" she said, understanding how important it was for him.

# Chapter 8
# Illumination

Playing back in his head those words he'd heard on the radio so many years ago, now Jack was walking in the actual palace where those famous armored tanks helped unify Vietnam, after ten long years of civil war aided by the US. As Jack and Linh walked the grounds, they came up to a series of posters on display. Jack explained to Linh the historical importance of those military tanks and what purpose they served. Linh, already knowing about her country's history, still appreciated Jack's detailed explanation of those vehicles. Jack noticed several old gentlemen in Vietnamese army uniforms. The soldiers served as tour guides. Jack, in a sign of respect for the officers, saluted them. One old soldier stared back at Jack, standing at attention, and returned the statue.

He asked the officer, "Is this the room where the president fell, captured by the soldiers?" The officer acknowledged Jack, smiled, and pointed to an adjacent room.

Jack thanked the officer again, showed Linh the famous place, and described the backstory.

She smiled. "I know, Jack—I am Vietnamese." Jack grinned back at her and gave her a loving wink. He was astonished that even after thirty-seven years, the same soldiers reported for duty to guard the old building.

Jack and Linh walked downstairs to the basement, which had also served as a communications room for the president and his military advisors. Hanging from the wall, a famous original picture stood out, and Linh stared at it. The image, with three gentlemen sitting somewhere in deep thought, intrigued her. After a few minutes, she called Jack over, "Jack, who is that?"

He stopped for a moment and took a deep breath before answering, "That has to be a one-of-a-kind picture." It was the late John F. Kennedy, before the

Vietnam War. JFK hadn't wanted to send troops to Vietnam but approved the Pentagon to send military advisors in 1960. The picture hanging on the wall showed JFK sitting next to Vice President Lyndon Johnson. "I have never seen the original in the United States. How did this picture get here?" The historical figures seemed to be in deep thought. Jack wondered if they were thinking about where to send troops in Vietnam.

"If President Kennedy survived the assassination, maybe America would never have sent troops to Vietnam, to begin with," he pondered aloud.

The tour group officer came over and asked Linh in Vietnamese, "Why is this man so interested in this picture?"

Linh replied, "He would like to know where this picture came from?"

The officer stared at Jack and then led them outside where the president's escape helicopter still rested on the palace grounds.

He pointed at a building to the east. "There—the picture is from that building."

Jack began to walk that way, wondering what the building was. Linh thanked the officer for his help. The officer nodded his head and went back inside the palace.

"Jack, let's go, love—my feet are hurting."

He froze for a moment, realizing. "Could this be the missing embassy? Yes, love, let's get some tea."

They walked out of the palace. He stopped and looked at a series of pictures on the wall. One image stood out from all the rest. On April 30, while the North Vietnamese Army took the president of South Vietnam into custody, a lone young officer had led the president out of the palace. Jack looked again, realizing that the young officer was the old gentleman he'd saluted earlier in the day. Linh looked confused. "Jack, what is it?"

He held his hand up for a moment. "I will be back."

Jack hurried back into the palace only to find the officer standing at attention once more, saluting. Jack, in complete astonishment, returned the salute back to the proud military man. "You are the person who escorted the president!"

"Yes, that was me—those men over there, the ones who opened your door, they were the first tank crew."

Jack, overwhelmed with joy in this heart, couldn't believe his luck. On a single day, he'd found an answer to an old question by coming to the palace.

Jack thanked the gentleman and then walked out to catch up with Linh.

After thirty-seven years, Linh's countrymen still went to this place as a memorial to all the Vietnamese people who'd suffered to unify their country. Jack remembered traveling to Washington, DC, to see the Vietnam War memorial, displaying the names of the fifty-seven thousand Americans who died. Jack remembered what Chi had told him: *Vietnam lost three million people during the war.* The feeling of watching these soldiers report for duty at the Saigon Presidential Palace each day after so long became an uncontrollable emotional moment for him.

Jack, unable to control his emotions, cried openly. Linh, feeling the need to comfort her lover, violated Vietnam's local law and held Jack's hand, kissing him softly on his lips. Knowing this could spell trouble for them later, Linh still forwent the risk. "Jack, let's sit down here in the park and relax for a moment." They walked to the nearby park bench overlooking the independence park and the reunification palace.

Jack, attempting to steady himself, explained to Linh why he was so emotional. "My love, thank you for being here on this journey; I never believed after all these years I would ever be here."

Linh, still a bit confused, replied, "Thank you for taking me here. I have lived here my entire life and never have been inside the palace. I am so proud of my country."

"Yes, I understand how you feel." Now filled with a renewed sense of strength, Jack noticed Linh's high heels. "How are your feet feeling in those?" He realized how much pain he must have put Linh through with all this walking around.

Linh gave him a warm smile. "Jack, I am fine. I can survive—let's continue! Where to?"

Jack, thinking about what the old officer had pointed at, walked back toward the palace. Once they reached the front gate and turned right, they both noticed the road leading east past a series of buildings and shopping areas. Jack grabbed Linh's hand and gave her a quick loving squeeze before letting go.

As they walked east of the palace, several local people looked at the couple. Some would smile and wave. Others would bear a frown. Jack saw the building the officer pointed at. To his amazement, it turned out to be several single-story units behind a guarded iron gateway.

*Welcome to the United States Consulate, Vietnam.*

Jack believed he may have found the lost embassy, but in his research as a young man, the embassy had several buildings with multiple floors. They captured the helicopter pad picture on one of the rooftops in those Time-Life photos. At the end of the war, when people tried to escape Saigon, American Marines guarded the embassy, creating barricades to protect the building and only allowing some personal to reach the helicopter pad.

Jack turned to Linh. "I don't believe this is it; I don't see the tall buildings or helicopter pad."

Still not understanding the importance of this building to Jack, Linh commented, "Let me ask."

She walked toward the consulate gate and began a conversation with a Vietnamese guard. Within a few minutes, she returned. "My love, my feet are hurting. Let's sit down and have a beer. I will give the story of this place."

Directly across from the US Consulate in Saigon stood a refined American restaurant. The Hard Rock Café, long known in America for its great food, glorious music, and musicians' artifacts, was the perfect place to go. They went in for an early dinner. "Okay, my love—what did the guard tell you?"

"Oh him? He knew nothing. I only wanted to get off my feet and have a beer with you."

Jack, rolling his eyes, couldn't believe what Linh was saying. "Come on, Linh. You are killing me here!"

"The guard told me when he was a little boy after the war, the entire embassy was torn down completely. Many of the building materials, artifacts, and cars all ended up down the street and placed inside the unification palace and war remembrance museum. The guard mentioned that in 2004, when relationships between the United States and Vietnam became better, our government allowed the US to put the consulate here and the new embassy in Hanoi."

Jack felt so excited with the news from Linh that he couldn't thank her enough. "How can I thank you? In one day, we have found the palace and the missing embassy. How can I ever thank you?"

Linh always appreciated such loving words from Jack. "Please don't forget me or this moment we have shared." Jack wanted to reach over and give Linh a loving kiss. However, he knew many people in the restaurant were staring. Instead, he reached into his pocket and removed an object from his keychain.

"This angel has been with my family for thirty years—please keep it as a symbol of our love and our time together."

"I could not accept this, Jack."

"Please," he insisted.

Linh placed the object in her hands. "I will forever keep this with me."

Jack reached under the table and squeezed her hand.

As they finished their dinner, Linh reached for her cellphone and discovered that she had missed several calls from Vo. "Oh, Jack, I need to call him back."

Jack, always understanding of the complex spouse issue, smiled. "Please take your time."

Linh stepped away from the table and went outside to call her husband. After about twenty minutes, she returned with a flushed and unsettling look on her face. "Jack, I need to go home—something is wrong, and I need to be there."

"No worry, my love. Let me get you a taxi."

Jack and Linh headed out of the restaurant. While waiting for the taxi, Jack continued to stare at the consulate complex. Replaying the scene from 1975, with all the refugees trying to get through the embassy gate and being held back by barbed wire and soldiers, Jack said to himself, *Here is where all that happened.* Soon afterward, as the taxi pulled up, he gave Linh a hug and watched her depart toward the bus station.

"Be safe, my Jack," she said as she left.

Jack, deep down, questioned how this relationship would impact Linh's other life. Being a wonderful mother, she had many of the same problems as he did.

As she walked, Linh received a phone call from her mother-in-law. "Linh, you need to come home now! An unknown woman is here in the house waiting for you and Vo!"

Taking a deep breath, Linh knew that this strange woman could only be Niu. "Yes, Mom, on my way!"

She reached the bus terminal in Saigon, where she received another phone call, this time from Vo. "Linh, don't come home. I will take care of everything."

Linh felt her blood boiling to the point of internal explosion. "What is she doing in my house near my daughter?" Vo, at a loss for words, hung up the phone. Linh, shaken, boarded the bus toward Bien Hoa.

# Chapter 9
## Detachment

After a bumpy forty-minute ride, Linh stormed into the house to find Niu sitting on the couch next to Ngoc and Vo. "Get up and get out. Now!" shouted Linh.

Vo was shocked at his wife's temper. "Linh, she can stay. You can go!"

Linh, beside herself, reached over and grabbed Ngoc's hand. "Come on, dear. Let's have some dinner."

"Okay, Mommy."

Liu came in. "Niu, get out of my house now!" Niu, not knowing who to listen to, continued to sit frozen on the couch.

"Mom, she needs to stay," added Vo.

Liu, completely upset with her son, yelled, "Leave now, both of you!" Within a few moments, Niu and Vo got up and left the house.

Linh was relieved that her mother-in-law threw the two of them out. "Mom, thank you."

Liu was still upset. "Sit down. We need to talk."

Over the next hour, while Ngoc enjoyed some dried fish with oil, Liu expressed concerns to Linh. "Look, I don't want my son leaving you and Ngoc, but he will make his own decision. I would suggest you look for some place to live."

Linh, shocked by Liu's request, cried. "All right." She continued to cry as she left to go into her room.

Within a few moments, Ngoc came in. "Mommy, please don't cry. You are my mommy." Both Ngoc and Linh cried themselves to sleep, not knowing what the future would hold for them.

After the Monday sun rose, Linh told her mother-in-law, "Mom, I will be back; I need to go to government services."

With an approving nod, Liu smiled. "That girl, she is tough," she whispered.

Linh jumped on her 110cc scooter and headed into town. Within a few minutes, she pulled up at the government services office to apply for a government apartment for her and her daughter. While Linh sat in the office waiting for her turn, a young homeless man snuck quietly around the building and spotted Linh's scooter.

"Ha! No lock!"

After a few twists of wires, the scooter came alive, and the crook spun the bike around, taking off.

Within a few hours, Linh received a non-approved status for government housing because she was a married woman. Government apartments were only open to unmarried mothers.

Feeling frustrated, Linh stormed out of the building in tears. Just a few moments later, Linh noticed her scooter wasn't where she left it. She began to run around the building in sheer panic, crying with the knowledge that she lost her only mode of transportation. After searching frantically for an hour, Linh walked over to the local police office to report the bike missing. To her surprise, the police had caught the thief a few hours before and were holding him in a jail cell. "Yes, we have him; someone reported him stealing a bike from the services office," replied the officer.

Linh, feeling sincerely happier than before, said, "The bike is mine. Can I have it back?"

The policeman replied, "I am sorry. Before we could stop him, he sold the bike."

Linh felt miserable. "Okay, is there any money I can collect from him?"

"No, he is an orphan and homeless. He has nothing; he used the money from the scooter to buy drugs."

Linh walked out of the station, crying and feeling completely worn out from the day's events. She remembered her time with Jack and his beautiful smile and was overcome with missing him. She knew she already asked so much from Jack—the money when she was young, coming all the way here to see her, and taking her to places in Saigon. Linh walked back to her mother-in-law's house feeling very sad and without hope. Linh pondered her options to overcome her crisis. 'What would Jack do in a time like this? Did he leave early?' Linh, after careful consideration, decided not to call him and ask for more help.

As Linh approached the house, Ngoc saw her mother through a window and came running out. "Mommy, you are back!"

Smiling, with tears streaming down her face, Linh ran to her daughter. "Yes, baby, Mommy is here." After a long embrace, they walked into the house.

"Well, daughter, what happened?" asked Liu.

"The government won't help me because I am a married mother, and my scooter got stolen."

"Let me understand this—in the last twenty-four hours, you lost your husband to a younger lady, you are about to be homeless, your scooter was stolen, and you are low on money?"

Linh realized the depth of her crisis. "Yes, Mom, and it's only 5 p.m!" Both ladies laughed and smiled at each other.

"Linh, I have something for you." Her mother-in-law reached into a bag. "Here, dear, take this."

Linh couldn't believe the amount of money Liu was giving her—savings of over 40,000,000 Vietnamese dollars from over her lifetime. "Take care, and keep it safe, and don't show this to my son!"

Linh had never in her life felt close to her mother-in-law until now. "Oh, my mother, thank you!" Not one for much emotion, Liu smiled and looked away. With a new sense of hope, Linh hid the money in a secret place in her room.

After dinner, Vo came back into the house alone. "Linh, I want you to leave, but Ngoc stays, and Niu will be her mother."

Linh felt bolder after Liu's kindness. "Oh, Vo, I see; you want me to give up my daughter to your slut, and I should walk away!"

"Yes, now!"

Liu spoke loudly, "You have been drinking again, right? You get out of my house."

Vo wasn't prepared for his mother's response. "Mom, I am the man of the house, and I give the orders!"

Liu slapped him in the face. "Don't you talk to your wife or me like that again!"

Vo reeled. "Mom, she isn't my wife anymore."

Liu screamed back at her son, "Show me the papers, you worthless son, or get out now!"

Realizing that his mother wasn't his ally, Vo retreated to his room, gathered his clothes, and stormed out of the house.

"Never come back!" yelled Liu to her son. "Daughter, you stay here with my granddaughter."

Linh jumped into her mother-in-law's arms, crying uncontrollably.

"Linh, come now. Time to be your own person."

Linh took the words to heart, stopped crying, and finished her dinner.

After finishing her traditional rice and fish, Linh put Ngoc to bed and went outside to see the stars in the sky. The evening was cold, with a light touch of wind from the south and no clouds in the sky. Linh allowed herself to think about Jack and the love they shared. She could still remember the passion she felt lying in Jack's arms, kissing his neck as he stroked his strong hands along her back. 'My Jack, I love you wherever you are.'

Linh thought about the future—if she would ever see Jack again or if she could reach him via email. She wanted to know if he was safe at home and if things between him and the stick were getting better. After a few night-dreaming moments, Linh spoke out loud to herself, "Jack is gone but not forgotten." She would always remember him, and she hoped he would never forget her. Linh realized how much strength it gave her, having Jack in her life. She hated not seeing him. Linh's love for Jack was more than just a physical connection to her. Linh had felt so comfortable with him. She could even ask him about marriage advice and parenting ideas for Ngoc. Jack had become her friend, mentor, and lover. Could they become more? Would he ever consider coming back to Vietnam?

Did he get to see everything he was seeking? She realized that Jack may never return to her again and wished they could have made love one more time before he departed. After allowing herself that moment of thought, reality sat in for Linh. 'Okay, what am I going to do about Vo? Should I divorce him and allow him to run off with Niu? Where will I live? How can I raise Ngoc on my own? Too many questions for one night—better to see what tomorrow brings.' With a deep breath, Linh entered the house to say goodnight to Liu and Ngoc.

# Chapter 10
# Confession

After Linh's sudden departure, Jack walked back to the Reunification Palace through the park. Vietnam's most prestigious landmark, the Notre Dame Cathedral, stood at the entrance of the square. The centennial building had survived the Japanese invasion in the 1930s and the war with the French in the 1950s, among other armed conflicts. Jack could only wonder how many people sought refuge in that massive church during all those conflicts. Being a lifelong Catholic, he went into the church to say his evening prayers. Jack entered the historic cathedral with absolute amazement. It was unbelievable the building had survived for so long. Jack found a pew, kneeled, and performed the cross over his chest. *Dear God, thank you for this day, thank you for everything in my life, thank you for my family and friends, and thank you for putting Linh in my life. Please, God, look after those that need the most help, amen.*

As Jack was completing his prayer, an elderly priest came up and sat behind him. "Good evening, my son. What brings you here?"

Jack turned and faced the priest. "Giving thanks to God for everything in my life."

The priest seemed taken aback. "I see you are American. What brings you to Vietnam?" Before Jack could respond, the priest spoke in a straightforward tone, "Let me guess—you are here to find a wife and enjoy the parties and all the fine foods."

Despite Jack's faith, he didn't like priests. Since his days in Catholic school as a child, Jack had never liked the nuns or the priests. On many occasions, Jack had received several hits on his ass from the wood paddle or the rope from the head nun. Never a very disciplined student, he often found himself in trouble at school. On a few occasions, he witnessed a priest kissing another man and was confused, not knowing if this was allowed by the church. He learned later in life that many of them had lost their faith a long time ago. The Catholic Church had continued to cover up ongoing sex scandals dating back to the 1970s and 1980s. He was sure Vietnam was no exception to the crisis.

"Actually, I am here for several reasons. May I ask you a question, Father?"

"Yes, go ahead, son. What is your question?"

Jack asked if he remembered Operation Babylift in 1975. The priest seemed to be uncomfortable with the question.

"Why do you ask? That was a long time ago."

"I always wanted to find those nuns to see if they were still alive. I want to ask them what happened that day and why they didn't leave after the orphans departed on the planes."

The priest was not prepared to carry on the conversation any further. "Son, that event was a complete failure, and those nuns had no business doing what they did. I suggest you never bring that subject again, at least not while you are in Vietnam."

"Why, Father? Why can't I ask questions about such an important event?"

The priest, distraught by the line of questioning, got up from the pew. "Go with God, my son."

Surprised by the priest's attitude, Jack became even more interested in discovering what happened on that day. He remembered the news about how the massive airlift was coordinated. They'd wanted to get the orphans to a safe place.

"Is there something to hide? Why can't I talk about the nuns?"

The priest just walked away.

Jack finished his evening prayers and began to walk toward the hotel. He needed some rest. He arrived at the hotel, wondering what happened to Linh. *Why did she need to leave so soon?* He considered for a moment how their affair could do more harm than good. *What good could come from having a love affair? Could this relationship hurt Linh too?*

Jack considered his own fate. Having an affair would seal his outcome with Silvia and his children. It would result in a messy divorce where he could lose more than just money—he could lose respect from his family and everyone else in his life. Could the passionate love affair place Linh in a terrible and risky position and possibly impact Ngoc as well? He was sure the call Linh had received came from Vo. Jack wondered if Vo behaved similarly to Silvia.

*Does Vo verbally abuse her? Doesn't Vo appreciate Linh for everything she does? Isn't Vo romantically interested in Linh because of his affair with the girl in Hue city?*

Jack didn't stop at the bar on the fifth floor as he usually did. Instead, he went straight to his room. After having a very long, fulfilling day, he wanted to reflect on the day's events. Jack was worried that his depression could resurface. He prayed again, asking God for strength in overcoming his addiction and pain. After thirty minutes of quiet prayer time, Jack opened his eyes as the cellphone rang. Jack had set up the ringtone with a song from U2, 'It's a Beautiful Day,' if the call came from Linh.

As the music began, Jack picked up the phone, knowing it was her.

"My love, how are you? Are you safe?"

"Jack, I can't help with your project anymore. Please enjoy the rest of your trip here in my country. Please never forget me."

"My Linh, please, I need to see you again!" The phone line went dead. He sensed the trouble Linh may be in and chose not to call her back.

Another morning came. Jack missed the sunrise because of his worries. Feeling hollow, he felt the depression coming on again. To try to keep it under control, he prayed once more. Not long after, Jack's phone rang. He reached for it, surprised to see that his wife was calling.

"Jack, when are you coming home? William and Regina need to talk to you, and we need to discuss where our marriage is going."

"Yes, I can change my flight and come home early. Let me see what I can do."

Silvia saw an opportunity to put Jack down. "I guess you are stuck there, Jack. Good!"

Jack was unable to reply, since she hung up the phone quickly after her statement. He logged on to the travel site, changing his ticket's date and time. After moving up his departure, Jack went to the lobby of the hotel. He wanted to let the people at the front desk know he would leave earlier than expected. The front desk understood, agreeing to credit back the days.

Jack needed something refreshing to drink. "Van, please make a green ice tea with lime."

Van, ever happy to see Jack, said, "With a triple espresso as well?"

Jack smiled back at his friend. While he enjoyed his tea, he thought about the challenging discussions he'd face at home. Were William and Regina really having that many issues in life? Was he prepared to leave Silvia? Or was this another power trip Silvia was doing to keep feeling in charge? No matter how Jack felt, the trip home would be difficult. He wasn't looking forward to going back. After he finished his espresso coffee and tea, he thanked Van for always making the best green tea.

"Thank you, Van. I will never forget you."

Van smiled ear to ear. "Thank you, sir, for always making me smile."

Jack headed toward the entrance of the hotel. He planned to have the last green tea before leaving the country. As he turned right from the door, Tuan, racing on his scooter, pulled out.

"Jack, Jack, I need you!"

He realized that something had happened. "Tuan, stop here—what is going on?"

Tuan was entirely out of breath. "Please come with me. The water stopped flowing again!"

Jack considered whether he wanted to use the day, possibly his last day in Vietnam, to fix a broken water plant. As Linh had described to him, most of Vietnam was held together by a string and tape. Yet, things seemed to keep going anyway.

"Tuan, I would love to help, but I am leaving early tomorrow, and I may not have time."

Tuan was in sheer panic. "Mr. Jack, please an hour of your time."

Jack reluctantly agreed. "Okay." He jumped on the back of the scooter, heading to the water plant.

Sure enough, when Tuan and Jack arrived, they found the water pipe broken, with water gushing everywhere. Tuan had never experienced such problems before. The factory, for the most part, operated well with very few issues.

Jack jumped off the scooter, running inside the plant to find the emergency shut-off valve. Then he remembered that he was in Vietnam, where those didn't exist. He looked at the problem and realized how much damage had occurred. Like on a submarine during Jack's military days, he witnessed several pipes bursting. The factory broke the mainline from the water source with no means to shut it off. Jack cut a new line to place over the existing one to create an emergency seal. Within a few minutes, the pipe was fixed, stopping the water from flowing out of control. It started to fill up the tanks for processing again. Once the water flowed in the new tubes, the water treatment produced freshwater.

After almost an hour of repairs, Jack felt exhausted. Needing some distraction from his current and future conflicts, he appreciated the crisis more than most people would have. After a few more minutes, the water pH level balanced off, and new bottles were filled. Tuan hugged Jack repeatedly, thanking him for coming to the rescue.

Jack smiled. "Don't worry, my friend, anytime."

Jack chatted with the factory workers, asking them where they came from and where they lived. To his amazement, many of the workers were orphans; most had grown up on the streets of Saigon or in the Mekong delta region. All the employees slept on the second floor of the factory. They didn't have another place to go.

One worker, Tui, walked up to Jack. "Thank you for saving my home."

Jack hadn't really understood how important the power plant to those people was. It was their home, everything they had.

"I am glad I could help."

Afterward, Jack walked around the factory, noticing several things that needed to be fixed so the plant could run better. *Maybe in another life,* he thought. He made a list of items for Tuan to consider repairing after he departed for America. After finishing some last-minute tuning of the systems, Jack left, saying goodbye to the team members.

"Mr. Jack, will we ever see you again?"

"God willing."

Tuan added, "Thank you, Jack. How can I pay you back?"

"No need; thank you for giving me a purposeful today." Jack continued to have thoughts of Linh, and the memory of her voice shattered his emotions. Not having the strength to cope with the loss, Jack looked at the water plant problem as a much-needed distraction.

Tuan dropped him off back at the hotel.

"See you later, Tuan. Take care." Tuan turned with a smile and a small tear in his eye.

Jack thought about whether he wanted to take a walk or just go back to his room, and he became sidetracked when a familiar voice reached out to him.

"Hey, Jack, how about a tiger beer?"

Always the complete smart-ass, Tien seemed to find him no matter what. "Sure, love one or two or three."

Tien laughed out loud. "Classic American, not sure about anything."

As the two gentlemen headed to the elevator, Tien asked, "Where is Ms. Linh?"

Jack chose not to reply and instead just smiled at his friend. They drifted toward their favorite table in the fifth-floor lounge. Designed similar to the Marriott Marquis in Times Square in New York, the lounge had an indoor atrium that opened all the way to the twenty-seventh floor. It was beautifully designed, with high tables, comfortable couches, and a gorgeous glass bar with neon blue lights shining on the counter. Jack and Tien seemed to enjoy their time, sitting on their favorite table, close enough to listen to the beautiful piano player rendering several romantic songs. Tien, noticing his friend was quieter than usual, asked what was on his mind.

"One beer or three?"

"Four, please!"

Tien ordered ten beers on ice with a plate of Vietnamese rolls. Jack thanked his dear friend for the beers and sat quietly beside him. After a few minutes, Tien sparked up a conversation.

"Jack, thank you for coming to my country. In the beginning, I didn't trust you very much, but I can see that you are a fine American gentleman with good in your heart. I hope you come back someday and see us again. I ask, please, do not forget us."

Jack, holding back his tears, replied, "Absolutely, I will never forget you."

Jack, needing time away from his room and thoughts of Linh, decided to have dinner with Tien. They discussed the soccer world cup, the upcoming NBA basketball season, and the NFL. Vietnam was most well-known for badminton. Jack knew about this sport and had noticed, in America, many Vietnamese students playing competitively.

"I like that sport. It is fast and requires total focus and a complete sense of purpose with every movement," he said.

To him, other sports, like basketball, had become less team-focused. Jack explained that many of the pro players just didn't play defense anymore. Tien agreed, but he still loved to follow American sports. While finishing his last beer, Tien asked Jack a favor.

"When you get home, could you send this letter to my brother in Chicago?"

"Absolutely, I will be more than happy, my friend."

Jack took one last drink of his beer, thanked the man for everything, and rose to head up to his room.

"Go with God, Jack."

He smiled back at Tien. "You as well, friend."

As the day began, Jack chose not to look at the river below. He missed the feeling of watching the sunrise with Linh. Jack rose to take one last shower before heading off to the airport. Letting the warm water hit his body, he remembered the passionate moments with Linh in the shower and on his bed. Jack thought about the sound of her heart beating, feeling her touches on his face, and hearing her soft words in his ear. He realized that he needed to move on and away from this issue, as a very challenging time was waiting for him back at home. Jack finished getting ready and left his room, heading to the elevator one last time. Upon reaching the lobby, he headed to the checkout line where he was met by the hotel manager, Ms. Bui, who assisted Jack with his checkout.

"Mr. Jack, everything is in order. Thank you for staying with us. I hope we can see you again. My staff spoke highly of you and declared you were their favorite guest."

Jack replied, "See you again, Ms. Bui."

As he headed to the main door to retrieve a taxi, several hotel staff, led by Tien, lined up to wish him luck on his journey back home—Tien, Van from the tea bar, Trang from room service, Wei from the lounge, Nguyen from the restaurant, and Hoi from security. Jack thanked each of them individually and then stopped and gave Tien a big hug.

"Thank you, brother."

With tears flowing down their eyes, the staff waved at Jack as he headed to the airport. Jack, also with an acute sense of emotion, cried quietly. The taxi, in classic Vietnamese form, sped up and weaved through traffic. Jack noticed that next to the cab was a group of cyclists led by his friend Tuan. Jack, seeing them for possibly the last time, waved at his team and wished them well. Tuan stopped the group and extended a thumbs up to his friend.

# Chapter 11
# Digression

During the long flight, Jack could only think about what was waiting for him at home. Based on the last call from Silvia and his children, Jack needed to be the one to ensure his family stayed whole. They needed to find a way to overcome these challenges together. Jack had not only family issues but also a fulltime job in technology sales that needed his attention. He owned several client accounts within his firm and needed to produce sizable transactions to maintain his position.

He reflected on his life, remembering when he was the same age as his children. Jack had also made choices that his parents disagreed with. He had to try and miss so many times, learning it the hard way. However, years later, he made peace with his parents. Today, they had a better and open relationship. *I can expect my children to be in the same place as I used to be.*

Toward the end of the flight, the stewardess woke up the passengers.

"Everyone, thank you for flying ANA airlines. We are about to land in Los Angeles."

Jack still felt a bit tired and headed to the restroom for a splash of water on his face. Within forty-five minutes, the plane taxied to the gateway. He gathered all his belongings and headed to customs and passport control. *Finally, I am at home.* Jack texted Silvia and Regina, saying that he should be there soon.

Regina replied, *No worry, Dad. We are here waiting for you.*

After getting his bags checked, Jack headed to the curbside to look for his wife and daughter.

"Hey!" yelled Jack. Silvia stopped the car so Jack could load his bags and jump into the passenger seat. "Hey guys, great to see you. Thank you for picking me up!"

Silvia, showing a brief smile, commented, "You lost weight. Wow!"

Regina added, "Dad, glad you are home."

As Silvia spun the car away, Jack discussed his trip. Regina, ever close to her father, asked a lot of questions about Vietnam. Silvia, meanwhile, seemed to have zero interest in what he had to say.

During the drive home, Silvia asked Jack, "Are you going back?"

He was shocked by the question. "Not sure, why?"

Jack had sensed Silvia would most likely bring this up later that day. Silvia drove the car in silence. Regina spoke just to say something about the Los Angeles Lakers and Clippers trade in basketball. Jack, feeling jetlagged, closed his eyes for the rest of the journey home.

Around 3 p.m., Silvia's car pulled up next to their home. Jack woke up after the long drive. He got out first to move his luggage out of the vehicle. Silently, Silvia entered the house while Regina stayed behind, helping her father with his bags. Even though he had been a week in Vietnam, Jack realized that the house was the same. However, the mood was different. As Jack put down his bag, William came down from his room.

"Dad, welcome home. How was Vietnam?"

"Great, son. Glad to see you!"

William smiled at his father and walked into the kitchen to check on his mother.

"Everyone, thank you for the welcome home. I will go upstairs and shower. I will be back soon."

Jack went upstairs to clean up and gather his thoughts on what was about to happen. During the long shower, he remembered cycling in Vietnam and how he needed to maintain his balance at all times. Einstein once said, "To keep your balance, you must continue moving forward." Those words really resonated with Jack. The situation at home needed to be addressed openly. Yet, Jack also realized that his life needed to be in balance. To get better and live longer, he needed to think about the choices he'd made. After his shower, Jack headed back downstairs to begin the healing process with his family.

Jack allowed himself to think about the love and passion he felt for Linh and how much he missed her. Yet, he knew it wasn't right to think about his lover at the moment. Jack's overwhelming sense of responsibility for Silvia and the children drove him to not think about Linh anymore. "There is no way I will ever see her again," he whispered to himself.

"William, congratulations on Arizona State University! Where else did you get accepted?"

William, surprised by his father's happiness, was about to answer but was interrupted by Silvia.

"He got accepted at the University of Oregon and the University of Arizona."

Jack, already sensing his wife's attitude, said, "Silvia, thank you. Please let him answer."

William, sensing trouble between his parents, left the room.

"William, hold up for a moment, son."

William walked away from him.

"He doesn't want to talk to you," explained Silvia.

"I would prefer to hear it from him, Silvia. This is an important life decision."

Silvia showed signs of anger in her eyes. Used to her hostile behavior, Jack chose not to fight with her. She preferred to fight in front of the children to show them who ran the house. After a few moments, Jack opened a dialog with his daughter, Regina.

"I understand you need some help. What can I do?"

Before Regina spoke, Silvia answered for her.

Upset, Jack said, "Silvia, stop! Let her answer."

"Regina, please tell me what is going on."

Regina, tearful, said, "Dad, I got removed from college today. My grades have been poor for over a year and a half now. I have been struggling, and I wanted to tell you."

Always wanting to be a good and loving parent, Jack still couldn't believe his daughter's statement. Jack believed in trusting his children first. He'd tried not micromanage them once they entered high school, hoping that they would learn to be self-aware and responsible for their own lives. They needed to get ready for the actual world.

"What!? You told me you were doing great!"

Regina was shaken by her father's reaction. "I am sorry, Dad."

Jack was not in the mood to forgive. "Regina, leave for a moment, please."

She got up from the couch and moved upstairs.

"Silvia, did you know about this? And if so, why didn't you say anything?"

Silvia was finishing her third glass of wine. "Jack, they are afraid of you. You are a terrible father."

Jack realized Silvia had encouraged their children to hide things from him, telling them to be scared of his reaction. They had been brainwashed to hold hateful feelings toward their father.

"Silvia, you keep telling the children that, and you are damaging their ability to deal with their problems correctly and to learn to own them up!"

Silvia, stubborn as always, said, "Well, Jack, if you weren't always traveling, maybe the children would trust you."

Jack sensed the root cause of the problem. "Silvia, I work hard so you don't have to. Is this the thanks I get?"

He realized that the conversation was going nowhere. "You are so non-appreciative."

Silvia, laughing out loud, replied, "Yeah, so are you!"

# Chapter 12
# Dishonesty

After the brief exchange between Jack and Silvia, they retreated to their parts of the house; Jack went to his TV room, while Silvia got another glass of wine, sitting in the downstairs entertainment area. Jack considered the position he was in. William and Regina continued to be influenced by their mother. Even if William was a brilliant student, he hadn't achieved his goals. For some reason, he believed that leaving his home was the only course to see a better life. Regina, also an excellent student, didn't have a clear direction for what she wanted to do in her life. Jack, revisiting Silvia's comment, recognized the challenge of traveling for work so much and not being at home all the time. Years back, they'd decided Silvia would be in charge of the children, and Jack would work. As the children moved up in school and Silvia hadn't finished high school, she realized that she couldn't help with their homework. When the children's report cards came back low, Jack and Silvia would argue why they were struggling so much at school.

Silvia defended her decision, always saying, "I am helping!" Yet, Jack knew that Silvia drank more wine each day.

Letting the time pass, Jack got up from the TV and walked into William's room.

"Son, do you have a minute?"

William, putting down his homework, said, "Yeah, Dad."

"Son, why do you want to leave?"

William closed his eyes and stared at the floor. After a few minutes, Jack rose and gave his son a hug and then walked out of the room.

After attempting to discuss things with William, Jack went to sleep early. He would address these issues another day.

He slept for nearly fifteen hours. Then he got up to take a quick shower, only to find Silvia sitting in the bathroom.

"Oh, you got up now," said Silvia.

"Yes, thank you for letting me sleep."

"Happy to be home, Jack?"

"Absolutely, no better place to be."

Silvia rose and stormed out of the room, heading downstairs.

After a long shower, Jack came down to find Regina at the breakfast table, reading. He knew he needed to help his daughter work this problem out.

"Regina, how about we head out for some breakfast?"

His girl was always ready for breakfast with her father. "Absolutely, Dad."

Close to their house, Jack and Regina stopped for sandwiches and coffee. They used the time to talk.

"Dad, I am sorry. I should have told you early that I was having problems. I know you trusted me."

"Regina, I love you so much. I know you felt pressured to be successful. The pressure is everywhere, and you need to get used to it. My role as your father is to help you get ready for the road ahead."

Regina understood what her father said. "Yeah, I know, Dad. You always wanted to teach us accountability for our actions. I am sorry."

"Reg, let's discuss how to move forward." Jack considered for a moment giving his daughter ideas on what she could with her life. Drawing from his own life, Jack had also dropped out of college and joined the military. Years later, he did go back to college and finished his undergraduate and master's degrees in global engineering technology and administration. The decision to leave school did not sit well with his father or mother. They wanted him to and graduate. But deep down, Jack was not ready to sit in a college and learn about life. He wanted to see the world and discover a new life outside of his family surroundings. Regina also had troubles at home, watching her parents fight way too often. Jack felt a deep sense of responsibility for Regina's education crisis. Jack second-guessed himself on many decisions. Those mistakes had played a role in William and Regina having challenges in school.

Regina smiled. "Yes, I agree—what do you recommend I do, Dad?"

"Reg, this is about you and what you feel inside. You alone know what you are capable of. I can only give you some ideas based on experiences, but in the end, you need to be honest with yourself."

Reg, looking away from her father and taking a sip of coffee, said, "Oh, Dad, I don't know—what will Mom say in a time like this?"

Jack knew Silvia wouldn't bring many ideas to the conversation. "Your mother will have her own ideas."

Regina got the drift and rolled her eyes. "I know, Dad. Mom has her own ideas about a lot of things."

Jack nodded back to his daughter. "With that being said, what do you want to do, Reg?"

"Well, I do like to fight, me being the first female wrestler in my school and all. Maybe the army?"

Jack was shocked. "Maybe not the army, but you are heading in the right direction."

Over the next few hours, Jack explained to this daughter how he'd ended up in the Marine Corps.

"Dad, I never knew the whole story about why you joined; I am sure Grandpa wasn't too thrilled."

Jack looked down for a moment before answering. "Nope, Grandpa was not happy at all. Grandma wasn't supportive either." Regina realized how much her father loved her. Listening to him discuss his struggles in life and how he overcame them inspired her to consider the military as a career option. Regina and her father talked about the various options.

"Please consider the Coast Guard; I believe you need the discipline and an alternative to learn things outside of the traditional college setting."

Jack remembered making the same decision several years before. At nineteen, he'd also failed out of college. Much to the dismay of his parents, he'd signed up for four years' active duty.

"Regina, I have been there. Let's take this forward and see what happens."

Regina rose from the restaurant table and gave her father an enormous hug. Feeling somewhat relieved, Jack drove her home to share the news with William and Silvia.

"Dad, how do I break the news to Mom?" she asked on the way.

Jack could never come up with the right words to talk to Silvia. Most of their discussions turned into arguments. "Be honest with her, Reg—this is your decision, and you believe this is your path forward." Reg nodded at her father and agreed with his advice.

After entering the house, Regina walked in to find her mother and brother.

"Mom, I just finished having breakfast with Dad. Do you have a moment?"

Silvia had just finished her morning tea. "Reg, whatever your father told you, I would consider getting advice from someone else!"

Jack just shook his head. Regina, staring her mother in the eyes, said, "Well, I made the decision to join the Coast Guard."

William, sitting in the next room, came in to see his sister. "That's a good move, Regina."

Silvia didn't share the same enthusiasm. "Regina, are you kidding me? Stay here, and we will figure something out—your father does not know everything!"

Regina, feeling a sense of strength and pride, answered, "No, Mother. I got this. This is my choice, not Dad's or yours."

Silvia stormed upstairs to her room. Jack hugged Regina and William. "Guys, I mean this—life is your decision. I am just your investor. What you need to help you figure out the next part of your life, I am here for."

William reluctantly hugged his father. Reg turned to him. "Daddy, I will never forget his moment, ever!"

"Great to be home, guys. Any ideas for dinner?"

Both children replied, "Yes, Chinese!" Jack was smiling for the first time since arriving home.

Jack called upstairs to ask Silvia if she wanted to have Chinese food. "Silvia, are you coming?"

Within a few minutes, Silvia came downstairs and proceeded to the garage without saying another word.

During dinner at the restaurant, William asked his father about Vietnam.

"Well, Dad, did you get to see everything you wanted to?"

As Jack was about to answer, Silvia snapped back to William, "Can we stop talking about that place!?"

Jack, wanting to keep the peace, said, "Yes, another time, son."

Silvia felt betrayed and an outsider in her own family—she had become bitter for the years when Jack spent more time with other people, including their children, than with her. Silvia always looked forward to getting away with her sisters and friends as a means for her to feel the love and fun in her life that she didn't get from Jack anymore. While Jack and the kids enjoyed the Chinese dinner, Silvia wanted to find a way to get away for a while.

Silvia commented, "Jack, my sisters and I are leaving for France. Take care of our trip."

Jack, especially in front of the children, rarely raised his voice even when Silvia became overly demanding on him. "Hun, let's discuss later."

"No, we are discussing now."

William looked over at his mother. "Mom, let's enjoy dinner. Then you and Dad can fight in private."

"Embarrassed at your parents?"

William was about to answer, but Jack intervened. "Silvia, I will be more than happy to help you and your sisters to go to France."

Regina looked at her mother with total disgust and decided not to speak for the rest of dinner. Silvia, all too pleased to watch how fast Jack caved in, said, "Good, that's more like it!"

Driving home, Silvia and Jack did not say a word to each other. William and Regina chose to text each other.

*Will, Mom is such an alcoholic. I can't believe she drinks as much as she does!*

William responded, *Well, Reg, Dad makes her drink. Look how many times he isn't home. I bet he is out screwing a bunch of women behind Mom's back.*

Regina looked over at her brother in the car with a complete look of disgust.

*Yah, probably Dad has someone in Vietnam, I bet. I can't blame him.*

*Reg, Mom is the one that needs our support now, not Dad!*

Reg just shook her head and mouthed, "Whatever."

Jack drove the car back to the family house. After parking, everyone departed in complete silence. Jack considered calling a family meeting to discuss the problems everyone had on their mind but optioned not to because those meetings usually only made things worse.

Upon entering the house, Jack held the door for Silvia, William, and Regina. Silvia headed to the wine closet to open a fresh bottle. William and Regina headed to their rooms and Jack departed to this home office.

Arriving at his home office, Jack knew the problems with Silvia continued to create a bigger problem between William and Regina. The last thing he wanted was for his children to suffer as a result of his issues with their mother. Trying to take his mind off things, Jack started to plan out Silvia's trip to France.

After careful planning and organization, Jack arranged a fourteen-day trip to France, including a stop in London for twenty-four hours. He booked his wife up in a five-star hotel, providing first-class seats on the plane. Jack scheduled the trip in May, just before the tourist season hit France. Once he completed his trip planning, he emailed the details to Silvia. She was happy to travel with her sisters, party, and carry on like she was twenty-five again. Jack, understanding this, had no issues with Silvia leaving and traveling without him. He preferred not to travel with her due to her excessive drinking and emotional outbursts. During several trips to the family's house in Hawaii, Jack had found Silvia drunk at the beachside bar, talking to strange men and sharing with them her sad story of being married to Jack.

Even during their time dating, Jack knew Silvia was an alcoholic. During their marriage, Jack had asked Silvia to attend Alcoholics Anonymous meetings to help stop. Silvia didn't believe she had a drinking problem, nor that she was causing any of the problems at home.

After finishing the trip planning for Silvia, Jack headed downstairs to share the information with her. Already having finished a few glasses of wine, Silvia looked at him with despair.

"What, Jack?"

"You are booked for next Thursday. France does not require a visa. Only your American passport is needed."

Silvia laughed. "What if I want take a cruise while I am there?"

Jack sat down. "We don't have the money for you to take a cruise or stay more than fourteen days."

Silvia tried to see how much she could get out of him. "Come on, Jack. We only live once!"

"How many glasses of wine have you had?"

Silvia stood up and threw her wine glass at Jack, hitting him in the chest. The impact caused the glass to shatter into several pieces. Jack stood and headed toward her. At the last moment, he had a view of Linh in his mind.

Seeing Jack back off, Silvia laughed loudly. "Come!" she screamed. But he headed to the garage to retrieve the dustpan and brush to clean up the broken glass. Silvia just watched her favorite show on television.

Jack took extra caution ensuring every piece of glass was picked up. He used tape to rub against the floor to get even the smallest pieces. After he was completed, he walked over to Silvia. "I will email you the details of your trip."

Silvia, already passed out from the wine, didn't hear him.

# Chapter 13
# Cessation

On the day Silvia departed for her trip to France with her sisters, she walked downstairs to say goodbye to her children. "Guys, have fun. Don't listen to your father!"

William and Regina looked at their mother with mixed reactions. William said, "Mom, have a good time." Regina decided not to say anything.

Jack just said, "Be well." Silvia laughed as she exited the house. As Jack watched his children's reaction after their mother left, his heart broke. He knew that the problems with Silvia and him made William and Regina's lives miserable. While he watched his children head for their rooms, Jack started to think about things he could do with them.

He loved to travel with Regina and William. During the same week Silvia departed for France, Jack organized a vacation with the children to visit his parents in Virginia.

Jack arranged a trip to Virginia. He went upstairs to break the news to the kids. "Guys, let's take a trip and see Grandma and Grandpa!"

William smiled at his father. "I'm in."

Regina came out of her room and gave her dad a big hug. "Let's do it."

Jack went into his office and decided to call his father. Jack Sr., a retired engineer, loved to spend time with his grandchildren. "Dad, it's Jack."

"Son, how are you? How are my grandchildren?"

Jack knew how much his father loved William and Regina. "They are great, Dad; we'd like to come east to see you and Mom if you are open. Maybe sneak in a round of golf?"

Jack Sr. was a former top golfer in college and always welcomed a game with his son. "Of course, tell those children to bring their 'A' game!"

Jack laughed. "Will do. By the way, Dad, how is Mom?"

The old man hesitated. "Jack, your mother is slipping—let the children know before they arrive."

Jack nodded, a tear coming to his eye.

Jack emailed the plans to his father and his only sibling, his brother Pierce. For years, they didn't speak much. Both boys had a difficult childhood together and never got alone even when they were older. Pierce was a twenty-year veteran of the US Navy, never married, and chose to live near his parents in lieu of moving away. Jack had left years ago after joining the Marines and never gone back.

On the day of departure for Virginia, Jack loaded up the car with William and Regina's golf clubs and luggage. "All ready, guys?" Jack put the car into drive and headed to the airport.

Jack, William, and Regina landed seven hours later in Virginia. Waiting for them at the airport was Pierce, standing tall and proud. As both kids spotted their uncle, they ran to greet him.

"Uncle Pierce, what's up?"

"Look at you guys. Ready for some action?"

Jack walked up. "Pierce, thanks for picking us up!"

"Wife away on another trip with her sisters?"

Jack shook his head. "France this time."

Pierce nodded. "All for the better. Come on. Car's this way."

As Pierce loaded up the car, he said, "Jack, we need to stop and see our parents first."

Within twenty minutes, they were pulled up at their parents' house. Jack Sr. was sitting out front and rose from his chair to greet his sons and grandchildren.

"Oh my, you guys have grown!"

Both Regina and William gave their grandpa an enormous hug and kiss on his cheek.

"Jack, you look well."

"Thanks, Dad."

The children went inside to greet their grandmother. After the hugs, the family settled down for a delightful home-cooked meal cooked by Jack's mother.

"Grandma, the food is fantastic!"

Grandma Terry replied, "Always for my grandchildren!" She loved to hear her grandchildren's voices and to watch them eat her food.

While they enjoyed the meal, Pierce asked Regina what her plans were in the future.

"I joined the Coast Guard."

Pierce just stared. "You want to chase drug lords and boat people?" Jack gave his brother a strong look, but Regina chose to answer for herself.

"Don't forget I get fire guns and missiles, Uncle Pierce." She gave her father a playful wink.

"Well, be careful out there, young lady."

"William, I believe you have some college choices as well?" asked Jack Sr.

William felt cornered. "Yes, Grandpa. Let's chat later, okay?"

Terry's food always left smiles on people's faces. Her pot-roast was legendary among the family members. Jack appreciated his mother's cooking.

"Mom, thanks. Let me help clean up."

"Absolutely, son, have at it!"

Jack rose to clear the dishes. Regina interrupted, "I got this, Pops."

"Thank you. Let's do this together."

While they cleaned, William leaned in. "Grandpa, can we go somewhere to talk?"

Grandpa Jack, smiling, led his grandson to his office. "Shoot, young man."

William always felt he could share anything with his grandfather. Jack Sr. knew about his son and Silvia's marriage problems. He feared that their problems became William's and Regina's as well. William expressed the pain and tragedy unfolding at home between his parents.

"Grandpa, I know my dad means well, but he is in my life too much, and my mother is only trying to protect me."

Grandpa Jack nodded slowly as his grandson detailed what was troubling him.

"My father doesn't care about what I do or how I do it."

"William, when your father was young, I also traveled way too much for work. Japan, UK, Singapore, Bermuda, Iceland, you name it. I was gone for months at a time." He paused for a moment to let those facts sink in. "I never coached my sons in sports. I never attended back-to-school nights, and I never helped with homework."

"So what did you do when you came home after all those trips?"

Grandpa Jack hesitated. "I drank my beers, smoked my cigarettes, and read my books. I also yelled at my kids for not doing well in school!"

William took a step back and realized that his father didn't do any of those things. His father had coached him and Regina for seven years. They together had won two championships. His father had always helped with homework, even when he traveled far away. William didn't understand what his father went through. After a few minutes, William stood up and hugged his grandfather.

"Thank you, Grandpa. I have a few choices for college. I should ask my dad what he thinks."

Grandpa Jack smiled ear to ear. "Yes, I believe your father could speak with some experience."

Even though it was a cold morning the next day, Jack, Jack Sr., Regina, and William headed off to play a round of golf.

"Will, head down and hold your grip," said Jack Sr. William listened to his grandfather and hit the golf ball over two hundred and twenty-five yards.

"Crushed it!"

Regina grabbed her favorite three-wood club out of her bag. "Move, Will, let a real golfer hit!"

William always got the better of Regina on the golf course. "Hit it, lady!" With her head down, Regina lined up her shot and hit the ball perfectly. The ball sailed past him by twenty-five yards.

"Yep, the real golfer showed up!" laughed Regina.

While they rode ahead on their golf cart, Jack and his father followed behind. "Jack, hope you are well?"

Jack shook his head. "Silvia and I are done—been that way for a while, Dad."

"I know. Did you meet someone in Vietnam?"

Jack looked down at his feet. "Yes."

His father shrugged his shoulders. "You need to own that decision. What will happen next?"

Jack described his choice to stay with Silvia until the children were old enough to be on their own.

"Sounds like you have everything figured out. I will tell you that no matter how much you want to leave Silvia, the children need to come first."

Jack knew that. "Yes, that is my plan—no matter what, I need to be here for them."

His father nodded. "Well, what about this lady in Vietnam? Any future?"

Jack reluctantly looked away. "No, I don't believe so."

"I had a few of those in my day. I had a friend in Singapore once when you and Pierce were young. Nice lady, I don't remember much about her."

Jack shot a look back. "I never knew that. Did Mom know?"

"I think she knew, yes."

He was curious to know more. "What ever happened to her?"

Jack Sr. stopped the golf cart for a moment to answer his son. "I don't know—my company stopped sending me to Singapore after we lost the big contract. We didn't exactly have instant messaging back then, or emails."

They rode in silence until they caught with William and Regina. "Dad, come on. Putt out!" yelled William. Jack jumped out of the cart with his putter and headed up to the green to finish his putting. With a smooth stroke, Jack dropped the ball into the cup. "Birdie!"

Two hours and nine holes later, the weather was getting even colder, so the family headed to the local Clyde's restaurant in Tyson's Corner for some early lunch.

"Grandpa, you still play great golf," said Regina.

"Yes, you can thank your father—he really helped with my game!"

After a filling lunch, Jack drove the other three back to Grandpa's house to check on Terry. Recently, she'd been diagnosed with cancer in the throat. A quarter-century of smoking had finally started to catch up with her.

"Mom, are you home?"

Hearing no reply, he ran throughout the house, searching for his mother, only to find her not breathing, lying on her bed.

"Mom!" screamed Jack, running to his mother's side, checking her pulse and breathing. "Mom, wake up!" There was nothing in response. "Dad, dial 911!"

Within seconds, William, Regina, and Sr. ran into the bedroom and watched their father give his mother mouth-to-mouth.

"Stop!" yelled Jack Sr. "Let her be."

Jack didn't understand. "Why, Dad?"

"Son, this is how your mother wanted to pass." He handed Jack a document. "Last medical request. Read it."

His mother didn't want any form of resuscitation. She'd lived in too much pain with cancer, and she just wanted to pass when it was her time. Jack cried, knowing he hadn't gotten to say goodbye to this mother. William and Regina came over to hold him.

Pierce, hearing the news from Jack, rushed over to the house. He broke down at the sight.

"Jack, where were you? Why weren't you home with Mom?"

"We were golfing with Dad."

Pierce was furious. "You should have been here—you have never been here!"

Jack stepped up to him. "I have a life, and I made a life for my family. What the hell have you done!?"

Pierce leaned in and threw a punch at him. The fisted connected with Jack's face and knocked him back. Then Pierce charged toward him, but with a shifty move, Jack dropped to one knee and launched a punch into his brother's stomach. The force of the blow knocked the wind out of Pierce, sending him gasping to the ground.

"Stop it, both of you!" screamed Jack Sr.

William and Regina ran over and grabbed their father. Pierce started to cough up blood, while Jack's face began to swell up. Pierce got to his feet. "Get the hell out of here, Jack—go back to your lovely home."

Jack, not knowing how to comfort his brother, just said, "Yeah, you're right, Pierce."

Pierced walked over to his father. "Dad, please let me know if there's anything I can do."

Jack Sr. simply replied, "She went the way she wanted to, son."

Pierce called the funeral home to come for his mother. Jack Sr. and Terry had made arrangements several months before for the burial. Within an hour, the hearse pulled up. "Mr. Kendall?" asked the driver.

Pierce pushed Jack out of the way. "Here."

The funeral home personnel entered the house and began their process to remove Terry. Pierce stood over his mother. "I will take care of Dad. Mom, don't worry," whispered Pierce. Jack Sr. bowed down to one knee and gave his departed wife a kiss on her cheek. William and Regina did the same. Jack chose to wait outside for the funeral personnel to come out. As the stretcher departed the house, Jack walked over and touched his mother's face. "I am sorry, Mom; I should have been here more." After a few moments, they loaded Terry into the hearse.

Later on, Jack sat on the patio in the back of the house, reaching for his phone to call Silvia.

"Hey Silvia, I just wanted you to know that my mother passed away."

Silvia replied, with little regard for the moment, "Oh, honey, we are in France having a great time. Sorry about Terry. She was old!"

Jack, disgusted with Silvia's selfishness, hung up the phone.

"Kids, your mother is having a great time in France."

William stared at him. "Dad, she should have a great time—if Mom was here, she couldn't do anything to help Grandma."

Jack looked away for a moment. he knew that Silvia had no feelings other than for the kids and herself. "I expected your mother to be there for me similar to the time when I was there when her mother passed."

"I remember that, Dad. That just isn't Mom, not her style."

"Yep, I guess so."

After a few days, the family went to the funeral home and held a brief service for Terry. Pierce stood up and made the first blessings. "Thank you all for being here today. Mom was a loving woman and a great mother. She held our family together for so many years and always looked after my brother and me. While I served in the navy, Mom always wrote letters to me. Mom, I will miss you."

After pausing for a moment, Pierce returned to his seat. Jack got up and headed to the speaker podium. As he walked past his brother, Pierce mumbled, "Make it quick." Jack laughed under his breath and then took a deep breath.

"Mom meant everything to us. Without her words of encouragement, love, and cooking, I would not be here today. When my kids were born, Mom made the children their first blanket and first sweaters. I will never forget her smile and her words of love. I love you, Mom." Becoming tearful, Jack departed the podium and headed back to his seat. Jack Sr. rose up next and headed to the podium. Casting a loving glaze over his departed wife, he spoke in a very low tone.

"Terry, when you said yes to my marriage proposal fifty-three years ago, I knew this day would come. I hope the good lord looks after you in heaven, and please save a seat for me on the porch. I will miss you, my wife." Holding back tears, he walked slowly back to his seat.

William and Regina, both crying, sat next to their father without saying a word. After a few closing remarks, the family rose and departed the funeral home. Once they reached the parking lot, Pierce turned to the kids. "You guys take care of yourselves." They walked over and hugged their uncle.

Jack said, "Take care, Pierce. If you decide to come to California someday, you are always welcome." Pierce gave a half-smile and then jumped in the truck and drove off.

Jack looked at his father. "Dad, anything I can do for you before we head out tomorrow?" The man leaned over and gave his son a hug.

"Take care of these kids, Jack—please."

"I'm on it."

The next morning, Jack Sr. said goodbye to this son and his grandchildren before departing for New York to spread Terry's ashes off the Brooklyn Bridge—the same spot where he proposed to her, as per her wishes. William, Regina, and Jack headed to Dulles Airport and boarded a plane home to California.

While sitting on the flight, Jack realized his challenge in life wasn't that his children didn't love him; they did. Jack just needed to find a balance between helping others and helping himself. He'd always wanted to learn to develop a healthy and productive life and now realized that he could achieve both.

When Jack spoke about this with Silvia, he always got so much pushback because his wife wanted so much more from him regardless of if it made him sick or financially broke.

A few days later, after returning from the trip to France, Silvia, ever so happy from the vacation, didn't take a moment to thank Jack for the journey. She only mentioned that she ran out of money because of his poor planning. Jack, just recovering from his mother's passing, didn't want to fight with her. It only drove Jack's blood pressure and sugar level to the point of continued migraine and stroke conditions.

Jack thought about the past six months and realized that he could change his life if he really wanted to. Previously, he'd believed that God placed him here on this Earth to be a provider to his family, work hard, attend church, and help others in need. Doing something just for himself wasn't something he thought of. Jack didn't want to take away any more resources and time from Silvia and the children. He felt that by thinking of himself, he was being selfish.

Jack realized that his health, both physical and mental, was failing. Even with cycling, swimming, and running, Jack's sugar was above one hundred and seventy-eight and his ac1 over 7.5. Jack's weight hovered around two hundred and sixty-five pounds. Along with his health issues, after fighting with Silvia, he continued to suffer from headaches, causing him to throw up in the bathroom just to relieve the pain.

Silvia continued to show very little interest in Jack's wellbeing. She needed him to continue to work hard, bringing home money and sending her off on her vacations with family members. Silvia didn't love Jack anymore, but she loved her life so much that she would tolerate the situation. She would act the part, in front of friends and family, that her marriage was great. Yet, after a few glasses of wine, Silvia spoke negatively about her life. This adverse action, most times, began with exaggeration of the truth to gain sympathy from others.

In the weeks following more doctor visits, Jack was cycling near Camp Pendleton, California. He stopped to overlook the Pacific Ocean toward Vietnam. *My Linh, if you can hear me, I miss you, my love.*

Jack, allowing himself a personal moment, smiled as he remembered the passion between him and Linh, the long walks in Saigon and the romantic talks while lying in bed together. It had been eight months since the last time he saw or spoke to her. He didn't know if she was okay or even if she'd stayed married to Vo. He wondered if she was happy or sad. After a moment, Jack opened his phone and sent Linh a message.

*My love, it has been too long. I miss you, and I hope you are safe and happy. I am doing okay. I need to make a life choice or I will die. I hope in my lifetime, I can see you again.*

Jack continued his cycling adventure, peddling south toward Oceanside. While riding, Jack continued to think about his direction in life. He thought about the possibility of returning to Vietnam someday. While this dream seemed to be very farfetched, Jack was confident of having a better life in the future. He loved his children so much that he couldn't leave his wife when they were small. Jack was always deeply concerned that his children wouldn't turn out well if he wasn't a part of their lives. But Jack also realized that his life wasn't going well.

Upon reaching downtown Carlsbad on his bike, Jack stopped off at his favorite coffee place, The Coffee Grind on State Street, and ordered a triple espresso. Nothing helped Jack more than fresh espresso. While he continued to take a mental inventory of himself, his phone buzzed.

*Jack, so good to hear from you again, my love. I missed you so much. I am deeply sorry I couldn't see you before you left my country. Things are very challenging here in Vietnam, especially with my stick.*

Jack read each word in the message with a sense of joy and sadness. Linh closed the message with, *'My love, I promise I will see you again someday.'* Overwhelmed with emotion, he cried quietly in the coffee shop and then took a moment to compose himself before replying.

*My love, Linh, I miss you so much. I will find a way to return to you.*

Jack looked at his watch and realized that it was 4:30 a.m. in Vietnam. *She's probably going back to sleep.* Jack finished his triple espresso and headed out on his bike again. He needed to be home to take the children for dinner.

After a very uneventful dinner, Jack sat down next to William in the TV room.

"Son, any thoughts as to where you plan to study?"

William, remembering the conversation with Grandpa, asked, "Dad, where do you think I should go?"

Jack was taken aback by the openness of his son. "Son, this is your decision; I will support whatever you decide."

William felt a sense of peace between them. "Thanks, Dad. But what do you think?"

Jack thought before answering. "William, this is your decision. In life, we make good ones and bad ones. We also learn to own them. I have made terrible decisions in my life. However, I owned up to it. I also made great decisions and enjoyed the rewards. In the end, only you know what you are capable of and how far you are willing to challenge yourself. With that being said, son, I would recommend software engineering."

William was listening intently to his father. "Great advice, Dad."

Jack concluded by telling him, "Please remember, college is for a gain of knowledge. You still need to accept the knowledge and to do something with it."

William was an A+ student in computer science in high school. He also had excellent math skills. He would make a great engineer. After some further consideration, William thanked his dad again.

"I will let you know what I decide."

Jack hugged his son and told him how much he loved him. After William walked off to his room, Silvia walked into the TV area, screaming at the top of her lungs, "My turn, Jack!"

Silvia, never a loss for words, said to Jack, "Okay, Jack, I would appreciate you not giving advice to the children if I am not in the room."

She never would agree with him in front of the kids. She would, later on, instruct the children in private in many cases to ignore him. In many cases, her opinions would be the opposite of Jack's.

"Silvia, I believe it is okay for me to speak to my children on my own. You are always most welcome to sit and listen so you can contradict me after they leave the room."

"That is because you are always wrong!"

Jack, sensing another argument, retreated to his office. "Thanks for the pointers. Have another glass of wine."

# Chapter 14
# Frontward

In the office, Jack opened his laptop and set up a fresh excel spreadsheet titled: *Change of life, balance, and road to happiness*. He added a password to the file so only he could open it. Over the next two hours, Jack created several columns including health, happiness, job, William, Regina, and Silvia. He created rows, which included a scoring system of good, better, and bad, green for good, yellow for better, and red for bad. As he added some notes on each subject, he kept coming back to the word 'happiness.'

Jack wanted to still be the provider for this family. He also acknowledged that he needed to change course to become a happier and better person. He then created a new column for happiness today and listed things that made him happy. These items included ensuring the children were comfortable, safe, and ready for the world.

After a few hours, Jack took a deep breath to remember the formula of balance: *To maintain balance on a bike, you need to keep moving forward.* That really stuck with him. He added a column: *Happiness for Jack.*

With each item added to his list, Jack felt a sense of guilt. He never thought of himself first in his life. As he thought about this list, only one word kept coming up, 'Linh.' When Jack added words like 'cycling the world,' this thought led back to Linh. Like owning a business in Asia, presenting at a technology conference in China, or selling technology in Singapore, all those ideas led back to her. While this notion seemed to please Jack, he knew being married would present several impossible bridges that he couldn't cross.

He remembered the sunrise over the Saigon River with Linh and knowing that no matter how much he loved her, there would always be a space between them. Keeping that in mind, Jack continued to daydream about how he could go back to Vietnam. While Jack was typing away, his daughter Regina entered the office.

"Dad, I went to the Coast Guard recruiter today. He said I can qualify for ship radar engineer."

Jack was excited about this fantastic news. "Well done, what is the next step?"

After she explained, he asked her, "Do you think I am too much in your life? Would you prefer if I ease it up and let you act without so much influence by me?"

Regina replied, "You been drinking, Dad?"

"No, I prefer not to drink anymore."

"Good for you. Yes, I would love for you to let me do my thing. Let me make my own mistakes."

Jack realized that this was the first step in becoming a better parent. "I agree I am here to help and support you. Please consider me an investor in your life."

Regina was very excited to hear this from her father. "Great, Dad! Can I get a tattoo?"

Jack looked at his young daughter becoming a strong, independent woman. "It is up to you," he said.

Once Regina departed her father's office, Jack updated his happiness spreadsheet with details about Regina's future, including the tattoo. Smiling for the first time in a long while, Jack asked William to join him for dinner that night.

"What about Mom? Is she coming too?"

"How about you and I hang out tonight and chat?"

"Dad, no thanks, unless Mom gets to come along."

Jack sighed. "You are right. Let me go ask your mother."

Jack found Silvia opening another bottle of wine. "Hey, before you do that, I'd like to take you and William out for dinner to discuss his college choices."

Silvia was already feeling the effects of the wine she'd drunk earlier with her friends. "Jack, give it a rest! Let him figure it out. He doesn't need your input."

"Silvia, I should share with him my experiences, and hopefully, he can learn something from me."

"Jack, are you kidding me?"

Jack realized this was a no-win argument, so he took a fresh approach. "Silvia, you have years of education experience. Maybe you can share some ideas with our son."

Silvia was beginning to laugh. "Funny, Jack."

She had never finished high school. She'd spent most of her life working in bars.

"Okay, Silvia, I just wanted to ask." He went upstairs to his son's room. "Mom believes this isn't a good use of her time. How about we head out?"

William replied, "No need, Dad. I will figure it out."

Jack, taking a deep breath, nodded and walked back to his office. It was better to keep the peace at home as much as possible.

He realized that he was trying too hard with his family. After taking a moment for quiet prayer, Jack realized that his children needed to learn from their own mistakes. It was the only way to become adults. *I need to get used to this. Okay, Jack, what is next?*

He wrote for the next two hours in the spreadsheet, focusing on things he felt would lead to a new level of happiness, giving him a sense of purpose. Jack knew it was the only way to become healthy and to feel complete. He loved his children, but he also knew his current life would only lead him to his death.

Jack started with his data map, showing that all roads led back to Linh. He began by stating what he didn't accomplish when he went to Vietnam.

- *I didn't find the nuns.*
- *How can I help Tuan and Tien fix their water company and make it better?*

If he was an investor in Vietnam, he would get a long-term visa. He would also gain access to American companies in the country. Moreover, this would give him excellent work experience as to how to run a global company.

The thought of owning a company in Vietnam and making a difference to others appealed to Jack. If he found the nuns, then what? Maybe the nuns could use some water in some way? These ideas created an incredible flow of energy on Jack. Something he hadn't felt in many years. *Before you get ahead of yourself, Jack, ask what Silvia and the children would think.* As Jack crafted these ideas, he needed to realize that the more he spent seeking his goal, the less he would be there for his children. Before long, Jack closed his laptop to rest his mind.

After dinner, Silvia started her normal conversation. "Jack, I want to go back to Hawaii with my sisters. Please put it together."

"Absolutely," he said. "When do you want to go?"

Silvia mentioned a few dates, and Jack said he would work on it.

Later, while he was watching TV, William came up and asked for a favor.

"Hey, Dad, I want to attend college here in California, but I want to live at home for a while."

Jack understood William's thinking. "Are you doing this because you want to stay close to Tricia?"

Tricia Howard-Smith and William had been dating since middle school. Tricia's parents had also recommended their daughter to attend school in California.

"Son, what do you plan to study?"

"Software engineering, Dad."

"That's a great choice. I will support this, absolutely."

William was thankful to his father for giving him the space to make his own decisions. Deep down, he knew his parents wouldn't stay together, but he loved his family very much. He also knew he needed to live his own life.

"Dad, I want to be here for Mom, but I understand if things don't work out. I know you are still a great dad."

Jack didn't know how to react. "Son, I believe your mother and I will be fine. Please look after your life now, just like we have to."

William nodded in approval and walked back to his room to call Tricia. He wanted to let her know the glorious news.

Jack knew that leaving Silvia would create a complete disruption to his children's life. Yet, listening to William's comment gave Jack a look into his children's perspective about their home life.

Jack closed his eyes for a moment, seeing a loving memory of Linh, and asked God to look over her. *God, please help my Linh with her life journey and that she finds peace for herself and Ngoc, amen.* After Jack completed his prayer, he drifted asleep on the couch.

The next morning, Jack awoke to hear that the TV was still on, and he was still in the loft.

"I guess I must have slept here all night," he said softly.

Jack smiled, reflecting on the peace he felt being there alone and away from Silvia. Jack rose and headed to the bedroom to take a shower and clean up. Silvia was still in bed. Having been home from France for a while now, Silvia sensed a greater change in Jack. She felt many times a deep sense of regret for not being good to Jack. While in France, Silvia had felt several times that she should be with Jack and the kids and not out partying for strangers. Over time, Silvia knew Jack wanted something more than what she could offer him. Yet, she didn't know how to let Jack know she still cared.

"Jack, are we okay? I mean, is our marriage going to be fine?" she asked.

Jack stopped in his tracks for a moment and turned to her. "I just want to be happy; everything I am doing, and all that I plan to do, is to allow me to be happy again."

"What does that mean, Jack? Are you leaving me?"

"Silvia, we all have choices on how we live and behave. I need to make some changes, including being happy each day." Jack didn't want to carry the conversation any further. "William is going to school soon. He plans to attend the same school as Tricia."

Silvia didn't want to change the subject. "Jack, answer me!"

Jack knew she was more concerned about her life than their marriage. "Silvia, please be happy, and I will do the same."

He stripped off the clothes and went into the shower. After he washed and shaved, Jack retreated into his office and worked on Silvia's request for the Hawaii trip. After a few hours of checking his reward points, savings account, and airline mileage, Jack put together a trip for October. It was only three months away.

"Silvia, all done, dear. Please check your email."

Silvia was excited for the opportunity to travel again. "Thanks!" She needed Jack in her life as a provider, not as a loving husband anymore. While on the surface Silvia was all smiles in order to keep the peace at home, deep down she wanted nothing more to do with him. She loved being out and traveling without anyone telling her not to drink anymore.

"No problem, dear."

After completing the bookings for his wife's trip, Jack allowed himself to daydream about Vietnam and seeing Linh again. He realized that when Silvia departed for Hawaii, he would be left alone at the house. William would be with Tricia, and Regina would be heading to the Coast Guard training. So what now?

Out of curiosity, Jack looked at all of his airline points across several carriers, including ANA, Delta, and EVA. After reviewing his available points, he whispered, "Oh my God, I have enough." He also logged into his Marriott account and found that he also had plenty of hotel points.

Jack emailed his boss to see if he had available vacation days. Within a few moments, he found out he had fourteen days available. Staring at his computer screen, Jack took a long breath. "Okay, Day One of the new happiness." He started to book everything to head back to Vietnam.

# Chapter 15
# Advancement

Jack couldn't contain himself long enough. *How do I tell Linh I am coming back?* He realized that Linh's marriage life could be in disarray, and his sudden return to Vietnam could make matters worse for her and Ngoc. So he focused his efforts on the other reasons to go back to Vietnam—searching for the nuns and how he could become part of the water business. Jack knew that every step he made in this new journey would take him away from his current life. *Am I willing to risk losing my children's love and respect or will I gain something more that I need?* He meant better health and love in his heart. Weighing out the risks, he made his move to realize his path to happiness by contacting his friends back in Vietnam.

Jack opened his Gmail and wrote an email to Tuan and Tien.

*Tuan,*

*My friend, I plan on a return trip to Vietnam in October, and I'd love to take another cycle tour of Vietnam. Please, let me know if you have an open spot for me.*

*Jack*

Jack also typed a message to his friend Tien.

*Dear Tien,*

*I am planning a return trip to Vietnam in October. I have already booked the Renaissance Hotel, and I am looking forward to seeing you and the staff again. I ask for a moment, my friend. I need your help in finding someone.*

*Jack*

Jack told him the story of the Catholic nuns and Operation Babylift, explaining the event's timeline and when the planes stopped coming. After Jack finished typing the emails to his friends, he sat in his chair, considering for a moment how he would let Linh know he was coming back.

Measuring his words closely, Jack wrote to Linh.

*My love,*

*Linh, it has been twelve months since we saw each other. I plan to return to Vietnam again in October to take another cycling tour and continue my search for the nuns. I would love to see you once again. I miss seeing you, kissing you, and loving you.*

*I have realized that your personal life is very similar to mine here in America. Your stick and my stick are very similar. Hopefully, my trip won't bring any hardship to you or Ngoc. If I can only see you for an hour, that would be worth it to me.*

*Please, let me meet you if you'd like to see me again, my love.*

*Jack.*

Jack released a breath in relief. He could only imagine what Linh looked like today. He remembered her beautiful skin, perfect smile, and lovely hair. *Does she want to see me again?* He could only wait and see if she replied. He smiled again, thinking of going back to Vietnam. Cycling was still a vast passion for Jack. He couldn't wait to cycle through Saigon with the team. The thrill of cutting between cars and around a million scooters put such an enormous grin on his face. He turned off the light and headed into the TV room for some late-night movie time.

Morning came early for Jack. He heard his phone buzz, alerting him of incoming emails and text messages. The first message he received was from Tuan.

*Jack, absolutely, we welcome you back to my country. We will create whatever cycling tour you want, my friend. The entire team is ready to race again with you across the entire city. This time, we will cycle the city at night and stop for some snails and beers!*

Jack, already feeling more energetic than before, typed back,

*Tuan, count me in, my friend. See you in October!*

With a newfound sense of purpose, Jack got up and showered, getting ready for the day, wondering who else would reply.

Silvia, already up and starting her day, couldn't wait.

"Jack, the Hawaii trip isn't long enough. I want to stay longer."

"Silvia, let me figure out what I can do."

"Are you kidding me? How much did you spend in Vietnam?"

Jack, not wanting to spoil his already good mood, said, "Yes, Silvia. Let me finish getting dressed, and I will look at your trip again."

Silvia, smiling like she'd just won another battle, walked away proudly. Jack thought about his path and where his life could take him. *Live to fight another day.* Once Jack finished his shower and grabbed his morning coffee, he worked his way up to his office. He wanted to update his master spreadsheet, including Silvia's trip, along with Regina and William's plans. He realized that his entire life was about to unfold in a new direction. In a few months, William would start his new college, studying computer engineering, while living with Tricia. Regina had already left for the Coast Guard, and now Silvia wanted to spend more time away from him.

*I didn't realize how all of this was happening at once.* Overwhelmed with this near-future reality, Jack paused for a moment and asked God for strength and guidance. *God, please look after my children as they embark on their new lives into adulthood. Please watch over them.* Feeling a sense of peace within himself for the first time in a long time, he completed scheduling his projects.

Jack looked at Silvia's schedule. Based on what he already worked on, she was planning to go for two full weeks. *She wants to stay longer?* Considering that Silvia always overspent his money on her vacations, he added another two weeks. That would cost another $10,000.

*I need to make this happen.* He looked at his investment accounts and bank accounts. He sold off shares of stock and transferred the funds to his account. Jack knew he was spending his retirement money to go back to Vietnam and pay for Silvia's trips. He knew that spending his money now would impact his life later. However, he also was not ready to leave Silvia yet. These trips gave needed space to help with his personal recovery while giving Silvia what she wanted at the moment.

"Silvia, do you have a moment?"

"Yes, what is it?"

"I extended your Hawaii trip for another two weeks. I sold some stock to cover your trip."

Silvia, a bit shocked, said, "You sold our stock to pay for this?"

"Yes!"

"Well then, I guess I am going to Hawaii for a month. What about my spending money?"

Jack had learned to expect her selfishness. "That's part of the ten thousand."

"Jack, if I am gone, what are you planning to do?"

Quick and well-calculated, he said, "I am going back to Vietnam to cycle and hopefully, on this trip, find the Catholic nuns."

Feeling a rush of adrenaline, Jack couldn't contain his smile back to his wife. This news took Silvia a moment to comprehend.

"You are doing what? You're going back?"

"Yes, I am going back for three weeks. I will cycle again and continue to seek some answers."

Silvia thought about how to respond. "Well, Jack, I don't know if we can afford your trips like that."

"Silvia, any chance you can't go to Hawaii and maybe stay local here with your family? That could save money as well?"

"Jack, if you go to Vietnam, we will need to reconsider our marriage. I think you have another woman over there."

Jack wanted to come clean and tell Silvia, but he wasn't ready to deal with the financial impact nor the emotional toll on the children or himself. He knew that time would come, but not now.

"Silvia, yes, let's have that conversation when I get back. We need to talk about our marriage. Enjoy your trip!"

"Enjoy Vietnam, Jack."

After her departure, Jack began to daydream about his upcoming trip, hoping to see Linh again. After spending several hours updating all travel arrangements for their respective journeys, he noticed several new emails coming into his inbox but none from her.

One was from Tien.

*Good morning, Jack! You are always welcome in our country. The hotel staff can't wait to see their favorite guest.* He read further. *I don't remember the Babylift operation; this isn't something taught here in my country. Many things during the dark years are left out in our school education. They only teach about the importance of independence and reunification day. I am sorry I cannot help you more.*

Jack felt down at this but wrote back,

*Don't worry, my friend. I will see you in October.*

Already feeling a bit emotionally drained from the day's event, he took a nap on the couch, allowing himself some peace as he continued dreaming of his return to Vietnam.

William soon woke him.

"Dad, please wake up!"

"Yes, son?"

"I need some funds to pay for school, tuition, lab, and books. Mom just said that you spent this money on Vietnam and forgot to save for my college!"

Jack assessed the moment. *Geez, Silvia, how about all those trips to Vegas, Spain, and Puerto Rico!?*

"Son, I have your college funds ready. Let me show you."

He walked his son into his office and logged in to his computer screen. Jack opened several applications, including his banking and investment sites.

"Son, please see here. William's college fund, $95,000, available for withdrawing."

William was taken aback by what he saw. "Dad, wow! I never knew."

"I have been saving since the day you were born. Your car, your prom expenses…it all came from this account. Here is your sister's account."

"Dad, thank you, I didn't know."

"Don't worry—let's transfer the first thirty thousand now to cover your first-year expenses."

Within a few minutes, Jack transferred the funds to his son's account. Jack also gave William an American Express card.

"This isn't for partying—this is for emergencies in case I am not here and you need money in a pinch."

William couldn't believe how prepared his father was. "Thanks, Dad. I was just worried."

"Never fear. Dad will always be here."

They hugged each other and left the office. Jack went downstairs to confront Silvia.

"Hey, Silvia, I didn't spend any of the kid's college funds, whatsoever. That money is for them and their future. Stop telling the children false stories about me!"

Silvia dropped her wine glass on the carpet. "Jack, I didn't know. You never show me anything. I don't know what you are spending my money on!"

"Silvia, each quarter, we review our finances together, including investment accounts and banking. Don't you remember?"

"Yeah? That must have slipped my mind."

"Okay." This was pointless. "Please, can you ease up the political stabbing with the kids? Don't add to their anxiety up by saying things that aren't true!"

Silvia leaped off the couch. "Screw you, Jack. I am the only one saving these kids!"

Jack laughed out loud. "Yes, the big savior, Silvia." He turned around and walked upstairs, heading back to some more TV time.

Over the next few days, Jack continued waiting for Linh's email. He knew that even if he didn't hear from his love, he would still go to Vietnam in October. While he waited for her response, he started to think about the other items on his list surrounding Vietnam.

One thing that troubled Jack was the lack of detail around his search for the nuns. He thought about the history of Vietnam after 1975. The majority of individuals who supported the South Vietnamese government ended up in re-education camps or jail for a long time. *Did the nuns end up in jail because of their actions, helping the orphans leave? Why didn't the US president help them leave?* These were too many questions but ones that Jack knew he had to find answers for.

One notion that kept coming back was the priest in Saigon. Jack remembered his conversation and how the priest reacted when Jack mentioned the nuns. *What happened to that priest, and why didn't he like those nuns?* On the surface, trying to get the orphans out after the war seemed a very noble cause. Vietnam had many orphans from American GIs dating back to the 1960s. When men rotated home, the mothers of their children were outcasts in society even after 1975. Many Vietnamese abandoned their children on the streets. Catholics, living in Vietnam dating back to the French colonization, built several churches and cathedrals to protect those children. President Ford, a lifelong member of the church, appealed to the Roman Catholic hierarchy in Vietnam to help airlift as many children as possible. They airlifted fifteen hundred children during that operation.

A few years after the fall in Saigon, more Vietnamese came to America and lived very productive yet challenging lives. Some of those refugees lived in tents in Southern California. Later on, many moved north to Orange County to begin a life in Little Saigon, just fifteen miles from Disneyland. Many others moved to Northern Virginia. The journey of many of those people deeply saddened Jack.

Jack remembered his university days when he met some of those fantastic people, those refugees and orphans. However, he'd now lost the chance to ask them about the nuns. Jack thought about how he would approach Tien. The meeting with the priest continued to bother him. *Something must have gone wrong between them.* When he went back, he'd need to dig deeper.

# Chapter 16
# Envision

Linh spent several days reading Jack's email about his return to Vietnam. She wanted Jack to come back into her arms. "I love you. I miss you, my dear," Linh repeated those words quietly to herself. Her life, since Jack's departure, had only added more challenging and painful moments. Vo had left the house and moved up to Hue city with Niu. Linh, as such, had become a single mom. Luckily, she had the support of Liu.

She knew that her life revolved around Ngoc, and she needed to think about her future. Linh, already a professional in shipping and logistics, spoke and wrote excellent English. The shipping company she worked for was based in Toronto, Canada. She often connected via conference calls with the CEO, Royce Johnson. They talked about shipping requirements and cargo inspection issues. Johnson liked Linh and had promoted her recently to operations manager and chief logistic officer. Financially, Linh had plenty of money to support herself, Liu, and Ngoc. She knew all that could change, though, with any GEO crisis or problems with the Chinese or the Americans.

Each day, Linh was thankful for what she had. But she desperately wanted to see Jack again. She wanted nothing more than to love him and be in his arms once again. Linh had always felt at peace when sleeping in Jack's arms. Since his departure, Linh had never felt the same passion and love for anyone else.

After a few days, she decided that she would welcome Jack back into her life. She considered the impact on Ngoc and Liu, but she wanted Jack. She sat down at the computer and typed a response.

*My love, yes, I would love to see you again. I need you to know I need to be here with Ngoc and Liu. They are my family, and I need to take care of them. I have recently been promoted at work. I now carry a lot more responsibility.*

*Absolutely, let's make time to see each other again. Please remember I love you, Jack, but I also have responsibilities blocking my ability to spend more time with you.*

After sending the message, she walked through the single-story house in Bien Hoa to check on Ngoc.

"Ngoc? Where are you?"

"Here, Mommy."

Linh smiled when she saw how happy her daughter was, playing with her school friends. 'I have the most beautiful daughter.'

Then she went into the kitchen to help Liu with dinner. "Ma, may I help you?"

"No need. Dinner will be ready soon."

Linh stepped outside, sitting in her favorite chair while she daydreamed about Jack. She wondered what he looked like now. 'Did you lose weight? Do you still have gray hair?' Linh just smiled. After a few moments, her phone rang, letting her know a message had arrived.

Linh opened her device and felt her heart beating faster. All it said was:

*I can't wait, my Linh.*

Absorbing the moment, she leaned back in her chair and began to consider the impact this could have on her life. She loved Jack very much and yearned to make love to him again. She also knew that she was still a married woman in Vietnam. Vo, though living away, still came by to see Ngoc and his mother. She knew that this was not the life she wanted. Jack was a needed distraction for her. She hoped that Jack and she could have a normal relationship, but those dreams faded fast. "I love you, Jack, but my life is here with Ngoc," she whispered to herself. Linh started to cry knowing that this could be the last time she would ever see him again. She looked up at the stars. "I am here for you."

# Chapter 17
# Prevailing

Taking a day off from work, Jack took his bike for a fifty-kilometer cycling trip. He always loved challenging himself with long rides through the various cities in Southern California. He would start in Oceanside or Carlsbad, head down the 101 to the Del Mar, and then turn around to cycle back, twice. This was easy compared to the street racing in Saigon with Tuan and the team. *Here in America, we have different rules.* Jack couldn't wait for the chance to cycle there again. He pulled over at his favorite coffee bar to order an espresso. While enjoying the rest of the cycling with his favorite drink, Jack checked his emails. *Linh!* Feeling excited, he read the email, thinking about how much he loved and missed her. He wrote a reply to her message.

*My Linh, if I can only see you for an hour, I will make the most of the hour.* After sending off the details of the trip, he went back to cycling.

After completing his exercise, he grabbed a cold glass of water. Sitting in his office, he started to write a message to Tien.

*My friend, thank you for the response.* Choosing his words carefully, he wrote,

*When you were little, did you ever run into orphan children who were half American? Do you know where they were? My friend, the nuns in the church took care of old women who had no family. Are you familiar with a church that takes care of old people?*

After sending the message, he hoped that those clues would trigger some kind of memory. Tien and Tuan were born inside of the Chu Chi tunnels during the war. Jack remembered some stories that Tuan had told him about his life in the tunnels. Often, the soldiers would come there to cover themselves while under attack from the Americans.

Jack remembered Tien's story about his father dying of cancer because of the American's herbicide and defoliant chemical, Agent Orange. He looked in his notes to see some old photos of the Vietnam War, thinking about how they'd survived such dark times. Jack recalled walking into the Reunification Palace with Linh, reading the plaques with the names of the brave soldiers who fought for a unified Vietnam.

Jack also needed to set the groundwork for another goal in his life, working in Asia. Being a global technology sales professional, he'd always wanted to sell technology on that continent. He had worked for many international companies before, his favorite being with virtual team members from India, China, and Vietnam. Jack had accomplished so much in his professional career, but he has never sold or presented technology in Asia.

In his vacation in Vietnam, he was overwhelmed with the energy and passion of the people. Also, their dedication and work ethic were incredible. From the grandmothers working the markets to the students rising at 5 a.m. to cycle to school, the Vietnamese people believed in a strong work ethic to move their lives forward, without looking back. Jack witnessed this in Tuan's water company as well, watching these young kids with nothing but the clothes on their backs and a bed mat to sleep on, tirelessly working each day to create and deliver clean water. In many parts of Vietnam, younger people couldn't afford to drink clean water, so they drank pure sugarcane instead. That gave a short blast of energy but created diabetic problems and rotted their teeth. Jack remembered the advice Linh gave him: *We put together Vietnam with a string and tape.* Taking that advice to heart, Jack reached out to Tuan, asking for information about the water company.

Opening his Gmail, Jack drafted an email to his cycling friend.

*Dear Tuan,*

*Your water business impressed me. I would like to see if I can help to get certain things fixed or updated. You could have a very successful business, since water is one commodity that everyone needs. I appreciate the hard work of the employees and yourself. Please, let me know if you are interested in me becoming an investor in your business.*

Feeling a sense of accomplishment, he thought the new business venture could elevate his career, taking it in a new direction—building a water business with new products and new clients. He also wanted to have a profitable business. His goal was to help local temples and foundations assisting orphans in Vietnam. *Don't get ahead of yourself, Jack.*

The possibility of this new realm within his life excited him to a new level. He knew that Silvia would never agree to this new business venture. He also understood how much pain and suffering that will carry into his life. It was important that he understood the water business, how to do business in Vietnam, and how to establish an American company, knowing full well Silvia would never approve that. For that reason, Jack needed to create a win-win for both parties.

By the time he'd finished reading several articles about the water business, he became even more excited about his new venture. After a few hours of research, he took a rest and watched some TV. Within a few hours, Jack was already falling asleep.

The next morning, while Jack was typing a new email to Linh, he noticed several new messages coming in, including one from Tuan.

*Jack, they sent you from heaven! I would love your experience and investment to fix my water company. I will send you a spreadsheet of our current revenues and expenses where you can see where we need help. Any investment will be truly appreciated.*

*Your future partner, Tuan.*

Jack wrote back.

*Yes, my friend, let's discuss in more detail when I come there in October. I am very excited about the opportunity of investing in your water company.*

Feeling excited, he saw his road to happiness plan was starting to take shape. In three weeks, he'd booked a month away from Silvia, he'd helped William with what was needed to start college, and he'd gotten to see Regina off to the Coast Guard. Now Jack was heading back to Vietnam to see Linh, to invest in the water company, and hopefully, he would find the nuns.

# Chapter 18
# Culmination

October came sooner than expected for Jack. Just a month earlier, William had headed off to college and moved into a condo with Tricia. Jack was very proud of his son taking on adulthood in the best possible way. He had always been fond of Tricia, even back when she and William had dated in middle school.

"I am happy for you, son," he told William over the phone.

"Dad, are you going to be okay? I know things with Mom are getting worse. Anything I can do to help?"

Jack paused for a moment. "Yes. Live your life to the fullest. Please be happy and own all your choices. You are a man, and I will always be here as your father. The rest will take care of itself."

William wasn't happy with his dad's response. However, he chose to listen instead of arguing with him. The boy had finally realized that his father was a good man and that he worked hard to support the family. He loved his mother, but he also knew she hadn't always been good for his father.

"Dad, be good to Mom. I know she is not perfect. Neither are you or me."

"Yes, son. I provided for your mother for many years and supported her ideas and goals, even though I don't agree with them."

William appreciated his father's upfront discussions. "I'm glad you understand that, Dad. Mom comes to me with all her problems, and most of the time we are talking about you."

Jack felt terrible that Silvia took their problems to their son. "I am sorry your mother is coming to you—our issues are not yours."

William agreed. "Thank you, Dad. I love you. Be well."

"I love you too."

William hung up and turned to Tricia.

"Honey, are you okay? How is your dad?" she asked.

"My dad is heading in a new direction. I can't stop him; each of us has a life to live."

Tricia smiled at those words.

While Jack was reviewing his last preparations for the Vietnam trip, Silvia came into his office. "Hey, Jack, I need more money. Ten thousand isn't enough! Can I just charge the card, and we pay for it later?"

"Yes, let's do that. Enjoy!"

Feeling like a conquering queen, Silvia spun out of Jack's office with a smile on her face and without a thank-you. Jack checked his passport, visa, and Vietnamese currency; all was set and ready. He locked all his documents in his safe to avoid losing them. After taking care of the business items, he went into the bedroom to check his luggage and cycling equipment. Silvia was chatting with her sister Rose.

"Look, we have a ton of money, Rose. I will deposit a month's salary in your account if this will help."

Rose considered Silvia's generosity. "No thanks, sis. My husband and kids are fine. I will stay for a week. Lupe is going and Mary Ellen too. You will have plenty of people to party with."

"Oh yeah, that's true!"

Not realizing Jack was standing behind her until that moment, Silvia quickly hung up the phone.

"Oh, spying on me again, Jack?"

"No, Silvia. I was just checking to see if you needed anything else before I head out tomorrow."

"I am good."

Thankful that Silvia didn't ask for more money, he went back to rest in the TV room. Drifting in and out of dreams about Vietnam and Linh, Jack woke up, realizing he was the only one in the house. Silvia had left early to spend the night with her sister.

"Oh well, the shape of things to come for sure."

Jack felt a painful sense of anxiety and experienced trouble breathing, taking a moment to pray, trying to keep his depression under control. After doing a last check of the house, he moved all his luggage downstairs, preparing for the cab to take him to Los Angeles international airport. Within an hour, the driver showed up and loaded Jack's bags and cycling equipment. He was ready for the full day of travel ahead of him. *Linh, I will be there soon.*

# Chapter 19
# Reoccurrence

Resting comfortably on the plane, Jack thought about what he should do when he saw Linh. *Should I hug her? Kiss her? Shake her hand? I don't know! I just need to let it happen.* Jack closed his eyes, sleeping for the rest of the flight. During his sleep, the plane continued on course for Tokyo and then Ho Chi Minh City. Finally, the aircraft made its last approach into Tan Son Nhut Airport on time. As the plane bounced on landing, Jack woke up and realized that he'd slept the entire flight. He was full of energy. After a few moments, the aircraft rested at gate 102b. He disembarked and moved to the passport control. Customs and passport control in Vietnam were like in many Pacific countries—once the visa was verified, the passengers moved to pick up their luggage. Lastly, they moved to customs.

Within a few moments, he headed to the international gallery to retrieve a taxi. Walking through the International corridor in Vietnam was like being an artist entering the Oscars award show, with cameras and flashes going off, people wanting to talk to you, and drivers hustling for the next trip fare. Jack, already accustomed to this from his previous trip, headed straight for the white taxi line.

Once Jack made it outside, the humidity of Vietnam hit him directly in his face. *It is hot here!* After taking a moment to wipe the sweat off his brow, he collected his things and moved toward the taxi line. Suddenly, Jack's heart started to race out of control. Standing ten feet away from him was a beautiful Vietnamese woman in a traditional pink and yellow Vu Dai dress.

"Linh!" Jack called out.

Walking slowly up to Jack, she said, "Miss me, my love?"

Jack couldn't believe his eyes. "I didn't know you would meet me here."

"Surprise," Linh said, smiling back at her lover.

"Come, let's get to the hotel."

With the help of the taxi driver, Jack loaded his luggage and opened the door for Linh.

"Thank you, my love. Please remember we are in public."

Jack remembered the custom and rules and understood. But during the taxi ride to the Renaissance Hotel, Jack let his hands and finger drift slowly on Linh's legs. Linh touched his legs in return.

"Patience," she said. "I can stay tonight, my love."

Jack felt so excited and patiently waited until they arrived at the hotel. After the thirty-minute taxi ride, they stopped at the entrance to the Renaissance Hotel in District One. Jack departed the vehicle and extended his hand to Linh to help her out.

"Oh, I miss your gentlemanly ways, Jack."

He could only blush at Linh's playful comment.

"Mr. Jack, back from the hood, my brother!"

Only Tien would call out to Jack like that.

"Tien, my brother from another mother, father, and country. How are you?"

Tien walked up and gave his American friend an enormous hug.

"Oh, Ms. Linh, welcome back."

"Thank you, Tien," replied Linh with a small bow of her head.

"Jack, come in. We will get your bags to your room. Not to worry. Everyone is waiting for you at the bar!"

Linh, Jack, and Tien boarded the elevator and headed to the fifth floor.

"Ms. Linh, this is your key to the suite. Please remember to use separate elevators when coming and going."

As the elevator stopped, the three of them departed and headed into the bar. Several staff members got up to welcome Jack and Linh, including Ms. Bui, the manager.

"Mr. Jack, compliments of the house," said Bui.

Jack shook her hand and thanked her and the staff for a great welcome.

"Thank you all!"

Jack, Tien, Ms. Bui, and Linh sat on the top table filled with seafood and cold tiger beers.

"Welcome, Jack. We are glad you came back."

"Thank you, it is great to be here again."

Over the next few hours, Tien, Jack, Linh, and Ms. Bui drank, ate, and sang songs with the piano.

"Everyone, thank you for everything!" Jack couldn't stop smiling and laughing with his friends. After a few hours, he reminded himself that he'd just flown twenty-three hours and felt jetlagged.

"Everyone, I need to crash, please—long day."

He tried to pay the bill, but Ms. Bui took the bill from him.

"Compliments of the house."

He smiled and walked to the elevator to head up to the room. Linh followed Tien's recommendation and took the elevator down to the lobby first and then headed out the south entrance near his office. She noticed the private elevator that only went up to the club level. *Thank you, Tien.* Linh moved into the elevator and pressed the only button.

As he entered his room, Jack found all of his luggage and cycling equipment stacked safely next to the bed. He felt a bit tired, so he stripped down, jumping into the shower before Linh arrived. As Jack felt the warm water and steam coming from the glass shower, he felt a soft touch on his back. "Room for two?" Linh was smiling back at Jack with a playful yet sexy expression.

"My Linh, I promised you I would come back."

Linh, full of love for him, slowly embraced Jack under the water and kissed him gently.

"Welcome back, my love."

Enjoying the beautiful moment of passion, Jack laid Linh on the floor of shower. Placing a good amount of soap on his hands, he began to rub them slowly over Linh's body. Enjoying the soap massage from her lover, Linh also placed some on her own hands and began to massage Jack. After helping each other climax, Jack and Linh climbed into the bed together, staring out the window.

"Jack, thank you for being here again."

"Linh, thank you for being in my arms again."

With a few small breaths, Linh and Jack fell asleep together.

Mornings were always special in Vietnam for Jack. Feeling a bit jetlagged, Jack was still on west coast time. After going to the bathroom, he found Linh still asleep, with most of the covers removed from her body. Jack, seeing the sun was about to rise again over the Saigon River, slipped quietly back into bed. He was looking forward to seeing the morning sunrise touch his lover's skin. As the morning sun overshadowed Linh's body, Jack couldn't believe how beautiful she was. Linh, starting to wake up, opened her eyes to see Jack sitting next to her.

"My love, you are so handsome. How did I get to be so lucky as to meet you?"

"No, my love, I am the lucky one."

Jack slid down on the bed, hugging and kissing his lover.

"Linh, I love you!"

"I love you, my Jack."

After a morning of soft words and gentle touches, the lovers rose to get dressed for a morning breakfast.

"Jack, I will need to go home after breakfast."

"I understand, my love; I am here for two weeks. Please let me know how we can see each other again."

Linh smiled. "Jack, thank you for understanding."

They left the room and headed to get some breakfast in the lobby.

"Good morning," Tien greeted them. "Plans today, my friends?"

"Linh needs to head home. I will be cycling with Tuan today."

"Oh yes! Enjoy, Mr. Jack. Let's chat when you get back."

Jack, after finishing his breakfast, walked Linh to the taxi.

"Until we meet again, my love."

"I will see you again."

Without a kiss in public or even a hug, Linh entered the taxi and gently waved to Jack.

*I hate to see her leaving*, Jack said to himself. He entered the hotel but paused on his way in, realizing that the rainstorm had come a day earlier.

"Oh man, no cycling today. Tien, please call Tuan and ask if we can cycle tomorrow."

Tien was already on top of it. "Yes, I texted him."

*Day off. What should I do?* Jack realized that he'd arrived on a Saturday night. After a beautiful romantic evening with Linh, he discovered it was

Sunday. He decided to head off to church. Grabbing a hotel umbrella, he headed toward the Notre Dame Cathedral. Jack, remembering his last exchange with the priest, attended a mass in the grand church. He prayed for his family and Linh's safety.

The church was only five minutes away from the hotel, and it hosted a 10:30 a.m. English-speaking mass. Jack couldn't have timed the arrival any better. Following Catholic protocol, he dipped his hand in holy water and performed the cross from his forehead to his stomach and across his chest. Jack found an empty pew, kneeled, and prayed for a few moments until the mass started. He noticed several westerners sitting in the church. Jack believed many of them were probably from France or other European countries. Within a few minutes, the pipe organ in the back of the church came alive with opening music.

"All rise," the priest barked out.

The church came alive with singing and more handshakes, with everyone welcoming one another. After the opening prayers, Jack listened to the gospel messages from the priest.

"Thou shall not commit a sin, thou shall not commit auditory, thou shall not covet thy neighbor's wife." Jack remembered these very words from the Old Testament in the Bible.

Jack took stock of himself—*yes, I guess I have committed a terrible sin.* A lifelong practicing Catholic, he knew he wasn't a perfect member of the church. Since he was having an affair with Linh, he was a sinner according to the church. Jack accepted this, knowing that the decision to go forward had been his choice. Because of his sin, even with confession, he couldn't receive the bread and blood of Christ as part of the religious ceremony. Jack had long accepted this as a loss in his spiritual life, but he took the joy gained in his personal life. *Choices in life need to be owned, not passed on.*

After the gospel, the rest of the mass continued, and then the priest made some announcements.

"Today's second collection is for the nuns at the Mai Am Linh Me orphanage. Please give generously."

Jack was startled. He couldn't believe his ears.

As the basket for a collection made its way to him, he dropped several Vietnamese Dong bills into the donation basket. Reflecting on what he'd just heard, Jack thought these might be the nuns he was seeking. After the mass service ended, he walked to the exit of the church, stopping only to appreciate the unique beauty of the basilica. Walking with the rest of the crowd, he shook the priest's hand and then strolled into the park next to the church. Not wanting to waste any time, he walked over to the tea shop and researched the church he'd donated money to.

After enjoying his favorite Vietnamese espresso, Jack started to type on his phone. The internet, still running slow in Vietnam through Jack's secured internet connection, didn't return any web search results for this church. *Strange.* He started searching for Catholic nuns again and orphanages in Saigon. His search found several orphanages, but none of them had anything to do with nuns. Giving up, Jack headed back to the cathedral to find his favorite priest.

"Father! I am back."

The priest was not happy to see him again. "Oh. You."

"Hey, Father, question sir, why to do a collection for a church that doesn't exist in Saigon?"

"What are you talking about?" asked Father Flannagan.

"Father, the collection today—are these the nuns that helped with Operation Babylift?" The priest looked at Jack and then turned away and headed for the exit of the church.

"Father, I need your help to find the nuns."

The priest continued to walk away from Jack without saying a word.

"Go with God? How about you, Padre?"

The priest, stunned by Jack's remark, charged back to the American, slapping him across the face. "How dare you come back here and question me!?"

Jack, picking himself up off the floor, moved closer to the priest. "Father, please forgive me, for I have sinned. It has been five hundred days since my last confession."

The priest wasn't impressed with Jack's attempt. "Go, American, find a new country to confess your sins in."

The father walked out of the church, leaving Jack to his own thoughts. Never one to take a hit in the face, Jack found the needed self-control and compassion for the priest. He decided not to return the slap. Turn the other cheek, as they say. So, Jack listened to his inner voice and left the church. I was still raining, and he toured the remaining parts of the city while remembering the beautiful evening he'd spent with Linh.

Jack allowed himself to dream of better moments. Still, he couldn't shake the feeling he had when the priest hit him. *There is more to that guy.* He spotted a small tea shop and got out of the rain. The café had superb internet access, and he used the time to search about priests. Several queries came back regarding a scandal that happened ten years ago. Several priests were arrested for molesting boys in the church. The Vietnamese government imprisoned the priests. Some of them died of old age, while others were deported back to their home countries. One priest claimed his innocence—he was sent off to Hanoi and was never seen again. Jack felt a higher sense of compassion for the church in Vietnam.

He believed that Father Flanagan was probably here at the end of the Vietnam War and a survivor of the church's latest global sex scandal. Jack realized that this priest, during the war, was probably a new bishop in training and got caught up in the mess after April 30.

*I bet he witnessed the great humanitarian crisis that followed the war, and the Americans and the Vatican probably abandoned him and the church. I would be a little pissed off myself.* After a few rounds of coffee, Jack proceeded to walk back to the hotel.

As he approached, Tien came out to his friend. "Jack, they are here for you."

Jack wasn't surprised to see policemen asking for him.

"You!" yelled one cop. "Stop!"

Jack was already having a bad day. "I am here, officer."

Within a matter of moments, the police surrounded Jack and placed handcuffs on his wrists.

"In the car, now!"

Jack followed the orders and moved into the police car. After a brief exchange with Ms. Bui, the police drove off, taking him.

Several stops later, he arrived at the police station in downtown Saigon. Jack, confused from the entire event, held his words until the right time to speak. The police led him into the station, placing him inside a room with no windows. Still handcuffed, Jack started to think about what could have triggered this. After a time of self-reflection, he realized it must have been something with Linh. Jack began to consider the damage he may be causing over his lust for the woman. The hotel workers being questioned by the police only made Jack feel even guiltier. "I really need to think how I got here and the problems I am causing others," Jack whispered to himself.

After two hours, the lead police officer came into the room.

"Mr. Jack Kendall, you are under arrest for people's code of unacceptable public behavior and in the custody of a Vietnamese citizen. You broke our law protecting our women from foreign men taking advantage of them!"

"Yes, sir, I understand the charges. May I make a phone call?"

"No! This is not America," sneered the officer.

"Okay, what happens next?"

The officer punched Jack's stomach. Jack, already hurting from the slap earlier, doubled over in pain. He knew the Vietnamese police didn't treat westerners well, not ones who broke their laws.

"Now shut up!"

"Okay, officer," Jack whispered.

The man left the room, and Jack considered what options he had. *Confess and spend the next four years in a Vietnamese prison or shut my mouth and say nothing?* Jack started to think about Linh. Had she been arrested as well? He tried to speak to the guard outside the integration room, as he was beginning to become dehydrated.

Two hours later, Jack's luck changed for the better. After hearing a series of commotions outside his waiting room, he spotted two United States Marines in full uniform and a well-dressed man entered the room.

"Mr. Kendall? Forest Adams with the US Embassy."

Jack felt a sense of relief. "Thank you, sir, for coming."

Forest Adams's official title was an undersecretary of trade. But Jack sensed that there was a lot of more to this man.

"Mr. Adams, do you know why I am here?"

"Yes," proclaimed the embassy officer. "I know what is happening between you and Ms. Linh. I also know that the hotel's management and staff are protecting you. However, not everyone at the hotel is happy with your relationship with this Vietnamese woman."

"Did someone turn me in?"

"There is a 270,000 Vietnamese dollars reward for turning in Americans caught with a Vietnamese woman in a hotel. Yes, Jack, one of the hotel workers turned you in."

Jack looked away in shame. "Any word on Linh?"

Forest glanced at his notepad. "Yes, they have detained her as well at a separate police station. She is being questioned as well."

"Is there anything I can do?"

Forest gave him a very serious stare. "Don't say another word about her."

Jack nodded. He realized that he'd gotten Linh in terrible trouble in her own country. "What if her husband finds out? Look, I screwed up. I need help here, Mr. Adams."

"I am working on it, Marine. Now here is what I know so far."

Forest sat down next to Jack.

"Someone at the hotel sent a detailed the report including a leaked video to the Saigon police. In the film are images of your arrival, when you met Ms. Linh. In short, you have broken a few rules, Kendall. The cops want you to stay here for a while."

Jack wasn't feeling happy. "How long?"

"Maybe three to five years," replied Forest. "Sit tight and say nothing. We are making a few calls."

Jack understood what that meant. While he was waiting, one Marine guard came to ask him some questions.

"Sir, are you Corporal Jack Kendall, Marine Corps special operations team, 1982 to 1988?"

"Yes, that is me. Why do you ask, son?"

"You saved my dad's life in Beirut."

Jack remembered when he was deployed to Lebanon—a lifetime ago. After completing military communications school in the Marine Corps, Jack was deployed after the terrorist attack the US Marine Barracks on October 23, 1983. Along with several other radio communications specialists, he was flown into Lebanon to assist in the recovery of the fallen Marines.

"How is your father?"

"My dad passed away years ago from cancer, but he showed me a picture of you and him together."

"What is your name, son?"

"Reed Carson, sir. My dad was Bill Carson."

"Oh, yes, I remember him. I am sorry for his passing."

The other marine guard was interested in learning more about Jack too.

"Corporal, did you hack a Russian radio system while swimming near North Korea?" asked the second marine.

"Where did you hear that one, son?"

"Radio school twenty-nine palms, California."

"Well, yes." Jack smiled back at two young Marines.

"How did you do that, sir?"

Jack looked at the young soldier. "Well, I was on the DMZ separating North and South Korea. We knew the Russians were testing a new radio system along the border. I spotted a jeep with a large radio antenna sticking out near the river on the North Korean side. I stripped off my uniform down to my shorts and jumped in the freezing cold water and swam upstream. Once I got close to the jeep, I sneaked up and grabbed the radio and ran across the section of the DMZ that had no fence."

Both Marines stared at Jack in complete amazement. "Holy shit! Mr. Kendall didn't freeze your ass off?"

Jack laughed. "Yes, I still have frostbite on my ass even today."

The Marines smiled back. "What will happen to you, sir?" asked one.

"I am not sure—I am more worried about my friend at the moment than myself."

The Marines nodded in agreement.

After an hour, the lead police officer walked into the room and removed Jack's handcuffs.

"You can go, American."

Jack rose up from his chair. "What about Linh?"

The police officer stared back at Jack. "She has been released as well."

Jack, feeling a sense of relief, thanked the Marines and Mr. Adams.

"Jack," the man warned, "while you are here, follow the rules and don't get caught again." Mr. Adams handed Jack his card. "Look, if you need anything, please call me. Thank you for your service."

Jack nodded back to the embassy official.

"Need a ride, son?"

"No, I can humpback."

The sheer response put a smile on the marine guards' faces. "Once a Marine, always a Marine."

While walking back to the hotel, Jack tried to call Linh to see if she was okay. After several attempts, Linh texted him that she was.

# Chapter 20
## Adversity

After coming back to the hotel, Jack walked into the lobby. Ms. Bui and Tien were waiting for him.

"Mr. Jack, are you all right?"

"Yes, I am fine. I need to rest, thanks."

Without saying another word, Jack headed upstairs to his room. Still exhausted from the day's events, he sat by the window, watching the boats sailing along the Saigon River below. After a few hours, he ordered some room service, and after an hour, it arrived at his room.

"Mr. Jack, dinner," said Tien.

Jack didn't expect his friend to personally deliver his room service.

"Don't expect a tip, bro!" snapped Jack with a smile.

Tien entered the room and placed the food on the table.

"I am sorry about earlier; anyone in Saigon catching an American with a Vietnamese girl is rewarded with a lot of money."

Jack, settling in to enjoy his dinner, invited his friend to stay.

"Tien, want a beer?"

"I am working, but maybe later."

Tien showed himself out. Jack finished his meal and placed his tray in the hallway for someone to pick it up. After a delightful dinner and a few beers, he opened his laptop to continue his search for the missing nuns. *Okay, why is it coming up blank?* After a few moments, he remembered having a similar experience in China. *Wait, they are removing all reference to this at the firewall level.* Jack, a seasoned information technology expert, realized the Vietnam government had a similar firewall setup as China.

So he started up his secure secured internet and connected back to his home system. Many people traveling to Vietnam or China would order a secured service in order to connect outside of the government internet systems. For years, Jack used to help traveling executives with his capability.

Within a matter of minutes, Jack ran similar queries against the orphanage mentioned during church. *Yes, I knew it!* He found a story about a group of Catholic nuns that ran an orphanage north of Saigon, but he also found the story of the priest—*Father Michael Joseph Flanagan, a fine Irish name*. After reading for almost an hour, he could understand why the priest didn't like Americans at all. The priest's background didn't mention having any connection with the orphans or the order of nuns. However, the article did talk about the priest spending time in prison after the war. Jack read for several hours, trying to find more.

Jack read until after midnight and then realized he hadn't messaged Linh once. He stopped what he was doing and opened his phone app.

*My loving Linh, I am glad you are safe. We will be more careful.*

Jack woke up listening to raindrops hitting his window on the high floor of the hotel. Feeling drained from the last two days, he stayed in bed longer than usual. After an extended sleep, his phone rang.

"Incoming, from Tuan."

"Oh crap, cycling. Tuan, I am sorry I overslept. Are we still on?"

"Let's go. Your team is waiting!"

Jack, excited by the possibility of cycling in the rain, got quickly dressed and hustled down to the lobby.

Tuan felt excited to see his friend again. "Mr. Jack, here is your team jersey—let's move!"

On the beautiful rainy morning, Jack and the team enjoyed cycling on Saigon's streets. The cycling team turned to the hotel's right, down a major road that headed out of the city.

"Where are we going?" Jack called out.

"To the factory—the rain is causing a ton of flooding," replied Tuan.

"Absolutely, let's go!"

Within an hour, the team rolled out to the factory to find the machines underwater and the power off in the building.

"Oh my!" screamed Tuan.

"Don't go in. Electricity is still active," said Jack.

The team backed away from the door until it was safe.

"Tuan, let's continue cycling for now. We can come back when the rain stops."

Tuan was upset at the destruction caused by the storm. "We have nowhere to go, Jack."

Jack understood this wasn't America. He knew the building was their only home. It was imperative to find a place for them to stay and to get some food to eat. He took a seat and stared back at the workers and Tuan. The sheer devastation that showed in their faces made Jack sick. They had nothing. Jack took a moment and looked at the water damage to the plant. One good storm and this place would be wiped off the earth. Part of Jack wanted to get up and just head back to the hotel and mind his own business. "Not your problem," he whispered to himself. But seeing the workers all cling to one another for support made Jack consider other options.

"Team, follow me!" Jack yelled. He told the workers to climb on their bikes and head off to a safe place.

Jack and the workers rode back to District One, toward the Renaissance Hotel. During the cycling, they stopped several times to help others in need. Vietnamese have a history of typhoons that have destroyed the country many times. Once Jack and the group helped as many people as they could, they mounted their bikes and kept cycling to the hotel. After an hour of traveling, they safely made it the grand entrance of the hotel. Jack leaped off his bike and asked the team to join inside.

"Guys, hang here for a moment," Jack requested.

"Ms. Bui, may I talk to you?"

"Yes, Mr. Jack, how can I be of service?"

"Ms. Bui, my cycling team lost their home in the storm—we can't perform any repairs until the rain has stopped. Do you have eight rooms for the night?"

Ms. Bui checked on her computer system. "Yes, Mr. Jack, I have eight rooms on the eleventh floor." Jack opened his wallet and pulled out a few credit cards. Even though his financial situation was better than before, he still didn't know if he had enough to cover eight rooms. "Ms. Bui, how much will the rooms cost, please?"

Ms. Bui glanced at the eight boys sitting in the lobby, most of them orphans. "Mr. Jack, let me check your reward points." After checking his account, she realized that he didn't have enough to cover it all.

"I will deduct seventy thousand of your hundred thousand points available—I will cover the rest." Jack became emotional at the generosity of Ms. Bui. "Thank you," he said.

Ms. Bui, maintaining her calm, professional composure, responded, "My pleasure."

Ms. Bui handed Jack the eight keys, he walked over to the workers. "Tuan, team, here is your hotel key. Please, go upstairs and dry off. We will stay here tonight."

The team, most of them orphans with nowhere else to go, couldn't believe they would sleep in a hotel like the Renaissance.

"Team, shower, dry your clothes up, and let's meet for dinner at 6:30 here in the lobby," said Jack.

"Mr. Jack, we could never pay you back."

"Don't worry, team. Please thank Ms. Bui." As the team walked toward the elevators, the young boys stood and bowed to Ms. Bui. She tried to maintain herself but started to be tearful. She bowed back at the young men and motioned them to the elevators.

After a few hours, the team came down with clean hair, clean faces, and dry clothes provided by the hotel. Ms. Bui sent up clothes and additional cleaning items for the boys to use.

"Thank you, Mr. Jack."

He waved his team on into the lobby restaurant for dinner.

Tuan felt so appreciative of Jack's hospitality and friendship. "Mr. Jack, I know you wanted to invest in the water business, but I fear this isn't a water business anymore."

Jack had come to the same conclusion. "Tuan, don't worry. Let's look at the factory tomorrow. We will discuss it then."

Tuan could only smile at the possibility of Jack being an investor. While enjoying dinner, Jack got up and headed back to the lobby, where he found Ms. Bui.

Jack nodded to the woman and then headed back to finish dinner with his team. The group was already full of all the food, and they couldn't wait to get back to their rooms to sleep in proper beds for the first time. The boys slept in one another's rooms, watching movies together all night. Jack, even with the pain and challenge of the last two days, smiled again.

# Chapter 21
# Reprise

The next morning brought several surprises to the cycling team. Ms. Bui ordered a private breakfast on the top bar for the whole group. The rain finally stopped pouring after four days. The city, still reeling from the flooding and water damages, showed signs of life again. People were out in the open markets shopping for the day's fresh food. The flower stands displayed colorful arrangements, and the teenagers filled the curbside tea shops, chatting with their friends. Jack stepped outside the hotel to see the morning energy from the city.

"Mr. Jack, breakfast!" yelled Tuan.

He realized how special this breakfast was for the team, so he headed to the elevator to join them. Ms. Bui set up a breakfast arrangement of traditional and western food for the boys. Even though Ms. Bui was a very professional woman, deep down, she seemed to have a soft heart for helping people.

"Thank you, Ms. Bui. I am sure the team appreciates everything you have done for them."

"Thank you, Mr. Kendall, for everything you have done for my staff."

He joined the team for breakfast. As he enjoyed the moment with the group, he checked his messages, hoping to see something from Linh. Since her departure four days ago, he had heard very little from his lover.

"Patience," Ms. Bui expressed.

"Huh?"

Ms. Bui only could wink and smile at Jack.

After eating as much as they could, Tuan and the team cleared their plates, thanking Ms. Bui for everything. While the crew departed, the hotel staff handed out new backpacks. They included fresh clothes, soap, shampoo, snacks, water, and sandwiches.

"Goodbye, little brothers," the staff called out to the boys.

The boys didn't know why the staff had treated them with those gifts. Grateful, they bowed and said, "Thank you."

"Thank Ms. Bui," said Jack as the team headed down the elevator and out the main entrance.

After a few minutes of bike adjustments, the team rode off, heading back to District Thirteen. After cycling through the continued flooded road and mud holes, the team arrived back at the factory. Tuan dismounted first to unlock, pulling back the doors.

Jack was second. "Jack, hold on for a moment. Let me check the electrical system."

He listened to his friend and stepped back from the door.

"All clear. Everyone, come inside," said Tuan.

They all surveyed the damage to the plant. "I have seen worse, Tuan."

Tuan didn't know what to say. The storm had ruined the factory and their living area. Jack understood the situation, removed his laptop, and started drafting ideas to fix the place quickly.

"Tuan, I am your partner now. Let me start by wiring some funds to you so we can start fixing this place."

Tuan stared at Jack for a moment, showing no emotion. Tuan remembered the days when he was a boy in the tunnels, seeing American soldiers coming in to kill everyone in there. Now, years later, his American friend was here, offering to help him.

"I trust you, Jack—please trust me too."

Jack looked at his friend and partner. "I do trust you very much."

Jack thought about Linh's words. *Tape and string.*

He and Tuan shook hands and began the journey of fixing the plant. They broke the team up into three groups: repair, replace, and construct. The repair team would begin pushing the remaining water out of the building, slowly assessing the various parts of the plant that needed repair. It seemed most of the equipment needed to dry out, but the water tanks seemed to be okay.

The second team would focus on the replacement of all broken items in the plant. If the plant was down, why not make everything better before turning on the water flow system again?

Jack walked across the street to the local tea house to access the internet.

Once Jack connected via secured connection, he accessed his investment account and his bank records. He executed a stock sale in order to get access to cash to wire to himself in Vietnam. After the sale was completed, he had access to $35,000 US dollars minus tax withholding. Jack created four different transfers to Tuan via Western Union, one for $2,500 and the rest for $1,000 each. All were to arrive the next business day. Now that he'd created some working capital, he made a list of things the factory needed.

The third team would focus on constructing the new floor and living quarters for the whole team. Jack checked to see how much cash he had available. Then he asked Tuan where they could purchase items such as wood, nails, and tools.

"Tuan, is there any store nearby where we can purchase some wood and tools?"

Tuan looked confused. "I don't know. Let me ask Tien."

Tuan reached for his phone to call his brother, and after a few minutes of yelling and insults, came back. "Tien said you can send him an email, detailing what you need. He will have it all delivered."

"Outstanding!"

Jack went back to the tea house and sent Tien a shopping list. While he sat, he watched the team working hard to get the factory back up and running. Then two policemen entered the factory. Jack didn't know if it was a good idea to go in. Within a few minutes, they walked over to Jack.

"Are you the owner now?"

Jack was surprised by the question. "No, I am only helping a friend."

"You need to pay a fee now." Jack started to question the police on why he needed to pay. But Tuan nodded frantically from behind them, so Jack reluctantly paid the fine.

He paid the officers twenty thousand Vietnamese dollars each and sent them on their way, realizing that he was an investor now. He was starting to think that he'd made a colossal mistake. While the team continued working on their respective assignments, the delivery scooters began showing up with the tools and supplies they needed.

"Over here!" Jack yelled at the deliverymen.

He paid for the supplies and helped the team unload the wood and tools. They needed to start by fixing their sleeping area. Jack texted Tien and thanked him for the supplies and help. Tuan spent most of his time cleaning and drying the factory floor along with stacking the bottles to prepare for the next production run. Jack thought hard about what he was doing.

*I just sold off some of my retirement stock to invest in a water company that could be washed away at any time.*

He needed a moment with Tuan and asked him to step out.

"Tuan, I am helping here as your investor, but you are still the owner of this place."

Tuan, understanding Jack's concern, said, "Yes, Jack. This is my place, but this is your place too."

"In America, there would be a contract, lawyers, transfer of tax, and licenses. I am sure in Vietnam they have something like that too. Do you have a license of record, tax forms, and tags for everything?"

"Yes, I have everything."

Jack was still feeling cautious about Tuan's business. He remembered what Linh had told him about who to trust in Vietnam and who not to. "Okay, after we fix the factory, let's sit down and figure out how much I can invest in. I need to understand what this will mean to the ownership record."

"Sure thing."

After returning to the tea house for more drinks, Jack packed up his laptop. Lastly, he went on to help the construction team fix the sleeping area. The group used to sleep on the floor with rice and straw mats. Jack walked a few blocks down the street from the factory, discovering there weren't any shops that sold sleeping mats for the team. With each step, he realized more how impoverished the district was if he were to compare this district to other ones in Saigon. Many shops in this district only carried simple items like food, sugar, and some meats. After an hour of walking around, Jack spotted a lady sewing in a small store.

"Excuse me, do you speak English?"

"Yes, I do."

"I am looking for new sleeping mats for my workers. I am an investor in the water company down the street."

The lady rose from her chair and looked at the water plant. "Oh, that is Tuan's house."

Jack smiled. "I am sure everyone knows everyone here."

"What do you need, sir?"

"I need eight straw and rice mats for the boys to sleep on tonight." Jack could not afford to have the workers stay at the hotel again, so he needed to get the factory repaired quickly.

"Please, come back in four hours. I'll have your mats ready."

"Four hours?" He was surprised at the speed. "Okay, I will be back."

Jack bowed and walked out of the store, heading back to the water plant.

"Tuan, do you know the sewing lady up the street?"

"Yes, she was my teacher in school. Why?"

"Well, she is making us new sleeping mats for the team."

Tuan was proud. "Mr. Jack, well done!"

The next major part of the construction was the floor leading up to the second level where the team slept. The stairs needed repair, and the roof had some serious leaks. The rain wasn't in the forecast for quite some time, so Jack focused his attention on the stairs. Within two hours, Jack and Tuan ripped out the old wood, replacing the stairs, making it better and safer for the team.

"Mr. Jack, you are amazing. Thank you," said Tuan.

Jack smiled back at his new business partner. Still troubled by the financial arrangement between himself and Tuan, he knew deep down he wanted to own this factory. He also remembered that this wasn't America. *Don't expect the organization and work stream, Jack.* Now that the construction team was completing the floor repairs and sleeping areas, Jack and Tuan left the factory. They walked down the street to pick up the mats.

"Good day," Jack called out to the sewing lady.

The sewing lady and Tuan talked in Vietnamese.

"You guys must know each other," Jack called out.

"Yes, he was my student," she explained.

After a few moments more of conversation, the lady gave Jack the mats.

"These look amazing, thank you!"

The sewing lady smiled in appreciation. "That will be 250,000 Vietnamese dollars."

After paying her for the sleeping mats, Tuan and Jack carried them to the factory. When they arrived, the repair team was completing the window replacements, and most importantly, they were fixing the roof.

"Oh, no more leaks!" Jack exclaimed. "Are we ready to test power?"

"No, Mr. Kendall. We still have power problems," explained one of the team members.

"Okay, let me take a look," said Tuan in Vietnamese.

Tuan quickly found the problem. One fuse wasn't correctly set.

"Okay, try it now."

Within a moment, the factory came alive with power. All the systems, including the control computer, booted up.

"Jack, let's let this run for twenty minutes. Please check all seals, pipe connectors, and drain system before we take on fresh water from the city."

Jack felt a sense of accomplishment and pride and believed he was making a difference. Jack always found a way to help others. If a friend or family member needed money, he would help. If a niece of nephew needed money for college or trade schools, Jack always helped and never asked for anything in return. Jack felt for years that he was so blessed in life with a great career, money, and his wonderful children that helped others who needed the most help. The water company became a part of Jack's deep connection with the people and country of Vietnam.

After he reflected on the moment, he checked his phone, noticing a message from Linh.

*My love, I can come tomorrow at 8:00 a.m. and stay the day with you.*

Jack always felt wonderful to hear from and see Linh.

*Yes, my love. See you in the morning.*

Jack knew though that someone at the hotel had turned him and Linh to the police.

*Please remember to use the north elevators near Tien's office.*

He turned his attention back to the plant. While the power systems were restarting, Jack noticed an older lady sitting outside.

"Hello?" Jack said to the lady.

"Hi."

"Tuan, who is this gracious lady?"

Tuan spoke to the woman, asking her who she was and what she was doing there.

"Mr. Jack, she is the neighbor next door and wanted to see if she could have a job."

"What can she do?"

"She said she is a superb cook and could feed the workers breakfast and dinner." Jack wondered how the workers ate each day. He'd noticed up the street near the factory several food tables and mini markets. He wondered if the workers had enough food to eat. Jack started to calculate in his head. "Okay, for ten workers, times six days, two meals plus a morning coffee. How much would she charge per day?"

Tuan translated the question to the lady.

"65,000 Vietnamese dollars per day."

Jack did a quick calculation. "That's $30 per day times twenty-one days—$630 per month. Can we afford that, Tuan?" Jack didn't know the current financial picture of the factory.

"Yes, we can afford this."

"Okay, she can start tomorrow. Please let her and the team know."

After a very long day rebuilding the factory and the living quarters for the team, Jack pulled Tuan aside for a moment.

"Tuan, I need to go. Please let me know that the team knows they can sleep well tonight. The meal lady will be feeding them, starting tomorrow in the morning. I will meet Ms. Linh tomorrow, and we will be back at the factory in the afternoon. Please wait until I come back before we restart the water flow."

"Yes, Jack. See you tomorrow."

Jack said goodbye to the team, heading off back to the hotel.

*Good day today. Where will this go? Who knows?* After thirty minutes of cycling, he pulled up to the entrance to the Renaissance Hotel. Feeling tired, Jack stopped at the lounge for some western food and a cold beer.

"Here you go, Mr. Jack. Your favorite beer," said Wei.

Jack smiled at the waiter. "Thank you, Wei."

Jack opened his phone to check his emails. *Nothing. Good, I can rest now.* After finishing the meal and beer, Jack retired to his room for some much-needed sleep.

As the sun rose in Saigon, Jack awakened to the loving touch of Linh.

"You must have arrived early, my love," said Jack.

Linh smiled. She always did when she saw him. "My love, I couldn't wait to be here again."

As the two lovers embraced and connected with a passionate kiss, the morning sun glazed across both of their bodies. Linh, wanting deeply to feel Jack's loving passion again, began to kiss his knee softly. She then proceeded to lift up Jack's shirt and run her tongue up and down his chest. Hearing Jack moan softly, Linh began to remove Jack's sleeping shorts. After slowly pulling them off, Linh ran her tongue up and down Jack's member slowly. Seeing the pleasure in Jack's eyes, Linh whispered into his ear, "I love you."

"My Linh, I love you!" Placing her hands on Jack's member, she stroked gently until her lover released. Jack leaned down to Linh and picked her up off her feet and carried her to the bed. Caressing her long hair, he asked, "Where will our love go?"

Linh shook her head. "I don't know, Jack." She was still trying to come to grips with her feeling. "My Jack, I love you, but please remember you'll need to leave someday. What would I do then?"

Jack realized the reality of Linh's speech. "Let's remember now, my loving Linh. Let tomorrow happen as it comes."

"Absolutely, my love."

After an hour-long rest, Linh woke up to a phone call from her CEO. "Yes, I am here."

She got off the bed and headed to the next room for a private conversation. After a few minutes, Linh came back into the room.

"My love, I will need to leave today and head back to work. This is a busy week for me."

"I understand."

After a long and passionate shower, the two lovers dried each other with a towel only to make love again on the floor of the bathroom. Linh, feeling Jack inside her, also climaxed greater than ever before. With both lovers drained from lovemaking, Jack covered Linh with a towel and held her closely, and they both fell asleep.

# Chapter 22
# Dawn

During the night, as Jack woke on the floor of the bathroom, he gently lifted Linh up and carried her to bed. He covered her beautiful body with the bed sheet. Jack leaned over and gave his love a kiss on her lips. Linh, awakened by Jack's passionate kiss, stroked his cheek with her hand. "My Jack, my love will always be here for you." He became tearful and held Linh close to his body.

In the morning, Jack ordered room service for Linh and himself. He looked outside his room window, seeing a beautiful morning with the sun already rising in the sky.

"Do you remember Tien and Tuan from the cycling tour? They also own a water company, and I decided to become an investor."

Linh was startled by the news. "Jack, please don't do that. Many Vietnamese cannot be trusted."

"Linh, Tuan and Tien seem to be straight guys. And they need help."

Linh wasn't happy with Jack's decision. "Jack, please let me look into this company for you before you send them money."

Jack knew the water company was a huge risk not only financially but emotionally. "Okay, my love, do you have time to help with this?"

Linh thought about what this meant for her. She was already spending too much time away from Ngoc.

"Jack, yes. I can help, but please listen to my advice."

He listened to his inner voice and realized that Linh was deeply concerned about his project.

"Yes, my love. How about we head over so I can show you the water plant?"

"Yes, my love. Let's go before I head home."

The two lovers got dressed and headed out to the taxi. Linh copied the address from Jack's phone and gave the instructions to the driver. While they traveled to the water company, he received a phone call from Silvia.

"Jack, what the hell are you doing!? I just received an email from our financial broker; you sold more stock. What are you planning!?"

Jack realized that Linh could hear Silvia screaming.

"Look, someone has to cover your expenses in Hawaii—I assume you are already hitting the credit card heavy with expensive foods and tours, aren't you?"

"Well, if you would have planned it better... You know how I am."

"I am doing this to avoid additional debt. Have a great time!" said Jack and hung up on his wife.

Within a few moments, the taxi arrived at the water plant. Linh stepped out of the cab first and walked into the factory. Her expression was a complete blank look of fear and confusion back at Jack.

"Jack, this place is a mess. Please tell me you aren't investing here."

Tuan said, "Hey, who are you, lady?"

Jack realized the tension. "Guys, chill out for a moment. Tuan, this is Linh She is a friend of mine, and she will help me work things out."

Tuan seemed unimpressed. "Jack, she isn't my partner. Only you are. And I only will answer questions from you."

"Fair enough. How are the repairs going? Are we ready to test the water flow system?"

"Yes, we are," replied Tuan.

After an initial false start of the electrical system, the water flow injection system received water and started to fill up bottles. Within an hour, the factory filled the production orders and inventory for the delivery teams.

"Jack, let's talk," said Linh.

They stepped away and walked across the street to the teahouse, ordering two green teas.

"My love, what do you think?"

Linh decided how to choose the right words. "Jack, this won't work. Look at the building and the pipes. I bet he doesn't have a valid license either. That place is a mess, and I suspect that Tuan isn't telling you the whole truth."

Jack had already felt a bit of the risk when discussing financial matters with Tuan.

"You are right, my love." He realized that he had already spent close to $13,000 fixing the plant.

"Linh. I thought I could purchase the factory. I could run this for a year to recover my investment and then sell it off."

Linh, thinking like a businesswoman, took a sip of her tea. "You will need to come back to Vietnam to run it."

"I can't do that, Linh—I have a life in America."

Linh knew that crossroad of reality was not the only one Jack and she would face in their relationship. She started to think about a way to help Jack manage this business better.

"My sister could run this!"

"Your sister?"

Linh explained, "Yes, I have an older sister, Chau. She is running my parents' coffee farm and she is ready for a change of scenery."

"Do you really think we can do this?"

Linh stepped away to have a conversation with her sister. While Linh discussed things with Chau, Jack walked to talk to Tuan.

"Let's chat."

Tuan sensed Jack's tone wasn't a positive one.

"Tuan, Linh feels strongly that this business isn't going to work. Can you tell me the truth? How is your business?"

Tuan had already considered telling Jack the truth. "The business is good. We have customers and partners. We make clean water in two products at a good price."

Jack could see the opportunity to expand into several new products, including sports bottles and a green tea offering.

"Okay—do you have a valid license and the tax reports?" asked Jack.

"Yes and no."

Linh came over to join them.

"Tuan, let's meet tomorrow. Please bring me the license and the tax reports. I need to see what you have."

Tuan nodded and headed back to the plant.

"Jack, my love, I need to go."

He knew Linh needed to get home and back to her life again. "Thank you. When can I see you again?"

"Next week maybe. Ngoc needs me, Jack." Linh didn't want to tell him that Vo had come back from Hue city the day before.

Jack, troubled by Linh's answer, realized that this was the reality of their near future.

"I understand."

Linh smiled gently at her lover. "My sister will come tomorrow to look at the business. She speaks good English and will be thrilled to get away from my parents!"

Jack smiled. "Thank you, my love."

Linh smiled and picked up her bag, walking to get a taxi. "Be well. Call me if you need anything."

"I will." As the taxi drove away, they waved goodbye to each other.

"Tuan, let's meet tomorrow at 10 a.m.," said Jack.

Tuan understood Jack was now taking more charge of the water business, but he didn't understand why Linh had to be here.

"Will Linh be coming back?"

"Probably not, but her sister needs a job. She will be here tomorrow."

Tuan was upset at this. "She needs a job? Who is she?"

Jack started on the plan for him and Ms. Linh to own hundred percent of the factory. "Let's discuss it in more detail tomorrow in the morning."

Tuan, shaken by this recent development, walked away and headed back to his house. Jack waved down a taxi to head back to the hotel. The taxi ride took longer than expected because of the traffic in District One.

Jack's phone rang. "Jack, what the hell are you doing? The bank records show a wire transfer to Vietnam for $13,000 US dollars. I didn't approve this!" screamed Silvia.

"Silvia, I am investing in a water company."

Silvia couldn't believe what Jack was saying. "You did what? Without my approval?"

"Yes, without your approval, Silvia. What is this credit card bill at some club last night, $4,500?"

"You told me to have a good time!"

Jack couldn't believe how irrational his wife could be. "Yes, Silvia, enjoy!"

Within a few minutes, Jack arrived back at the hotel to see Tien waiting for him.

"Jack, we need to talk."

Tien explained to him that Tuan had called and complained.

"This is Tuan's company, not yours. Yes, you are an investor, but Tuan still needs to run it. You will be leaving soon. I appreciate you helping my brother out, but don't take away his company."

"I am trying to recover my investment and to fix the company."

Tien was visibly upset. "Jack, like the Americans before you, don't take over!" He got up from the table and headed back to his office.

Jack, exhausted, took a walk and let the cold Saigon air help relax him a bit. Needing to feel a spiritual lift, he walked to the Notre Dame Church for evening prayer. As he sat in his favorite pew, Jack began, "Dear God, please look after everyone on my prayer list. Please look after my children William and Regina, my father, my brother, and please look after Linh. Please also look after those who need extra help and love, amen." After performing the cross on his chest, Jack sat back and reflected on the day's happenings.

"Well, the sinner has arrived," said Father Flanagan.

"Yes, Father, I have arrived."

"Well, let's begin, shall we?"

Jack and the priest headed to the church's corner, where the confessionals were located. Jack entered the screen room while the priest went through the adjacent door.

"Bless me, Father, for I have sinned. It has been five hundred and three days since my last confession."

"Proceed, my son."

"Father, I have committed adultery in my marriage. I knew this to be a sin. Yet, I broke this commandment, knowing that I would hurt my wife and children. Why? I can come up with a thousand good reasons to have committed this sin. I realize that in the eyes of the Lord, I can only be forgiven after confessing and asking for forgiveness."

"My son, let's step out of the confessional and have a seat somewhere else." Jack was shocked by the priest's request. However, he welcomed the newfound kindness from him.

Jack exited the confessional and followed the Father outside of the church. Within a few moments, Jack and Father Flanagan sat down in Unification Park.

"Okay, Jack. Let's talk man to man for a moment. God appreciates your confession and effort to repent. But unless you plan on never cheating again, I suggest that you save the confession for some other time, once you have decided you won't cheat anymore. Jack, I believe if you decided to do this, it means your marriage is far gone. You need to consider resolving that before repenting."

Jack had never heard a priest offer such a suggestion before. "You are right, Father. I need to solve that issue before I could consider never sinning again."

"Jack, when the priests got arrested for molesting boys, the first thing they did was try to confess after each sin. Those priests weren't forgiven because they didn't stop what they were doing. The Vatican didn't hold these men accountable for their actions. The Vatican built the Catholic faith on the foundation of repentance, where the sinner swears to never commit the same sin again. Protestants believe that each time you sin, you ask for forgiveness. The fundamental foundation of our faith is the intent to change our ways. After each Lenten season, Catholics who have sacrificed something for forty days and forty nights hopefully have learned to do without whatever they gave up just so they can start fresh."

Jack nodded in agreement with the priest. He knew the man had made great sacrifices in his life. Jack had also sacrificed in his life by choosing to stay with Silvia in order to give the children a family life and stability. Jack suspected that Father Flannagan could have left Vietnam once he was released from prison. Yet, the priest, similar to those nuns, apparently had also stayed in Vietnam. Jack felt a deep respect for the man.

"Jack, resolve your marriage issue first. The church doesn't condone divorce for several reasons, but we all have to make choices to move forward."

Jack saw the reasoning behind the priest's words. "Thank you, Father."

The priest placed his hand on Jack's head. "Dear God, look after this young man as he departs on his new journey, amen."

Jack was overwhelmed by the blessing. "May I buy you a tea, Father?"

"No, I prefer a beer, Jack; I am Irish."

Jack and the priest headed back to the Renaissance hotel to enjoy a beer.

"Oh, Ms. Bui," the priest called out as they arrived.

"Father, what brings you to my door?"

"Jack here needs some saving; let's say he is a work in progress."

Ms. Bui nodded and smiled at Jack. "Yes, I feel the same way, Father. I will meet you upstairs for a beer."

Jack, Ms. Bui, and Father Flanagan laughed as they headed up to the bar. As they entered, Tien walked up to the group.

"There goes the neighborhood!"

Jack could not help but laugh. "Tien, the Father was here in the neighborhood and stopped in for a nightcap."

Tien looked confused. "A priest, a nightcap?"

Jack smiled and ordered some beers for everyone.

"Father, how do you know Ms. Bui?"

"Jack, that's a long answer that I choose not to give to you."

"Ms. Bui, is it really a long answer?"

The woman just changed the topic. "Jack, I see you have bailed out Tuan and the water company?"

Jack, recognizing the change, rolled with the conversation.

"Yes. After the massive rains, the factory and water systems were damaged. We worked on rebuilding the plant. We also fixed the living spaces for the workers. Also, we hired the lady next door as our cook. She will prepare meals for the employees each day."

Ms. Bui was impressed with Jack's generosity. "Jack, thank you. These beers are on me."

Father Flanagan, feeling lightheaded from the beer, said, "Friends, time for this man to head home."

Ms. Bui stood up. "Father, I will have my driver take you home."

The priest bowed his head in thanks.

Tien, also finishing his last beer, said, "Yes, I need to close up the bar upstairs."

Jack gave everyone a hug, thanking the priest.

"Jack, you are the only one who can make that decision. Come to see me later, and we can finish our conversation."

Jack bowed his head as the man departed. Upstairs, after taking a long shower, Jack opened his laptop and researched the tax laws and license transfers in Vietnam. While reading for hours, Jack got a text from Silvia, threatening him with court orders and divorce procedures. Jack knew the day had come. "Look ahead, Jack, not back," he whispered to himself.

When the children were little, Jack was afraid to divorce Silvia because he didn't want them to grow up without a family. Jack had spent most of his married life biting his lip in the name of being there for his kids. Now, he reflected on the last twenty-five years of his married experience, knowing his life was about to change.

Jack silently prayed, thanking God and Father Flanagan for this blessing.

# Chapter 23
# Acquisition

During his morning breakfast, Jack received an unexpected guest—Forest Adams from the embassy.

"Well, if it is American 007. Good morning, Forest."

"Funny Marine, order me some coffee!"

Jack requested two coffees. "So, Forest, what brings you here?"

Forest wasn't the most patient man in the world. "I see you have met our Father Flanagan. Jack, do me a favor; please stay on his good side."

Jack was confused by Adam's comment. "Yes, the Father and I had a rough beginning, but we made peace last night."

"Good," proclaimed Adams. "Jack, the padre has been an asset for the Central Intelligence Agency since before the end of the war. He attended seminary school in a church up near Sapa. As the NVA pushed south, Father Flanagan came to Saigon to help the refugees. The Father was only seventeen years old back then. He used to feed us intelligence on the NVA and VC locations throughout the Saigon offensive. After the fall of Saigon, the NVA captured him and placed him in a re-education camp for three years."

Jack listened in great detail to Forest's story. "So, why did the US try to get him? Didn't we see value in getting him free with the rest of the South Vietnamese people?"

"We tried, Jack, but he did not want to leave Vietnam."

Jack began to see a parallel track between the priest and the nuns that stayed behind as the orphans were flown out.

"Jack, one more thing, please stay out of trouble," pleaded Forest.

Jack looked back at his friend. "I invested in a water company here in Saigon. That should keep me busy!"

Forest smiled. "Jack, make sure the embassy gets free water for a year. Oh, one more thing—the thing you are looking for, try to attend Sunday mass at 10:30 at 94/1 Phan Van tri, Pio, 9 GO VNP District Nine. I believe you will find what you are looking for there."

Both men stood up and gave each other a handshake before Adams departed. Watching at a distance, Ms. Bui could only smile at the exchange between Jack and Forest.

"Oh, the memories," she whispered.

After finishing his coffee, Jack made his way down the elevator to catch a cab to the water company. Chau, Linh's sister, planned to arrive at 10:00 a.m. sharp to review the plant. Jack jumped into a taxi heading to the factory. While checking emails, he noticed a letter from Silvia.

*Dear Jack, stop selling stocks until I have a better understanding of what you are up to. The stock is fifty percent mine, and I am entitled to my share.*

He shook his head.

*Well, Silvia, sounds like you are planning for a divorce.*

He knew that the day would come. In his heart, Jack also wanted to leave her and move on to a healthy and happy life. Divorce had been on Jack's mind for years, and now was the time.

Trying to keep his mind focused on the factory, he started running through the entire checklist of things he needed from Tuan.

*Tax book, license for water processing, vehicle certifications, and employee tax forms.*

Suddenly, his phone rang. "Hello, this is Jack."

"Dad, this is William. I hope you are well. I need to tell you something." William told his father that Silvia had been arrested in Hawaii last night and needed bailing out. "Dad, she is in real trouble."

"Son, I will take care of it. Don't worry."

"Thank you, Dad. How is Vietnam? Are you now an owner in a water company?"

"Yes, son, I am helping a friend here and getting some real-world experience in doing business in Asia."

"Strong move, Dad!"

After a few more words with this son, Jack called his sister-in-law Rose.

"Hey, Rose, are you okay?"

"Yes, Jack, I am fine. Silvia is a different issue."

"I can imagine. What do you need?"

"Jack, we will need $5,000 for bail and $25,000 for damages. Silvia got drunk again and started breaking things at the bar. She hit a few people as well. The police locked her up, and we are trying to get her released."

"Okay, Rose. I will send the funds now via the secured link to your account. Please give me an hour. Pay the damages and get her out of jail."

"Thank you, Jack."

After accessing his global bank account, he transferred the $30,000 US dollars. Within an hour, Jack received a text from Rose, telling him that the issue was solved.

*Not even a thank you.* Jack realized the money he sent to Rose was the investment fund he planned to use for the water company. Even though Silvia told him not the sell any more stock, Jack sold more to cover the $30,000 US dollars needed for the water factory.

"Mr. Jack, welcome back," said Tuan.

He smiled at his partner and workforce as he entered the water plant. "Did Chau show up?"

"Yes, but I sent her home. I told her I didn't need her here."

Jack was upset. "Tuan, she will manage my portion of this business while I am not here! Please call her back."

"Okay, Jack."

Chau showed up at the factory upset and asked Jack to join her for tea across the street.

"Jack, thank you for this job. My sister thinks wonderful things about you."

"Yes, Chau, I think your sister is a wonderful woman."

"Mr. Kendall, Tuan is hiding something. I don't know what, but please be careful with your money." Chau had started to ask around the district if Tuan was an honest businessman. To her great surprise, many people seemed to love Tuan. Chau decided to check inside the factory to see if she could find any financial records and license books for Jack.

"Yes, that's why I want to hire you to be the manager of this business. I will buy out Tuan's part and remove him today."

Chau, smiling with excitement, reached over and gave Jack a hug.

"Let me talk to Tuan and get this going."

They walked back to the factory. "Tuan, let's have a tea."

Tuan, sensing something was wrong, walked with Jack across the street. "Tuan, thank you for allowing me to invest in your business, but I get the sense that your business is quite a mess at the moment. I am deeply concerned about my investment."

Tuan didn't want to disclose the truth about the water business out of fear of losing him as a friend and investor. Tuan's business had lost money for years, and he'd failed to pay his taxes and his water license fees. The local government had threatened to take away the plant if Tuan did not come up with the money soon. Tuan spent most of the money on his cycling tour business while letting the water business collapse.

Tuan realized where Jack was going with this. "Jack, I see you don't trust me. Okay, what do you want to do about it?"

"I will buy you out for 12,000,000 Vietnamese dollars. I will get the factory, water, clients, trucks, scooters, and funds in the bank." Jack knew the only way he could have any hope in recovering his investment would be to control the entire factory.

"When can we do this?"

"How about today? Please, I need the license and tax information to review them with Chau."

Tuan couldn't wait to get rid of the water business and put the money back into his other company. "Thank you, Jack."

Jack knew he was taking a massive gamble, not only with his own money but with upsetting Silvia and his delicate balance at home with the children. He continued to doubt his own choices. When he felt the depression coming on, he tried turning his attention to the love he had for Linh. Jack wouldn't stop remembering the beautiful moments they had shared, like when they made love, or the fabulous walk in the park, and the time when they enjoyed tea and coffee. *Why are you doing this, Jack?*

Feeling empty, Jack excused himself for a moment and walked around the district. Seeing the neighborhood near the water plant gave Jack a sense of purpose and worth. *I have so much at home in America, and these people only have what they have. No mortgages, no college funds, no 401k.* Deep down, Jack always tried to help others in any way he could. The deep emptiness he felt inside as a result of being married to Silvia drained his ability to see a brighter light in his life. Already having witnessed the departure of his children heading to their own lives, Jack saw a purpose for owning the water plant. "I'd use the profits to help the orphans here in Vietnam," whispered Jack. He knew that the only person who truly understood this consciousness was himself. Linh, Chau, and others thought Jack was crazy to do this. "Yes, in five years, I will look back on this as one crazy idea," Jack said to himself.

While walking, Jack noticed street vendors selling food, toys, and small tools. Others were inside their shop, calling him to get in their shop. Jack, who wasn't in the best mood, waved at his neighbors. After spending thirty minutes walking, Jack found a bench to sit to reflect on his life. *You have spent over $40,000 of money you saved for your retirement. You lied to your wife about what you are planning to do. You have committed adultery and attempted to confess your sins to a priest. Moreover, you are putting your working career in jeopardy because you are four thousand miles away from your clients. Yep, that's the path for success.*

Jack took a few deep breaths, standing up. He headed back to the water plant. As Jack arrived, he noticed several kids sitting around, drinking sugar. Jack stopped and bent down to look inside their mouths.

Jack couldn't believe the condition of their teeth; they were completely ruined by what they drank.

Jack hurried up to the plant to find Tuan. "Hey, why does no one drink water in this district?"

"They can't afford the water, Mr. Jack, so they drink pure sugar liquid instead."

"Ms. Chau, as the new manager of the water plant, come with me, please."

Jack and Chau departed, heading back to the street corner. He noticed a small park at the intersection where old and young people hung out and passed the time. Chau saw a space between the part entrance and the sitting areas.

"Chau, starting tomorrow, please have two of the workers assigned to bring ten five-gallon containers to the park. Please, let these people fill their bottles with fresh water."

Chau looked completely surprised. "Mr. Kendall, that will cost us money."

"So I heard. Let's do it anyway."

Feeling inspired by this gesture, Chau assigned two of the workers to focus on 'park duty' starting the next day. Jack continued to walk around the plant, looking for better ways to do business under Vietnam terms. *This isn't America, Jack.*

Jack nodded and headed off to the teahouse for an afternoon tea. Chau, feeling more empowered, started giving direction to the workers, including better ways to clean the bottles, how to put the labels on correctly, and how to package the large ones in a container.

# Chapter 24
# Association

As Jack headed back to the water plant, he noticed several children running by. "Oh, to be young," said Jack. After arriving back at the factory, he noticed several workers getting into an argument with one another. "Hey!" yelled Jack. As he approached the workers, all moved quickly away and headed back to work. "Chau, what was that all about?"

Chau, with a look of shock on her face, said, "Mr. Kendall, some things are very troubling here in Vietnam."

He pulled her outside. "Chau, what is it?"

Chau began to cry. "Many of these workers were street orphans when they were young. Some of them were sold off by their parents."

Jack knew about the problems with human trafficking in Asia. "Yes, I heard many stories about this." Chau nodded. "During some of our water deliveries, many of the workers have stumbled upon factories, houses, and warehouses full of children being sold off to foreigners."

Jack, with a look of horror on his face, could not believe what Chau had told them. "Where?"

Chau, still crying, said, "Three factories here in the district and a couple of houses in District Seven."

"Chau, let's go out with the after deliveries to see for ourselves."

Chau shook her head frantically. "No! Those men are very dangerous."

Jack, sitting back on the bench, knew he could not just turn a blind eye to these events. "Chau, we need to at least get some pictures and share with the police."

Chau kept telling Jack, "No, the police protect those foreigners."

He understood her concerns and gave Chau a hug. Not wanting to let this emotion go, Jack decided to walk over and visit with Tuan.

"Hey, Tuan, you got a minute?" Tuan looked up from cleaning his bikes, getting them ready for an upcoming tour.

"Sure, Jack."

Jack walked over and sat down near him. "Chau and the workers have been delivering water to several factors and houses that seem to be selling off children to foreigners. I guess everyone is scared to report this?"

Tuan put down his tools. "Mr. Jack, stay away from that issue."

"Okay, did you know about this?"

Tuan stared at him. "Yes. I am a business owner with three kids. I am not going to report something that will hurt my family!"

Jack understood Tuan's dilemma. "I know. I would do the same thing."

"Look, you are leaving soon. Don't make trouble for us!"

Jack nodded and headed back to the factory. While walking back to the factory from the bike shop, Jack noticed the same children running earlier all were sitting perfectly still outside of a home. All the children had blank looks on their faces and stared straight ahead.

Within moments, a large man in his late seventies came out of the house and grabbed three of the children and led them into the house. The rest of the children started crying. "I have to get this on film," Jack whispered. Jack positioned himself around the corner and began to film using his camera phone. Several minutes passed, and the same older man came out and retrieved several more children. Jack zoomed in his camera to get a good look at the man and the children. While filming, Jack got a good look at the man. He wasn't Asian.

After the second bunch of kids were taken into the house, the remaining children got up from the ground and began to run away. Noticing the children running, the older man screamed in Vietnamese, "Stop!" Soon after, several men came running out of the house and began running after the kids. Jack, still filming, moved around the back of the house to see if he could get a look at what was happening inside.

After going through a broken fence, Jack noticed a half-covered window to the house. *Let's see what these bastards are doing.* Being stealthy, Jack positioned his camera on the edge of the window, hoping to record something. After a few moments, Jack leaned over and looked inside for himself. Immediately, Jack noticed several men sitting in the middle of the room with the children standing against the wall. "These men must be Pakistani or

Indian," whispered Jack. The children, all crying, were being told to shut up by the older man.

Jack, after completing his filming, moved quietly back through the fence and headed back to the front of the building. Walking as if nothing had happened, he headed back to the water plant.

"Chau?" asked Jack. "Who lives in the house three doors down from us?"

Chau looked over at the house Jack was referring to. "I don't know. They don't buy from us."

Jack nodded. "Okay, I will be back later."

After saying goodbye to the workers, Jack rode off on his bike and headed back to the hotel. While cycling, Jack decided to message Forest.

*Message: US_Consulate_HCMC: Encryption: Forest Adams: Jack Kendall: Marine, spotted possible human trafficking near the factory, need assistance.*

*Jack.*

Leaving a meeting with the Mayor of Saigon, Forest noticed the secured message and stopped for a moment. "Jack, Jesus!"

Forest stopped off at a bench near the consulate building.

*Message: US_Consulate_HCMC: Jack Kendall: Forest: Leave it alone, Jack, signed: Forest.*

Jack, while cycling, felt his secured communicator vibrate and pulled over and checked his message. A moment later, two men on the back of a red scooter raced by Jack and struck him with a lead pipe. Feeling the crushing blow from the pipe, Jack hit the ground hard and smacked his head on the road.

Even with wearing a helmet, Jack still got knocked out cold. After lying on the road for a few moments, he suddenly woke up and noticed his head bleeding. "What happened?" Several people noticed Jack lying on the road, but none came over to help him.

Jack, still very dizzy from the impact, sat up and leaned across the curb on the road. He dialed his phone to try to reach Tuan. "Hey, it's Jack, on the road heading back to the hotel—someone hit me with a lead pipe."

Tuan was in total shock. "I am on my way."

Jack, staying still in case of a possible concussion, started to throw up on the road. Within a few moments, Tuan arrived. "Jack, holy shit!"

"Help me up, pal."

Tuan grabbed a towel from his car, placing it on Jack's head to control the bleeding. "Come on, stand up if you can."

Jack tried to get to his feet. "This hurts."

Tuan walked his friend to the wall near the road. "Did you see who hit you?"

Jack shook his head. "No faces. Two guys on a red scooter."

Tuan pressed the towel against Jack's head to try to stop the bleeding. "Can you continue to cycle?"

Jack tested his balance. "Yes, I am good. Hey, Tuan, check this out." Jack took his camera out and showed the video. "Who is this asshole?"

Tuan shook his head as he watched. "Oh, no, you have to delete this."

"Who is the hell is it?"

Tuan removed the towel from Jack's head. "Be careful cycling back to the hotel; those men are very dangerous. We see them from time to time in our district, taking children away." Jack got up and thanked his friend for helping him stop the bleeding from the pipe hit. Tuan proceeded to climb back in his car and head off.

Jack realized that this mystery man in the video must be someone very dangerous for Tuan to run off like that. He messaged Forest again.

*Message: US_Consulate_HCMC: Encryption: Jack Kendall: Forest Adams: Uploading video, possible foreigner, need ID, signed: Jack.*

It took nearly twenty minutes to upload the video, during which time Jack continued to cycle back to the hotel. The headache continued to impact Jack's ability to stay on the bike. Once he noticed the tall Renaissance Hotel in the distance, Jack hopped off his bike and decided to walk the rest of the way.

"Oh my God, Mr. Jack," said Van, the tearoom lady at the hotel. "Are you okay?"

Jack walked in with blood on his face and arms. "I am good, Van."

She ran over to the management desk. "Ms. Bui, come quick."

Bui, dropping her notepad, ran over to see Jack. "Oh, Jack, what happened?" She led him to a table in the lobby. "Van, get our medical team here!" Van nodded and ran off.

"Jack, what happened?" As Jack began to speak, Forest showed up at the door leading into the hotel.

"Jack!" yelled Forest.

"Glad you are here, Marine," Jack said with a laugh.

Forest instructed Ms. Bui, "We need to move him." She helped Jack to his feet and led him over to a private office behind the front desk. Van, with the medical team, entered the room.

"Here." Van pointed to Jack. The medical team checked Jack's eyes and the cuts on his head.

"Sir, does your head hurt?"

Jack nodded. The medical team checked for any open cuts. While they provided care, Forest and Bui stepped out of the room.

"He was filming someone selling kids to a foreigner—they must have seen him."

Bui asked, "Do you know who did this?"

Forest glanced away for a moment. "Yes, Boris Latcha."

Bui's eyes grew big with fear. "Oh God, I thought he was gone, left Vietnam."

Boris Latcha was known by many North Vietnamese army officers and Vietcong leadership during the war with the Americans in the 1970s. He served as a Russian military advisor to the North Vietnamese Army. After the war ended in 1975, Boris stayed in Vietnam and became one of the country's most wanted drug lords. His outfit controlled half of the heroin shipped out of Vietnam along with a great deal of the human trafficking of young children to other countries.

"Well, Interpol had him in custody three times. Yet, due to political pressure from the Russian ambassador, they had to release him. Last I heard he was still in Thailand."

Forest walked head out. "Jack, you all right?"

"Yes, though my back still hurts."

Forest nodded. "Okay, let's get you to your room." The medical staff and Forest helped Jack to his feet.

Tien, just coming on his shift, noticed everyone by the front desk and began asking what had happened.

Meanwhile, Forest led Jack around the back service elevator, so as not to raise any suspicion. "Jack, you need to back off this one," whispered Forest. When they arrived on the eighteenth floor, Jack and Forest exited the elevator and headed into this room.

"Who the hell is that guy in the video?"

Forest reached into the minibar to grab some beers. Jack took one from him.

"Look, this asshole is Boris Latcha, a real piece of shit. An ex-military advisor to the North Vietnamese Army during the war. He trained many Vietnamese soldiers how to torture American soldiers and kill South Vietnamese people."

Jack took a gulp of beer. "Damn, and I guess there are still some people today that see him as a hero of the people."

Forest nodded. "Yep, he is a protected asset even with the current Russian ambassador. Jack, he controlled a great deal of drug money here along with smuggling out children to third-world shitholes like Pakistan."

"Why doesn't this government do something about him?"

Forest looked out the window of Jack's hotel room, seeing the Saigon River below. "They are taking five-year-old orphans off the streets of Vietnam and getting them into a place where at least they are eating something once a day."

Jack, full of rage, threw his beer bottle against the wall.

"You mean that his human smuggling piece of shit is seen as a saint because he sells children to the highest bidder and makes the problem go away?"

"That is the third world, Jack."

Jack reached into the minibar for another beer. "So, I can assume the Vietnamese government or the United Nations or the American government will do nothing about this?"

Forest took out his phone to look at the video again. "Jack, these men sitting on the floor are part of a human smuggling group out of Karachi, Pakistan. In one month, these kids will be making sneakers with sports stars autographs in plain sight."

Jack had read for years how many clothing companies outsourced their manufacturing to India, Thailand, Vietnam, and Pakistan. "Look, you need to delete that video, and don't go near that house again."

Jack heard his friend. "I got it."

Forest, finishing his beer, added, "Stay out of trouble, Jack." Soon after, the man departed the room.

Jack, sitting on his couch, continued to stare outside of the window at the Saigon River. "And this guy is considered a hero?" He placed his beer on the table and headed off to take a shower.

# Chapter 25
## Skirmish

Heading off the elevator, Forest stopped off at the desk to check on Ms. Bui. "Thank you for helping him, Bui."

She smiled. "What time are you coming home, my love?"

Forest placed his finger over his lips. "Shh." Forest and Bui had been secretly married for several years since he returned to Vietnam in 2004. Bui smiled again at her husband and headed back to her office.

While getting back in his car, Forest was still troubled by Jack getting attacked by Boris's people. "I am going to get that bastard." Forest didn't want to tell Jack his plan to get revenge. He had a score to settle with Boris for all the terrible things he did to American GIs during the Vietnam War.

*Message: US_Consulate_HCMC: Encryption: Marine Corps Detachment Operations: Forest Adams: Need assistance: American citizen down: scramble Reaction Force Seven to District Thirteen, civilian protection package, signed: Adams.*

Inside the US consulate in Saigon, the state department deployed several US Marine Corps detachments, including security personnel, operations teams, and hostage extraction teams, better known as Reaction Force Seven. The team was under the command of Major Tyson Harrison, a fourteen-year Marine Corps officer with two tours in Iraq and Afghanistan before starting his assignment in Vietnam. "Hmm, Mr. Adams, what are you up to now?"

Reading the encrypted communication, Major Harrison sent a flash message to the reaction team:

*Message: US_Marine_Detachment_Reaction_Team_Seven: Scramble now. Muster in the motor pool in five mikes.*

As each member of the team received the message from their commanding officer, each of the Marines switched out of their military uniforms and changed into civilian clothes.

Within ten minutes, the entire Reaction force assembled for instructions. "Okay, Marines, you are heading into District Thirteen. Possible VIP terrorist. Mr. Adams will meet us at the location."

As Major Harrison finished, each of the team members loaded into their SUVs, and the team headed out the consulate gate and toward District Thirteen.

Forest, arriving first, stopped his car in front of Jack's water company. Walking in, he asked, "Who is Chau?"

Chau looked over at this western man. "I am, sir," she replied.

"I am a friend of Jack's. Get everyone out of here and lock the door!"

Chau looked terrified at Forest's request.

"Sir, these workers live here. They have nowhere to go."

Forest looked around. "Okay, get them in a safe place here in the factory."

Chau nodded and began to get all the workers upstairs. "Shut off the lines," she ordered.

Forest looked down the street. "Chau, which door did Jack ask you about?"

"Three doors down."

Forest nodded. He reached for his radio in his pocket. "Major Harrison, Forest Adams, come in."

"Go for Harrison," replied the major.

"Major, hold your position on Nguyen Hai AI alley."

Harrison acknowledged.

Forest, using the water company as cover, watched the house that Jack had inspected earlier. After waiting nearly thirty minutes, Forest noticed several men entering the building. "Got you!," said Forest. "Major, execute, roll in."

Major Harrison, hearing the order from Forest, ordered, "All teams, engage." Within moments, Forest ran up the door of the house and drew his weapon. Just then, Major Harrison and his team pulled up in front of the house.

"Major, send two units to cover the back."

With one press of the door, Forest busted into the house.

Startled, several men sitting on the floor jumped up and attempted to attack him with pipes. Forest drew his weapon and shot two of them, screaming, "Stay down!"

Then he felt the gun being pointed at his head. "You piece of shit," said Boris.

"Shut up!" Forest responded.

"Oh, fuck no!" screamed the major as he charged in and hit Boris in the head with his machinegun. Boris was knocked down and then rolled on the ground and sprang up, shooting. Forest, seeing Boris land, started to shoot first and hit Boris in the chest with two rounds. As Boris reacted to the gunshots, the remaining men on the floor attempted to escape the room, only to be met by the Reaction Five team waiting by the door. The team, armed with brass knuckles, started punching the escaping men.

Forest stood over Boris. "Stay the fuck down."

Major Harrison came over and knocked Boris in the face with his fist. Recovering the man's gun, Forest stared down at his nemesis. "And the Vietnamese government calls you a hero for selling off their children?"

Boris began to laugh. "You piece of shit Americans, I will be free in an hour."

The rest of the escaping men were getting beaten up by the Marine detachment. After several blows to their faces and bodies, the Reaction Team threw the men back into the house and on the floor. Bleeding, the men, all from Pakistan, pleaded for help. "Help! Stop! We are here as workers for our factories!" The Marines, hearing this, continued to punch the men and told them to sit down and stay in their place.

"Boris, you are coming with me," said Forest, binding Boris's hands behind his back and leading him outside to the car. The remaining Pakistanis were also tied up and left inside the house.

"Go ahead. Turn me in, asshole."

Forest threw Boris in the trunk of the car and slammed it closed.

"Major, you need to get your men out—the Saigon Police should be here shortly."

The major nodded.

Forest jumped in his car and started to drive west, outside of District Thirteen. After driving for several hours, he stopped the car.

Opening the trunk, he lifted Boris out.

"Okay, Boris, over here."

Boris looked around. "Where the fuck am I?"

Forest pulled Boris toward the river. "You are at Mekong Delta River."

"What the fuck are you doing? I am protected by the Vietnam government; I am a hero!"

Forest turned to Boris and punched him in the face, knocking him down. "You killed many Americans, asshole—consider this a payback."

Boris's eyes filled with fear. "No, you can't do this!"

Forest lifted him up and dragged him near the water. "See those cobra snakes?" asked Forest. Boris looked down at a small hole near the river.

Forest proceeded to push Boris into the snake pit full of king cobra snakes. After a few moments of screaming, Boris fell silent and his body rolled into the river. Watching the man float away, Forest could only think about how many Americans this Russian had killed during the Vietnam War.

Seeing the body completely sink into the river, Forest cleaned his trunk of any blood and proceeded to drive back to the consulate.

Soon after Major Harrison cleared out of District Thirteen, several Saigon Police cars showed up and with guns drawn entered into the house. The police, along with several news crews, began filming the inside of the house, including the Pakistani smugglers.

Heading back to his office in the Consulate in Saigon, Forest remembered his time during the Vietnam War. At the age of seventeen, Forest had arrived in Saigon on April 10, 1975, only twenty days before the fall of the city. Forest spent his entire time guarding the main gate at the US Embassy. With the war about to come to an end, Forest watched thousands of South Vietnamese people trying to climb the gate, hoping for a helicopter ride out of the country before the North Vietnamese army arrived. Forest, like many servicemen, knew the North Vietnamese Army had received military assistance from many communist countries including Cuba, China, and Russia. These advisors also brought advanced military technology including surface-to-air missiles, tanks, and intelligence information. Forest knew many Marines stationed with him at the embassy that spoke about these advisors. Many of these foreign fighters killed, shot down, or tortured many Americans during the war.

Forest sat in his chair, looking around his office, seeing old pictures of him and many of his comrades he'd served with both in the Marines and as an intelligence officer for the Central Intelligence Agency. "I miss you guys," he whispered.

Just as Forest began to pack up and go home, he got a call. "Adams, please report to Ambassador Orwell," said Julie Lasi, executive assistant to the US ambassador for Vietnam.

"On my way," said Forest.

Forest went down the hall from his office and into the outer office of Ambassador Orwell, where he knocked on the door.

"Come in," said David. "Adams, sit please."

"Yes sir, you wanted to see me?"

"Adams, I know you have been around these woods for many years—however, things have changed."

Forest nodded. "Yes sir, on and off for thirty-two years."

"I see. I received a call from the Russian ambassador this evening. One of their citizens has been reported missing. A Boris Latcha, name ring a bell?"

"Doesn't ring a bell, sir."

The ambassador rose up from his chair. "Oh, no? Hmm."

David continued, "You authorized a civilian extraction today with Reaction Force Seven in District Thirteen. I spoke to Major Harrison an hour ago. I guess you guys roughed up some Russians and a few Pakistan businessmen. Does this ring a bell, Adams?"

Forest looked up. "Come to think of it, I do remember stopping a child slave auction today in that vicinity."

The ambassador nodded. "Oh, yes, good work." He smiled. "Forest, I expect several formal complaints being filed by the Pakistani ambassador anytime now. I guess the Marines used brass knuckles and beat the shit out of them."

Forest looked up. "Look, they were selling children, not more than seven years old; the Russian is an old advisor to the NVA during the Vietnam War responsible for killing many Americans."

"That was thirty years ago, Adams!" pushed David. "Those men were taking those orphans off the streets and away from the drug monkeys and sex traffickers. This is the new world." He shook his head. "Look, Latcha brings these resource recruiters from all over the world to Vietnam. They exchange some funds, these orphans end up living in a home, safe and away from these streets, and we are developing commerce."

Forest was disgusted. "We profit from child labor and human trafficking!"

The ambassador walked back behind his desk and sat down. "Look, let me give you the real-world 2020 version."

Forest looked away from the ambassador. "I have ten companies a day calling me, wanting to relocate their manufacturing to Vietnam and away from China. Companies bringing jobs to Vietnam. Those brokers you beat up, they take these kids, place them into a home with supervision, teach them a skill, feed them, and give them clothes and medical care. In exchange, these companies move billions of dollars of product in and out of Vietnam at the lower cost point. Those companies need that cheap labor in order to break their supply chains away from China and be competitive. We, the United States, are here in Vietnam today to help this country, not become the next Colombia, Panama, or Laos. Vietnam is this close, Adams, to becoming the next failed state and hub for global narcotics and human trafficking. These jobs and these manufactures give people here a reason not to support the drug lords. We get a fair cut of the revenues, and our military and intelligence agencies now have a base of operation again. Big picture, Adams."

Forest, while listening to the ambassador's logic, began to understand. "I get it, David."

"Look, Adams, I could force you into retirement, but I don't want to do that. I need you to come full circle here."

Forest nodded. "Yes, sir, anything else?"

"If you hear anything about this Boris character, please let your pals at the Russian consulate know. That will be all."

Forest rose up and headed out the door without saying another word to the ambassador.

Heading back to his office, Forest could not believe how the world had changed. He was getting too old for this shit.

# Chapter 26
# Progression

Jack woke to a small amount of rain hitting the window in his room. Even eighteen floors up, the water sounded quiet. *Rainfall—the factory will be okay.* Realizing that the time was 9:30, he needed to get up to head off to the place Adams told him to go.

"Oh, Jack," he'd said, "one more thing. The thing you are looking for, try to attend Sunday mass at 10:30 at 94/1 Phan Van tri, Pio, 9 GO VNP District Nine. I believe you will find what you are looking for there."

After a quick shower, Jack got dressed and headed down to pick up an espresso before heading to the church. After retrieving his favorite beverage, Jack gave the taxi driver the church's address.

*"Mai Am Linh Me?"* The driver looked a bit confused. "This isn't a church."

Jack thought for a moment. "Okay, let's go anyway."

The traffic was prolonged on this Sunday morning because of the rain. The location of the church was in the northeast part of Saigon. After forty-five minutes, the taxi dropped Jack in front of a series of buildings.

"Thanks," Jack said to the driver.

After looking around for a few moments, he walked down a side road that seemed to run parallel to a series of old buildings, hidden behind a large fence. As he continued walking to the back of the area, Jack noticed a small gathering of nuns. *This must be the place.* Jack walked up to the community. It was then he saw that part of the building had been turned into a small outdoor church.

"Good morning," an elderly man greeted Jack.

"Good morning; I am here for the mass at 10:30 a.m."

The old man walked Jack to the open seat in the back of the church.

"Thank you, sir."

The man bowed and walked away. Jack noticed something very heartfelt; the younger nuns began walking out several old ladies. They were helping them to a seat in the small church. Most of the ladies looked well into their nineties, and most of them seemed very sick. After fifteen minutes, the church filled mostly with those ladies and the younger nuns sitting next to them. *Incredible.*

"Excuse me, could you slide down, please?"

Jack turned to the right to see Ms. Bui standing before him.

"Ms. Bui? Good morning!"

"Good morning, Mr. Jack. How did you know about this place?"

"Forest told me."

Ms. Bui took a deep breath. "I knew he couldn't keep a secret."

"What brings you here, Ms. Bui? What is this place?"

Ms. Bui, already upset, didn't want to answer him. "Jack, this is an orphanage for old ladies. Women who had been abandoned by their families. The Sacred Heart nuns look after them."

Jack shot Ms. Bui a look of surprise. "Sacred Heart?" Had he found them after searching for so long?

"The lady in the third row, to the left—she is my adopted mother."

"Your adopted mother?"

Ms. Bui cried quietly. "She doesn't remember me."

Jack felt Ms. Bui's pain. He knew she was an orphan after the war. "After she found me in the church in Saigon alone, she adopted me and sent me to the rice fields to keep me safe," she explained.

A few moments later, the priest walked into the church. Everyone stood up to greet him. The priest conducted the mass and praised everyone for attending. Jack had never met this priest before, but he liked his sermon and kindness. He went to bless each one of the old ladies individually. After ending the mass, the young nuns helped the old ladies back to their living quarters. The rain poured. Ms. Bui asked for Jack's umbrella and assisted to take her mother and others back to their rooms.

Jack stood off to the side, watching in admiration for the nuns and Ms. Bui. Once all the ladies were placed in their rooms, Ms. Bui came back out to Jack.

"Why did you come, Jack?"

Jack sat down with her. He told her the story about the nuns and babies at the end of the war.

"I have been looking after them for several years. I have read many stories about them and what happened that day. One of my goals was to find them and ask them things I always wanted to know."

Ms. Bui said, "Let me ask." She walked over to the old man. After a brief conversation, she returned. "He believes they may be in the front building."

Jack was shocked that his dream of finding the nuns might be coming true. "Let's go, please."

As the rain continued, Jack and Ms. Bui walked arm-in-arm as friends, under the umbrella. They headed down the road leading to the front of the building complex. Jack stopped at another building, noticing the sounds of children behind a fence and walls.

"What is this place, Ms. Bui?"

"This is a place for children with AIDS, abandoned by their families. The nuns take care of them as well."

Jack stopped for a moment to take in what he was seeing. He spent the next five minutes just listening to the children, knowing they wouldn't live much longer. *Yet, they still have a laugh in their hearts.*

"Thank you, Ms. Bui, for showing me this."

She squeezed Jack's hand as they continued to the front of the complex. Once they reached the road, Jack and Ms. Bui turned right, heading to an enormous iron door. He attempted to open the door, but it was locked. Jack knocked on the door, but the buildings behind the door were a great distance away.

"I believe they've locked it. What can we do?"

Ms. Bui looked defeated, but then she heard a voice from across the street. A man yelled in Vietnamese, "Put your hand through the hole and pull!" Once Jack did this, the enormous iron door opened. And beyond it, Jack saw an incredible sight. The entire wall and iron door led into a vast courtyard. It looked like a high school playground. Jack and Ms. Bui entered the complex, closing the door behind them. He walked ahead of Ms. Bui, wondering if that could be the place where the nuns lived now.

"Ms. Bui, what is this place, please?"

"I am not sure, Jack; I have never been here before."

Jack and Ms. Bui strolled through the massive courtyard. After a few minutes, they reached a building's entrance. To the right, Jack heard a voice calling them.

"Can I help you?" The nun spoke in Vietnamese.

"Yes, this gentleman is looking for the nuns," replied Ms. Bui.

The younger nun looked quite puzzled. "Which nuns does this man seek?"

Ms. Bui mentioned the orphan airlift at the end of war with the Americans.

"Ah, yes, those nuns are still here." She asked them to come upstairs to her office. "Let me get them for you."

Jack began to shake uncontrollably. "All these years, and those brave nuns are still here in Saigon," he mumbled.

Ms. Bui watched Jack almost lose his balance. "Are you all right?"

Jack sat down in a chair for a moment. "I am fine. I just need a moment, please."

Ms. Bui smiled and moved a few feet away to give him some space. No matter how Jack tried to compose himself, he could not calm himself down. "I am here, after all these years of wondering about these ladies—they are still here, God bless," said Jack.

"Hello, I am Sister Florence. What nuns do you seek, dear sir?"

Through Ms. Bui's translation, Jack told the story about when he was a boy and read about the operation, and he asked if those nuns were still alive and if she knew where they were.

"Oh, yes, they are here. I am one of them, sir—do you want to meet the rest of them?"

Jack dropped in a chair, drained of all strength. After more than four decades, he had finally made it to Vietnam and found the incredible nuns. Jack stood up and reached over to take the nun's hand and kiss it gently. Overwhelmed with joy from Jack's outpouring of emotion, she started to be teary-eyed.

"Yes, please, sister. I would love to meet the rest of your order."

Ms. Bui helped Jack to stand up. It was then when she realized that her friend was in a complete state of shock.

"Please come with me to the prayer sitting room. I will go get my sisters."

Jack held Ms. Bui's hand. "Thank you for being here with me."

Ms. Bui wiped away her tears. "No, thank you, Jack."

A few moments later, Sister Florence returned with three other ladies.

"Mr. Jack, this is Sister Nguyen, Sister Christine, and Sister Vu."

"Sisters, my deepest honor to be here meeting you." Jack's eyes filled with tears.

"Son," said Sister Vu. "Please sit. Thank you for seeing us."

Jack realized that Sister Vu spoke French.

*"Merci, beaucoup,"* he replied.

As the nuns sat down with Jack and Ms. Bui, Sister Christine spoke, "My son, why did you come all this way to see us?"

Jack told the sisters about his whole journey, starting from the age of eleven.

Sister Nguyen replied, "Not all the children got out, Mr. Jack. We needed to stay here and make sure the remaining children were safe."

Sister Florence added, "Yes, please remember, we had to get back inside these walls. The North Vietnamese Army arrived in the city and planned to shut down the airport."

Jack remembered seeing news films of the North Vietnamese troops running through the streets, fighting the remaining South Vietnamese Army.

"You stayed, knowing that the new government would punish you?"

Sister Vu replied in French. "Mr. Jack, that is our calling, my son. I have been here since the 1950s, and I have seen many babies die because of the various wars."

Jack understood enough and cried, *"Qui,* sister."

Sister Vu asked if Ms. Bui was Jack's wife. Jack replied, "No, she is my friend."

Everyone smiled. No longer in a state of shock, Jack began to relax and enjoy the life-changing conversation he'd sought for so many years. He took the opportunity to ask them how they got the babies back from the airport when the planes stopped coming.

"Oh, we had a bus driver that worked hard. He helped us to load the babies in the middle of the night and back to the orphanage in the morning for those that did not get out," said Sister Christine.

He realized that his complex wasn't a school. "Is this the same orphanage?" Jack asked.

*"Oui,"* replied Sister Vu.

He asked why the government didn't take over these buildings.

"Oh, I will show you," replied Sister Nguyen. The nuns led Jack and Ms. Bui to another room.

"This is our prayer room. Please notice the sacred statue of the blessed Mary," said Sister Vu.

"Yes, I see her. Why is this the prayer room?" asked Jack.

Sister Nguyen smiled back at Jack, took his hand, and sat him down in a pew. She spoke in a soft, kind voice. "On the day we rushed back from the airport, we got past the soldiers and armored tanks heading to the unification palace. Once we had the bus inside these walls, we heard soldiers running down the street. Several of us were still outside the walls trying to get the children back inside—"

Sister Nguyen became tearful, so Sister Christine finished for her. "As we were on the street in complete chaos, suddenly the tanks stopped and turned away from us."

Jack, puzzled by Sister Christine's story, asked, "They just turned away?"

"Yes," replied Sister Christine. "After the tanks turned away, we got all the carts filled with children and the bus inside."

Sister Florence smiled at Jack. "This is our prayer room, Mr. Jack. Here we witnessed an appearance of the blessed Mary herself on that day."

Jack knew the church's history well. "I am sorry, you said that they blessed Mary made an appearance in spiritual form? Where?"

"Here, behind you, exactly where that statue is. Her spirit came out from the wall but only for a few moments," replied Sister Florence.

Jack sat back in his pew and cried openly. The nuns took Jack's hands. "It's all right, my son."

He wiped away his tears and stared at the statue of Mary. "Thank you for sharing this with me." The nuns were overwhelmed with Jack's outpouring of emotion. After a few moments, Jack reached into his bag and pulled out some religious items.

"These rosaries were my grandmother's. I'd like to give them to you."

The nuns couldn't believe the gift. "My son, God be with you."

Ms. Bui sat quietly; she also could never believe this side of Jack. She squeezed Jack's hand and smiled at him.

"Sir, we would like you to come upstairs, please," the nuns requested.

Jack followed the nuns to a staircase leading up to their second floor. *These ladies use the stairs? Incredible.* After a few minutes of slow climbing, Jack and the nuns reached the resting room. Sister Nguyen waved Jack into the room. Jack couldn't comprehend the place before his eyes. Several people were dressed in white gowns, all lying on their beds in complete peace. The room was partially dark, and they couldn't hear anything. Sister Vu took Jack by the hand and walked them through to meet each person.

Jack realized why that room was the resting area. These people were waiting for their time to join God in heaven. Overwhelmed with emotion, Jack took Ms. Bui's arm for support. "Ms. Bui, I didn't expect to see this in my lifetime."

She wiped away Jack's tears. "God wanted you to be here, Jack."

"Mr. Kendall, this is another nun that was there that day," said Sister Vu. "And this gentleman was the bus driver who helped bring the remaining orphans back here."

Jack bowed with a deep respect for the man. As he walked around the room, acknowledging each person with a gentle smile, a man rose from his bed.

"This," said Sister Vu, "is the doctor that treated the babies."

When they reached the end of a row of beds, he noticed an elderly nun smiling at him.

He bent down and placed his hand on her cheek. "God bless you, sister," Jack spoke quietly to her. The aging nun warmly smiled back. Jack strolled to the exit, thanking the sisters for sharing this with him. He turned around, looking one last time at the people in their final resting place. He realized that he wouldn't be coming back to this place again. "I will never forget this place ever in my life."

Sister Florence guided Jack and Ms. Bui out of the resting room and into another room to continue their conversation.

"Mr. Kendall, what other questions do you have?" asked Sister Florence.

Jack needed a moment to steady himself.

"Yes, sister, I have been a Catholic for most of my life. Yet, I have never heard the story of the appearance of the blessed Mary in Vietnam."

Sister Florence repeated the question to the other sisters in French and Vietnamese. Both nuns smiled and looked down at their feet.

"Mr. Jack, the blessed Mary made an appearance here, as we mentioned. The church here in Vietnam and the Vatican didn't believe our account of the story. Many of the local churches here in Saigon and in Rome felt that the moment of terror that was arriving at our door triggered our imagination," said Sister Christine.

Jack understood the logic. No priests lived here, nor were part of the operation itself. "I see, sister. Why weren't the other members of the church helping with the endeavor?"

Sister Vu spoke up. "Our church, at the end of the war, was under so much pressure. They were forced to turn over the non-communist people to the new government. Many churches, including The Notre Dame Cathedral, had to send people away or risk being destroyed by the soldiers."

*That would explain Father Flanagan.*

"Mr. Jack," said Sister Vu, "many of the orphans were left here with the exception of some who were outcast because of their American fathers. The government took them away and we never saw them again." Jack remembered how many of these 'half-breed' children were sent to the Mekong Delta region to work.

"Mr. Kendall, another important moment after the appearance. Mother Teresa of Calcutta made six trips to Vietnam in her lifetime just to understand why the blessed Mary came here in our time of need and not to her orphanage," said Sister Nguyen.

"I didn't know that fact. I can see why the church probably doesn't believe in the Blessed Mary's appearance." Jack understood enough about the Catholic Church politics and their global view. "I am sure when Mother Teresa come, I bet she could not understand why the blessed Mary came here to Vietnam and not Calcutta."

Sister Florence spoke. "You clearly understand the world we lived in. Mother Teresa was a dear saint for her work she did in Calcutta, and she deserves the respect and admiration of all people on this Earth. God has a plan for all of us, and our day in April 1975, we needed God more than anything to protect these orphans. Our faith in God was reinforced on the sacred day. You, Jack, one day will have your sacred moment."

Jack looked over at Sister Florence. "That day, Sister, is today for me. Being here and seeing the journey fulfilled also enforces my faith in God."

The sisters all looked over at Jack and rose up from their chairs. "Please join us for a prayer."

Jack helped Ms. Bui up from their chair and proceeded to follow the nuns to the small chapel next door. Jack entered into the small chapel and took a pew, knelled, and held Sister Nguyen's hand. "Heavenly Father," said Sister Florence, "bless this man and his woman for being here today among us. Help him on his journey in life, find his peace and strength. Thank you, lord, for bringing him here into our lives, in the name of the father, the son, and the Holy Spirit, amen."

Jack also replied, "Amen." After the prayer, the nuns rose and lead Jack out the door to a sitting area overlooking trees behind the building.

"Mr. Jack, we spent close to six months behind these walls, after the fall of the city, trying to protect the children from being stolen and killed," informed Sister Vu.

Jack's admiration for the nuns grew even more with each word they said. "When did things get better for the orphanage?"

"Well," said Sister Florence, "in 1978, when the Chinese invaded us, and people spoke about the discovery of the killing fields. The government moved on from attacking the church and looked for ways to work together to keep people safe."

Jack knew that Vietnam was home to several churches, monasteries, and seminaries, all supported by the Catholic churches from around the world.

"So, after 1978, what happened to the children?"

Sister Christine cried, "Many of the children after the age of eight were taken to go to work in the rice fields and factories. Many of them ended up on the streets, to never be seen again."

Sister Nguyen added, "We have met a few children that got out on the planes. Some of them came back to Vietnam." That comment placed a smile on everyone's face.

Jack read about many Vietnamese, including many from the university, who were alive, thanks to this operation. All were safely living in America, thanks to these nuns.

"Yes, I went to school with many of those children in America."

The nuns smiled back at him. After a brief walk down the corridor, Sister Florence explained how the place survived all these years.

"Many times, the government considered taking this place away, but they always changed their minds."

Jack believed the Vietnamese government needed places like this orphanage to help deal with the street children, the kids with AIDS, and the older women abandoned by their families. The government wouldn't destroy it unless the place was a threat.

Jack asked Sister Florence, "Do you accept donations?"

Sister Florence smiled. "Yes, Mr. Jack, we do."

Jack opened his wallet and removed 30,000,000 in Vietnamese dollars and gave it to her. "I hope, in some small way, this could help."

Sister Florence went into the office. She came out with an item for Jack and Ms. Bui. "Here, please take these with you always. Please remember us," said the nun.

Jack smiled back to them all. "I will never forget you."

After a few hugs and handshakes, Jack and Ms. Bui departed to the main gate of the orphanage. He stopped a few times to wave back at the nuns, thanking them for the life experience. They stopped outside the main gate, before closing it, to take one last glance back.

When Jack heard the gate close, he began to feel a sense of loss. "I have waited thirty-seven years to find these nuns, and now that I have, I feel a deep sense of loss, of emptiness."

Bui walked over to Jack and put her arm around him. "Jack, what you are feeling is not emptiness—this is more like a fulfillment waiting for a new goal yet to be discovered. Life didn't end for those nuns in 1975; they kept on living to serve God and those children. You also have to keep on living your life and continue to discover your journey." Jack took a deep breath and gave one more look over at the iron gate of the orphanage.

"Ms. Bui, sincerely, thank you for being here with me."

She only smiled back at him. "Jack, I know a great Pho place nearby. How about some lunch?"

"Absolutely."

The rain had stopped, and Jack and Ms. Bui silently walked as they were lost in their own thoughts.

Jack reached out for her hand. "You are a dear friend."

Ms. Bui replied, "So, are you, Jack."

A few minutes after, they arrived at the Pho restaurant. The waiter sat the two friends near a window seat overlooking the orphanage.

"Mr. Jack, I need to ask you something. Why did you need to come here to see these nuns?"

Jack explained that during his younger years, the Vietnam War was a dark mystery for many Americans. "All we knew about the war was what we watched on television or read in the newspapers. Most of what we watched were people setting themselves on fire or being shot at pointblank range in the head. Life magazine even showed a naked girl crying because her clothes were burned off by napalm."

Ms. Bui sat quietly with no emotion. She also had her own share of horror stories from the Vietnam War.

"Vietnam has always intrigued Americans. We know now Vietnam to be a magnificent place."

Ms. Bui understood. "But why the nuns? America has famous nuns, too?"

Jack considered his words for a moment. "Yes, America has some famous nuns—most of them made history through their public service or by helping to save children."

Ms. Bui listened in great detail to Jack's historical background of American nuns.

"However, America is also filled with many Catholic priests and nuns that are very self-serving."

Ms. Bui looked up at Jack. "Oh, how so?"

Jack replied, "Well, many of the priests were later found to have molested boys going back fifty years, and the nuns did not say a word to protect these children."

She gasped. "Oh my, I do remember that in the news." Jack nodded. "When I read the story in 1975 about the Catholic nuns here in Vietnam helping to get the orphans out, I always wanted to know why they did not leave after the fall of the city. Today, I found that answer—thanks to you."

Ms. Bui smiled back at Jack. "My honor, my dear friend."

# Chapter 27
# Realization

"Ms. Bui, I wonder how is that every time I found myself in a bit of trouble, Forest Adams always finds out where I am."

Ms. Bui, already beginning to see where the questioning was leading to, answered Jack in the best possible way, "Jack, Forest and I go way back—to the time of the falling of the city."

Jack dropped his spoon in pure amazement. "You've known each other for that long?"

"Yes, Forest was a Marine here, at the end of the war. He was a seventeen-year-old private, assigned to protect the embassy gate. At that time, I was a seventeen-year-old street orphan trying to get out."

Jack could only imagine the chaos at the embassy at that time.

"I made it to the gate. Forest tried to lift me over the gate, but someone behind me grabbed me and pulled me back to the street. Forest tried to reach for me, but he couldn't," added Ms. Bui. "Anyway, once I was lying on the street, many people pushed toward the gate. Before someone could step on me, a young priest pulled me up."

Jack, starting to see the connections, said, "Let me guess. Father Flanagan?"

"Yes, he was a young man as well at the time, and he saved me."

Jack sat in complete shock. He could only imagine the moment.

"Then Forest yelled for the Father to save me," reminisced Ms. Bui as she gently sobbed. "The priest yelled back to the Marine, 'I will. She will be at the cathedral.' Afterward, I ran down the street and across the park to the cathedral. I could still hear the helicopters taking people away."

"Please, you don't need to say anything else. I understand how painful this is for you."

"No, Jack. It's okay. Anyway, I made it to the church. Forest and the rest of the Marines barricaded the embassy and stayed on the roof for seven hours, until the last helicopter landed to take them away."

They continued talking about the events while finishing their lunch.

"So, how did you connect back to Forest?"

Ms. Bui smiled. "Well, that is something you need to ask him. All I know is that one day in 2004, he showed up at a hotel where I was working, and he found me."

Jack smiled, realizing this was a once-in-a-lifetime chance for two people who barely knew each other to meet again.

"That is beautiful, Ms. Bui. So, you and Forest have been together ever since?"

"Yes, Forest had to leave to go back to America, but he always seems to find a way to be stationed back here."

They finished their lunch and went outside to grab a taxi. "Jack, I'd like to ask you a question please. Do you love Linh?"

Jack looked away for a moment before answering. "Yes, I do, very much."

Ms. Bui smiled. "What do you plan to do?"

Jack didn't have a clear plan for his future with Linh. "I don't know. I have a family back home, and I don't believe there is a future for us here in Vietnam."

Ms. Bui looked sad. "When Forest left in 1975, I had no idea that fate would bring us together again. He didn't even know my name. He only remembered my face and the last known place I was at. I always prayed that he would return and find me. To this day, he still doesn't know why. In the end, when he returned in 2004, he did. I only hope you and Ms. Linh will find each again someday."

After a thirty-minute ride, they arrived back at the hotel.

"Thank you again, Ms. Bui."

She smiled and headed to her office.

There, she picked up her phone and called Forest Adams. "Jack found the nuns from Operation Babylift, my love."

"I am sure he was very emotional."

"Yes, and it was my deepest honor to be there with him. He is a very special man. He is going to donate money from his water company and deliver free water for the nuns and the orphans each week."

186

Forest smiled. "What a good Marine." He took a moment before asking, "Did you see your mother today?"

Bui let out a deep breath. "Yes, dear, I did—Mother did not recognize me at church today."

Forest knew how painful this was for Bui. "I am sorry, my love."

Bui stopped herself from crying. "Don't worry. See you tonight."

Meanwhile, Jack went up to his room to get some needed rest. While lying on his bed, Jack checked his emails and voice email. *All quiet. Thank you, Lord.* He fell asleep for the next few hours. When Jack woke up, he noticed he had received a few messages from Linh.

*My love, I can come to see you on Wednesday and stay until Friday morning.*

Jack replied, *Fantastic, my love. I can't wait to see you.*

Jack felt happy knowing he would see Linh long before departing back to America. He finished returning messages and headed back to the fifth-floor bar. Jack wanted to catch up on some sports and to have some dinner. When he arrived, Tien was helping his team to clean and set new tables.

"So, Mr. Jack. Are you a religious man as well?" said Tien.

Jack knew Tien always loved to get under his skin. "Yes, I even pray for you, Tien."

Both men laughed and sat down at the table.

"Mr. Jack, what can make for your dinner tonight?"

"Can I have Vietnamese steam fish with rice and oil? I also want a nice cold beer, please."

While Jack enjoyed his dinner, he heard a familiar voice.

"Marine, I will take that beer now!" yelled Adams.

"As we live and speak, the Marine 007," Jack replied.

Adams gave Jack a rip-your-lip look. "Easy, Jack, I am off duty now." He sat down next to Jack. "So, you know about Ms. Bui and me."

"Yes, so tell me, how did you end up here? How did you find her?"

Adams began talking after sipping a cold tiger beer. "Well, after the fall of Saigon, M.Sgt. Valdez, Major Kean, and I were the last US Marines here to guard the embassy."

Jack, being a former Marine, remembered reading the story from boot camp at Parris Island.

"Soon after we landed on the USS Midway, we steamed to Subic Bay with the refugees," added Adams.

"Did you help push those choppers into the water?"

"Yes, I did."

Jack realized that even after thirty-seven years, that moment still haunted Forest. The stony expression on Forest's face showed the continued pain he felt for leaving Ms. Bui behind.

"Sorry, man, didn't mean to go there."

Forest tried to contain his emotions. "Jack, Bui was so beautiful and determined to get over the gate that I had to try to help. I looked into her eyes and saw my life before here. Her passion, her drive, and her pain, trying to get out of Saigon. When she was pulled back into the crowd, I tried to climb over the people to get to her, and my Captain Wilson grabbed me and pulled me back. Thank God, the young priest witnessed this and saved her life."

Jack, while he listened to Forest, ordered more beers.

"So, after Subic Bay, most of us were transferred to Guam or Okinawa. After Oki, I re-enlisted again and tried to get back to Subic in case someday Bui got out."

"You hardly knew her Adams—why?"

"Geez, Jack, you are a married guy, and you flew across the world just to meet Linh."

"Point taken."

Forest sipped his beer. "So, why Linh, Jack?"

Jack realized it was his turn to confess. "Well, when I was online, my life and pretty much my marriage were headed downhill. I'd never looked around before, but when I received a poke from her and saw her face for the first time, I really felt a great sense of peace in her."

Forest understood this all too well. He'd only known Bui for a mere second.

"Well, after chatting with her and hearing her voice—I'd never felt that sense of passion or love before." Jack took a pause. "Anyway, we stopped chatting for a couple of years. Once we reconnected again, I promised her that I would come to Vietnam to meet her. Coming here also let me find the nuns and see where the embassy was."

Forest appreciated Jack's reasoning. Even after returning to America, Forest had rarely dated anyone and never married. In this heart, similar to Jack, he felt an unexplainable connection to Bui. That connection drove to him to always find ways to come back to Vietnam. "I see that, Jack. I don't know if you have any future with her, but at least you did what you came here to do."

Jack asked Forest more about his life. "How did you manage to come back to Vietnam?"

"After my twenty years in the Marine Corps was up, I got picked up by Diplomatic Security Services and later the Central Intelligence Agency. Then I got stationed in Tokyo, then Manila, and finally here in Saigon in 2004."

Jack couldn't believe Adams's commitment to finding Bui again. They only met briefly in a time of great peril. Yet, it had created a bond that lasted all those years.

"You never married?" asked Jack.

"Only to Bui," replied Forest. "I lived my life trying to get back here to find her."

Jack smiled in admiration. "For a tough guy, you have a soft heart."

"Stick it, Marine."

"So, how did you find Bui after all?"

"Well, I remembered Father Flanagan. I knew he would do his best to look after her, so when I finally landed here, the cathedral was the first place I went to."

Jack remembered the story that Ms. Bui had told him about the Father hiding her at the church.

"In 1976, the Vietnamese government sent Father Flanagan to a re-education camp. Bui was left alone at the church. One day, she was cleaning there, and an old woman found her. The woman took Bui home to live with her. The lady worked in the rice fields near Bien Hoa. Bui spent most of her young life living on the farm. When she turned eighteen, the woman sent her back to Saigon to go to school. Bui worked at a hotel, cleaning rooms. When they released Father Flanagan from the camp in 1979, he spent most of his years in the north near Sapa. In early 2003, the church moved the Father back to Saigon. When Bui found out that the church had re-opened, she started attending mass. It was then that she finally met her savior."

"So, you came back in 2004. Then, you started attending church, hoping to see her?"

"Pretty much," Adams replied.

"Did she recognize you?"

Adams laughed. "Not at first, but after church, the Father told her who I was, and she cried in my arms."

Jack also became tearful.

"Anyway, we went for a long walk to the old embassy grounds, reflecting on the happenings on that day." Forest took another drink of his tiger beer "Then Father Flanagan married us the next day."

Jack smiled. "That is beautiful."

Forest finished his meal and checked his phone for any messages. "Jack, I need to answer this."

Within a few moments, he returned. "Hey, I hate to eat and run, but there is an issue at the consulate."

Jack got up and gave him an enormous hug. "Later, Jarhead. We will do this again someday."

"Oorah! Marine."

Jack decided to order another beer. He wanted to reflect on what Forest had said about his responsibility and accountability in his marriage. *Square it away, Marine.* After a few more beers, Jack paid the bill and headed up to his room. Instead of going to sleep, he turned the couch around, facing the window to look at the Saigon River below. *What a sight!* Jack enjoyed the peace of sitting in there. There were no lights other than the hotel's neon sign reflecting on the water. He knew that when he arrived home, it was time to move on with Silvia with a proper divorce. Realizing that his marriage could not be saved, Jack needed to ensure that no matter what, he owed her a safe financial landing.

After watching the evening boats on the river, he decided to sleep on the couch, hoping to catch the morning sunrise hitting his face.

Jack had a very peaceful night's sleep on the couch. However, he missed the morning sunrise. After doing some stretches to relieve the pain in his back he showered and headed out for breakfast. Jack headed for the hotel coffee lounge to order his favorite morning drink.

"Oh, I see you were out late last night, Mr. Jack!" proclaimed Ms. Bui.

"Ah, I was with a fellow Marine," Jack replied, grinning.

"Yes, Forest came home under the weather."

"Please, forgive him. I made him drink those beers!"

Ms. Bui could only laugh while heading back to work. Jack was enjoying his morning coffee when his phone rang.

"Jack, are you coming on Friday as planned?" asked Silvia.

"Yes, I will be arriving at Los Angeles international airport at 8:30 a.m. I'll have a car to pick me up."

"Good, I will be out for the weekend with the girls." Jack was thankful that Silvia planned to be done. Jack had realized that he needed to continue to move away from Silvia and start planning his life separately. *Without her in my life, I will be able to be happier.*

"Silvia, we need to talk when you come back from your girls' weekend."

Silvia already knew what Jack wanted to talk about. "Good, I think I will be happy to hear your big plan, Jack." She hung up.

Jack, putting his phone down, sat in the hotel lobby and began to dream of life without Silvia. He knew the journey ahead was going to be painful and challenging. However, he also knew it was time for this marriage to end.

After the power of the espresso kicked in, Jack wondered, *What should I do today?*

He texted Chau and checked the water plant. *Everything is fine, Mr. Jack. Take the day off, please.*

Jack checked with Tuan. "Hey, Tuan, how is business? Did the new bikes show up?"

"Mr. Jack, yes, the new ones are here! And today, we have our first Saigon, Pho, and Beer tour. Four European tourists are here!"

*Well, maybe I should go and see a priest.* Jack rose and thanked the coffee ladies for the espresso coffee and walked toward the Notre Dame Cathedral. He took a moment to observe the statue of Mary and to have a private moment to pray. After a few minutes of personal reflection, Jack went inside the massive church to continue his prayers. He found his favorite pew, kneeled, and began to pray. After a few moments of self-reflection, Jack received a tap on his shoulder.

"Well, ready to finish your confession, son?" asked Father Flanagan.

"Sure, Father, let's do it."

They walked to the confessional area of the church.

"Bless me, Father, for I have sinned. It has been five hundred and twenty-five days since my last confession."

"Please continue, my son."

Jack confessed his sins, "Father, I know my marriage is over now. I need to move on and heal my heart and my soul. Silvia also is not someone I can care for each day of my life. It is time for me to move on and begin to heal myself. I can't help others unless I first help myself get well."

"Jack, in the church, we don't condone divorce. Doing so, you are going against the church and the word of God."

"Yes, Father, but staying in a toxic relationship with no real course correction can't be healthy or lead anywhere positive. Nor for my wife and me."

The priest had heard that before from many people in the church. "Jack, this is your choice. God will forgive you if you ask for penance and repent. Now, please remember what I told you. If you continue with your relationship with Linh, you will continue to break the church's rules and faith."

"Yes. To move forward in life, after my marriage, I need to be faithful to one person."

The priest nodded quietly at Jack, realizing that he understood what he had to do. "Jack, there is no timetable here; you have the rest of your life to decide how you live and what role your faith and the church have in it."

He sat in quiet prayer for a few moments before answering the priest. "I know, Father. My life seems to be a series of turns and reverses with minimal movement forward."

The priest couldn't contain his laughter. "Jack, let me ask you; are you a good person? Do you do good things in life?"

"Father, very much so."

"Please, remember we are all sinners here, in one way or another. Just try to live your life in the best way possible. For your penance, Jack, three hail Marys, four holy Fathers, and a quiet prayer of thanks to yourself for being the person you are."

"Thank you, Father."

He left the confessional and moved back to his favorite pew to perform his penance. After taking time in prayer and remembrance, Jack got up and headed to the east side of the vast church to light a candle for everyone in his family. Once he completed the prayers, he walked around the massive church and admired the stained glass and statues. *What a place!* After taking the day to pray, Jack walked back to the hotel. As he walked, he passed the Saigon River badminton courts. He always loved to see Vietnamese people playing badminton. He sat along the river bench area, watching the boats going by. *This must have been hell in 1975 when the war ended.* After a good hour of listening to the water and seeing the ships, he headed up to his room and fell asleep.

Tuesday morning came early for Jack. Calls from the water plant were coming in. Chau informed Jack that clients were coming to the plant today, and he had to be present.

"Mr. jack, please come and meet our clients. They aren't happy about the price increase," said Chau.

*Sales are sales, no matter where in the world you are.* Jack got up, showered, and headed downstairs to pick up his daily intake of a triple espresso.

"Good morning, Ms. Bui."

She was busy with a client. Still, she smiled and waved back at Jack. While in the cab ride over to the water company, Jack texted Tuan to see if he could borrow a bike for the day. He arrived at the water company to see about thirty clients inside the plant. All of them were yelling and waving their bills in their hands.

Overwhelmed, Chau motioned over to his arrival. "Here, he is the owner."

Jack, realizing that he was walking into a hornet's nest of trouble, smiled and shook everyone's hands.

"Thank you, Chau. Good morning."

Chau could only frown back at him.

"I got this. Please just translate."

Chau nodded and translated as Jack opened his speech, "Thank you all for being excellent customers. We appreciate your business, and we hope to continue selling more water to you."

Soon after Jack spoke, many of the clients screamed at the top of their lungs. He couldn't understand a word they were saying.

"Okay, I understand you don't like the new prices. I will tell you why that happened. We plan to fix many problems you have complained about in the past. Including poor water quality, bad bottles, and late delivery."

He took a drink of his espresso. *I can't fix these people's problems without more money. I need to raise the rates to restore the factory.* Some clients sat down on the floor, while others continued yelling at him.

"Please understand. If you want to do business with us, we will make the product better and try to keep our prices as low as possible. We are still cheaper than most brands while delivering an excellent product. If you don't want to do business with us anymore, please leave and have a good life!" Jack knew when Tuan ran the water plant, he spoiled his clients with low water prices. However, the factory fell apart and did not make enough money to support the operations. Jack was committed to only keeping clients that were worth having.

His statements shocked many of the clients. Out of the thirty in attendance, nineteen of them left.

"Chau, please give a twelve-bottle case of water for each client that stays."

She looked surprised. "Why?"

Jack smiled back at his manager. "Because they stayed." He explained that sales is all about building two-way trust and loyalty relationships. The clients needed to trust the water company to make a safe product at a reasonable price. Jack needed clients that were willing to help cover the cost of the product while buying more water when Jack and Chau offered a better price. "Chau, we can't lower our prices just to keep someone; we need to lower our price when they want to buy more."

Chau, realizing Jack's strategy, handed out fresh bottles to all the clients. Within minutes of receiving the fresh water, the clients got up, waved, and promised to keep buying more.

"Chau, losing nineteen clients now will make business more profitable." He continued discussing his plan with her. "We need to find nineteen clients that match the eleven that stayed. Please make more twelve bottle cases and use them as thank-you gifts for new clients."

As Chau handed out more water cases to the clients, twelve of them asked for better pricing. Chau offered a better price only if the clients increased their water purchases by ten percent each month. After having long conversations with them, Chau realized to her delight that all of them agreed to the ten percent increase in sales in exchange for a price reduction of five percent.

Chau, seeing the master plan unfold, could only smile at her boss. "Thank you, Mr. Jack—we now have ten percent more sales by giving away five percent discounts on new business!"

Jack smiled back. "Next month, offer a free case of water in exchange for them purchasing four cases."

Chau walked up to Jack and gave him a hug. "Thank you for being in my life and my sister's."

Jack had almost forgotten that Chau was Linh's sister.

"Jack, are you going to see my sister again?"

He remained guarded. "I don't know. She is very busy these days."

Chau gave Jack a small, sheepish smile. "Oh, yes, I am sure she is very busy!"

Jack also needed to discuss the water for the orphans and nuns. "Chau, could you do something for me while I am gone? Please deliver twenty cases of water to the orphans and fifteen bottles to the nuns each month. Please also donate 20,000,000 Vietnamese dollars per month." Chau slowly cried over Jack's offer to help those organizations. "Also, please donate 10,000,000 Vietnamese dollars to the local temple you and the team attend. I will send money each month to you. Please use the funds to help with the donations."

Chau burst into more tears and gave Jack an enormous hug. "Thank you, Mr. Jack."

"Chau, I will call you tomorrow. I will take the day off and go cycling."

"Enjoy, Jack!"

Jack walked over to Tuan's shop to pick up a bike. Tuan was busy with a new tour group from Europe. "Jack, please take the black one."

He smiled as he cycled back to the heart of Saigon. In all his cycling adventures in Vietnam, Jack had never cycled along the river. He picked up the cycling path near the Renaissance Hotel and badminton courts and then followed the river walkway on this bike, cycling for almost three hours and finally reaching the famous Saigon River span bridge.

Like other famous dual-span bridges, the river bridge was nearly a mile long and nine hundred meters high. He loved to cycle across bridges all over the world; he loved the challenge. At sunset, he made it to the midpoint of the bridge, stopping to admire the view. *This is incredible.* After resting, he decided it was time to head down the backside. Knowing the bridge had an eight percent decline, that meant cycling at night was a bit dangerous. Jack took it slow, enjoying the peace of the moment. After ten minutes of cycling down the backside of the bridge, he reached the other side. Jack searched for a way to get back to District One.

After consulting the GPS on his phone, he followed the roads leading into the jungle. *Maybe I made a wrong turn somewhere.* He followed his GPS, even though he realized the road turned into dirt. *Okay, Jack, this isn't the right way* After cycling for a full hour, Jack pulled over a small drink stand and tried to order some water. After showing water pictures on his phone, he realized that this stand, and many others, didn't have access to water, only sugar. Jack marked on his GPS where he was. He also made a note to ask Chau if they could use scooters to deliver water to these roadside drink stands. After cycling for another hour, Jack saw the lights of District One appear. He arrived at the hotel, feeling completely worn out from cycling but thrilled at the same time.

"Mr. Jack, is it beer time?!" Tien yelled in complete joy.

"Ah, yeah. Okay, Tien, beer time."

Jack gave his bike to the doorman and headed up to the bar with Tien.

"I heard you almost caused a riot at the water company."

"Yes, I almost caused a riot, but anyone who wanted to stay doing business with us got a case of water. The rest walked out empty-handed."

Tien saw the logic in Jack's plan. "Smart. You will probably be better off with fewer clients. At least you will be making some profit. Do you plan to save the water for clients who are willing to pay more?"

Jack looked back at Tien. "Yes, we need to create less water—our costs go down for that specific production run."

"Exactly," said Tien.

They started to talk about soccer and food as Ms. Bui, coming off a long shift, walked by. "No beer for me? Lovely, guys!"

Jack smiled and handed Ms. Bui a cold beer. "Here, lady, beer time."

Ms. Bui could only laugh. "So, Jack, is Linh appearing before you leave on Friday?"

"Yes, she will be here tomorrow and will stay until Friday morning."

Ms. Bui looked at him. "Wait here, Jack."

Within a few minutes, she came back.

"Jack, please have Ms. Linh see me for a room key when she arrives," said Ms. Bui with a warm smile. "Please have a wonderful time, my friend."

Jack got up and gave her a hug, "Thank you, Ms. Bui. But I don't want you in trouble with the police again."

Ms. Bui smiled and sat back down to finish her beer. "Jack, we found the employee who sent your picture and Ms. Linh's to the police—he has been taken care of. He is now working in Hanoi at another property. He donated the money he received for turning you in to a local temple before he left. It would be my pleasure for you and Linh to stay here together again."

Tien also smiled and asked Jack, "When will you come back?"

Jack thought long and hard before answering, "I am not sure. To be honest, I need to square my personal life when I get home and decide from there. But yes, I plan to come back again and see you all."

Ms. Bui, Tien, and Jack toasted each other, promising to meet back again to drink more beers. After a few hugs, Jack left to go upstairs to shower and catch some sleep before Linh arrived in the morning.

# Chapter 28
# Affection

Jack couldn't fall asleep even after his evening shower. He couldn't stop thinking about Linh. *How I miss you, my love. I know your life is challenging and full of conflict. Thank you for being here, for loving me in the only way you can.* Seeing the morning sunrise starting to come through the window, Jack looked away, promising not to see the dawn until Linh was there with him. He rose to take a quick shower and shave before Linh's arrival. Soon after 8:30 a.m., the door opened, and Linh entered the room. Jack rose from the bed to greet his love. Linh closed the door. Lifting her hand, she asked Jack to stop walking.

"Please wait there for me."

Jack froze, not knowing what she was planning to do, and waited in great anticipation. Linh, wearing a beautiful royal-blue dress, unzipped it, letting it drop to her feet. Dressed in lovely pink and white undergarments, Linh slipped off her shoes and strolled toward Jack.

"Please don't move, my lover; it is my turn," said Linh.

He listened to Linh, so he didn't move a muscle. She put her arms around Jack's neck, giving him a long and passionate kiss. While kissing her lover deeply, Linh unbuttoned Jack's shirt. Slowly kissing his neck and letting his shirt fall to the ground, Linh unbuckled Jack's pants. As she helped him get his clothes off, she kissed him on his chest while running her fingers down his legs.

"My love, how I missed you," proclaimed Linh.

"I missed you too."

Both lovers gently lowered each other on the bed and began a beautiful time. Linh, taking a moment to look deeply in Jack's eyes, said, "Allow me to please you."

Using her soft and wet tongue, she licked up and down his legs. Jack, feeling the passion from Linh, ran his fingers through her hair and rubbed gently on her ears. Listening to Jack's soft moans of pleasure, Linh flipped Jack over on his back and began to kiss very gently. Jack, lying on the bed in complete peace, spun around on his back and began to press Linh close to his body. Running his hands along her back, Linh also moaned in pleasure at Jack's loving touch. Jack rose his hips gently while whispering into her ear, "You are wonderful, my Linh."

Hearing those soft words, she began to kiss Jack softly on the lips. Feeling his passion and energy, Linh began to climax more and more. "Oh, Jack," cried Linh in pleasure.

They spent hours gazing into each other's eyes while making love. Without having to say a word, they were deeply connected to each other's heart. Linh pressed her body next to Jack's, feeling his love and strength, while Jack stroked her hand with a soft, playful touch.

"I will always love you, Jack, no matter where you are."

"My love, you will always be in my heart." Jack knew there was a chance he may never see Linh again. He wanted this moment to never end. Struggling with the conviction of his love for her, Jack gently kissed Linh while stroking her face with his fingers. "I will never feel this way again," Jack whispered. "I waited my whole for a moment like this. Only now I have found the passion my heart deeply craved."

Linh also knew that their time might be short. Yet, in her own life, she had never felt this much love before.

After making love for several more hours, Jack and Linh held each other while they took a long rest. Linh got up to use the bathroom, trying to not wake Jack up. Linh softly came back to bed, only to see that Jack was awake and smiling.

"What are you smiling at?" Linh asked.

"You, my love. How are you?"

"I am good. Ngoc is doing great. Stick is being stick."

"Yes, my stick is waiting for me."

Both lovers nodded but dropped the subject. Jack placed Linh on her stomach while on the bed. He dripped some massage oil he'd purchased in Hawaii on her back and gave Linh probably the best massage she'd ever had in her life. Jack used enough oil to see her beautiful tone shine while relaxing each muscle in her body. Before long, Linh fell asleep again. Jack also got up to use the bathroom while checking his messages. Jack realized he had several emails from Silvia but ignored them for now.

Jack returned to bed and closed his eyes, trying to get some more rest. After a few hours, they both woke up, realizing it was close to 5 p.m.

"Jack, darling, I am hungry for you," said Linh.

Jack also felt the want and need to make love to Linh again. He kissed her soft neck while gently rubbing his hands on her chest. Linh, moaning with pleasure, ran her fingers through his hair, whispering in his ear, "You are wonderful." Jack could only smile; he had never felt this loved before. He chose not to think about the future—he wanted only to enjoy the loving moment.

Jack and Linh took a long shower and bathed together. While lying in the tub, Linh asked about what would happen when he was back in America.

"My love, I know you are leaving soon. Do you plan to come back someday?"

Jack kissed Linh softly before answering. "I need to get my personal life fixed first. Then, I will need to see what direction my life is going. But yes, I will come and see you again."

"Jack, no matter where I am, promise me we will make love again someday."

"I promise, my love."

After they finished their bath, Jack helped to dry her.

"Allow me one more kiss," Linh said.

"Absolutely."

They embraced and kissed passionately for several minutes, allowing themselves to lower to the floor to make love again. "My Linh, please allow me to pleasure you once again." Linh, lying on the floor, closed her eyes and began to moan softly. Using the softness of his hands, Jack began to massage Linh's chest while running his tongue along her neck and down to her waist.

"Jack, you are incredible!" Linh said, feeling a climax coming and screaming in pleasure.

After cleaning up and getting dressed, Linh and Jack departed the room. With one last kiss, Jack said, "Linh, please never forget me."

Linh, weeping softly, said, "Never, my Jack."

She let out a deep breath. "I need to go a different way. I will see you in the taxi."

Jack smiled at Linh and proceeded to the elevator. He went to the main desk to say hello to Ms. Bui.

"Hey lady, beer time?"

Ms. Bui hit Jack playfully on the shoulder as he walked to the taxi. Within a few minutes, Linh arrived through the south entrance to meet Jack.

"Let's go to the plantation, Jack—they have great sushi."

Jack had never eaten sushi in Vietnam. "Yes, perfect!"

He kept his hands to himself and didn't say a word to Linh until they arrived at the restaurant. Linh glanced over at Jack and gave him a small kiss and wink. "Thank you for following the rules."

The loving couple departed in the taxi, and to Jack's amazement, the restaurant looked like an old French plantation house.

"You weren't kidding; this is a beautiful house."

"Yes, this is the French Embassy from the 1950s. I hear the food here is wonderful."

Jack and Linh walked into the restaurant. Linh briefly touched Jack's hand and gave him a loving smile.

"This way, please," the waiter said to them. He placed them at a lovely table with a window view.

"This is perfect," Jack proclaimed.

Linh was ordering in Vietnamese for Jack; she seemed to know the menu well.

"I ordered you a plate of tuna, my love, and a nice cold beer."

Jack smiled at the order and asked if they could have oysters.

"Jack, you don't need oysters, my love, ever."

Recognizing the moment, though, Linh ordered a dozen oysters for both of them anyway. "I may need them too, my love," she said with a beautiful smile.

Jack couldn't have been any happier. *This is living.* They were having a great time at the restaurant, the food was delicious, and the conversation was lovely.

"Linh, my love, where do you see yourself going with your life?"

Linh took a sip of wine. "Jack, my life is Ngoc. I want the best for her. My life with the stick will continue because I need Ngoc to have a father in her life. I want to go back to school, get smarter, and maybe come to America someday."

Jack was shocked at Linh's comments. "Come to America?"

"I would love to see you again in America." Linh smiled at Jack, but she knew deep down that her future with Jack wouldn't be possible.

Jack knew the same. They stared quietly at each other.

"Jack, let's discuss later. Let's enjoy our time together."

He nodded in agreement.

After dinner, they called the taxi. "Where to, my love?" asked Jack.

"I know a great tea place that is open late."

Jack knew the place and smiled. After a fifteen-minute ride, they arrived at their favorite tea shop, in Unification Park.

"Ah, I love this place," Jack commented.

Linh smiled in approval. After ordering drinks, she asked, "Jack, do you regret our relationship?"

Jack took her hands. "No, my love. I have never felt this much love and passion for someone in my life, ever. I will never forget this feeling you make me feel."

Linh smiled and then cried after Jack's words. She felt the same way. After finishing their evening tea, they walked back to the Renaissance Hotel, a beautiful and quiet stroll.

"Jack, here please." Ms. Bui was calling him over. "The airline called; you will need to leave tomorrow. They had to cancel all flights on Friday because of the upcoming storm."

"What storm?" Jack asked.

"There is a category-four typhoon coming to Vietnam. It is supposed to land here on Friday. You will need to leave sooner than expected. The airline already updated your ticket. You will depart at 9:30 a.m. tomorrow."

Jack, turning to Linh, whispered, "Linh, I need to leave."

Living in Vietnam her whole life, she knew how destructive the storm could be. "Jack, I understand—these storms have destroyed many cities here in Vietnam."

Ms. Bui spoke to Jack again. "Please have some drinks on the fifth on us with Ms. Linh."

Jack thanked Ms. Bui and headed up with Linh. They sat at their favorite table, listening to the lovely piano for one last time. Jack knew he would no be returning to Vietnam until his marriage to Silvia was over and the legal proceedings were completed. He knew this part of his life could take years before any final resolution. Sitting quietly, Jack became heartbroken knowing this could be the last drink with Linh in his lifetime.

"Jack, please never forget me," Linh asked.

"I will never ever forget you."

Tien arrived with Ms. Bui and sat down at the table. "Let's all drink one last time together."

The four friends toasted one another one last time before Jack and Linh departed.

When they reached the room, Linh turned to Jack. "Before we make love, can we watch the river one last time?"

Jack hugged and kissed her while moving her to the couch, facing the window. They sat for almost an hour without saying a single word to each other. They chose to only communicate through their gentle touches and soft kisses.

"I promise we will meet again," whispered Jack.

Linh began to cry. "I never cry, Jack, ever."

They embraced in a deep kiss, never wanting to let go of each other. In a moment, the lovers were exchanging passion, lovemaking, and sweet words for each other. They promised that they would meet again.

After making love, Linh fell asleep inside of Jack's arms. As the morning sun came through the window, Jack woke Linh up to share it together one last time.

"My love, the sun is rising over Saigon."

"Jack, hold me, please."

The sun's rays reflected a lovely beam of light off their bodies. The light stayed on them for only a brief moment. Jack knew all too well how life's moments end suddenly. Embracing her, Jack leaned over and kissed Linh on her lips.

"My love, I will be here again. I promise," he proclaimed.

Time couldn't stand still for them. No matter how much they tried, the clock kept moving closer to his departure.

They drifted into the shower one last time. Jack couldn't stop himself from crying in front of Linh.

"Happiness in life isn't a commodity," said Jack.

Linh could only weep in his arms. After dressing and packing, Jack departed as planned. He went to the left and Linh to the right.

"See you downstairs, my love," said Linh.

Jack went to the main desk to check out. "Jack, thank you for everything. Vietnam will never forget you, and neither will we," said Ms. Bui.

"Thank you for coming to my country; you are an honorable American," replied Tien.

Jack stopped and hugged both of them. "Thank you both. I hope to return again to Vietnam someday."

After the long goodbyes, Jack met up with Linh at the taxi. Seeing tears in her eyes, Jack knew he couldn't reach out to her in public; he could only whisper to her how much he loved her.

"Let's go," Linh stated.

During the taxi ride to the airport, they allowed themselves to touch hands and whisper 'I love you' to each other. After a forty-five-minute ride, the taxi pulled up to the Delta Airlines gate. The taxi driver, in a rush, ran over to open Jack's door. The driver motioned for him to get out quickly. As he did, he never took his eyes off Linh. As the backdoor closed on the cab, Jack could only stand and stare at his love. Linh, holding back the tears, continued to gaze back at Jack. Slowly, as the taxi moved away, they never broke contact. He walked toward the departing taxi, only to get one last look at her. Linh looked back at Jack with a soft smile and tears in her eyes.

As the taxi left, Jack grabbed his bags and sat down on the curb, reflecting on their every moment together.

# Chapter 29
# Vanished

The ride back to Los Angeles had always been eventful for Jack. Having a typhoon crashing into Vietnam made the ride very rough. Jack normally slept on the plane ride home. However, this time, with the incoming storm, the plane just made it out of Saigon. He strapped into his seat and felt every bump and drop in altitude. Prone to airsickness, Jack kept using the throw-up bag near his place. Trying to cope with the rough air, he could only think of his friends and workers back in Vietnam. They had to deal with this storm. Jack was on his way back to Los Angeles, which included changing planes in Tokyo. He tried to catch a few cycles of sleep. He took a moment and began a series of prayers, asking God to look after everyone in Vietnam. Within a matter of five hours, the plane ride smoothed out, and he could finally get some rest.

The plane descended into Tokyo. Jack woke up just in time for the landing. Immediately, he connected to Wi-Fi to check his messages. He could only pray that everyone was safe back in Vietnam. Much to Jack's dismay, he started receiving flash messages on this phone from the water company and emails from the hotel.

*Mr. Jack, if you are receiving this message, please note the entire District Thirteen has been wiped out. Emergency crews posted on the internet the entire district washed away. The rain won't stop for another thirteen hours,* said Tien.

While changing planes, Jack rushed to see if any of the TVs had any news on the storm. *Nothing.* With only thirty minutes to change gates, Jack needed to get moving to not miss his plane.

Jack tried sending messages to Chau and Linh. He needed to know if they were safe. *The internet must be down.* He thought about what Tien wrote and then closed his eyes and cried quietly on the plane. Within a few moments, the aircraft was airborne for the eleven-hour flight back to Los Angeles. Jack couldn't fall asleep, so he opened his laptop to plan his *path to happiness*. He remembered what Adams had told him: *Get it squared away, Marine*. Jack put together a list of things that would lead him to find happiness. He also understood that the more he moved in that direction, the farther he would get from Silvia and his children. Being out of balance for so many years, Jack knew this was the right time to make changes. He needed to be happy and healthy and wanted to have the chance to have love in his future. He made some notes and, after a while, finally fell asleep.

The plane arrived on time, precisely at 8:30 a.m. Pacific Standard Time on a Friday morning. It was April 24, 2016. Jack turned on this phone, fearing the worst had happened back in Vietnam. He'd received well over twenty emails and texts from Tien, Tuan, Linh, and Chau. All of them reported the devastation of the storm in many parts of Vietnam.

Linh's shipping company had lost three containers filled with materials heading to Long Beach. Tuan's bike shop, with all the new cycles and helmets, washed away in the storm. Chau reported the roof and the water systems were ripped apart because of the winds and rain. But the entire team was safe. Most of them had headed to the other districts, seeking shelter. Tien reported the Renaissance Hotel had minor flooding—the Saigon River had breached the seawall, and water was flowing in all the roads near the hotel. Normally a peaceful sight at sunrise, the water became violent and unforgiving to several boats carrying cargo. Most of these boats began to take on water, and some of them even capsized.

The Vietnamese government declared a national emergency. Thailand, Cambodia, Singapore, and Laos all suffered damages on a smaller scale. Ms. Bui confirmed that the nuns were safe, and many people had found shelter in their convent. Jack started messaging back to Linh.

*My love, are you safe? How is Ngoc?*

Realizing the time change, he figured Linh was already asleep.

Back in Vietnam, Ms. Bui attempted to find Forest. She received a flash message from him.

*My Bui, I, along with the Reaction Force Seven team, went out into Saigon to offer any assistance to help rescue people trapped in the storm.* She was relieved that her husband was safe.

Forest looked around at the devastation. "Major Harrison, let's head over to the water plant and check on things."

The major acknowledged and proceeded to drive to District Thirteen.

After several stops due to flooding and damage to the road, Forest and the marine detachment arrived outside Jack's water plant. Seeing the damage for the first time since the storm moved off the coast, Forest could not believe the destruction. Walking over to check on the building, Forest called out, "Ms. Chau!"

Chau, still trying to get the workers to safety, turned to see him.

"Oh, Mr. Adams."

Forest walked up. "Oh my God! Is everyone safe?"

Chau was crying at all the damage. "Our home is destroyed. The plant is ruined. Mr. Jack got out in time, but his investment is ruined."

Forest gave Chau a hug. "Don't worry, young lady. We are here to help." He waved over the Marine detachment. "Men, please help this lady—this water plant is owned by a friend of mine." The Marines acknowledged and proceeded to enter the structure. Seeing the factory workers sitting around the floor, soaking wet from the storm, the Marines placed blankets on them and fed them fresh water and began to offer food they brought from the embassy.

"Ms. Chau, I am going to relocate your workers to a safe house in District Two. The US government uses the building in case of emergency. We will house you and your team there until we figure something out."

She walked over and gave Forest a huge hug. "Thank you, Mr. Adams."

"Major, let's relocate Ms. Chau and her team to the Annex Seventeen—we will let them go back there until we can figure something out for them."

The Marines loaded up the workers from the water plant inside the SUVs and proceeded to transport them to the safe place.

*Message: US_GOV_Consulate_Saigon: Encryption: Forest Adams: Jack Kendall: the storm destroyed the water plant, Jack. I am moving your team to Annex Seventeen in District Two for safekeeping. I will look after them and help get them settled once the storm passes and cleanup has started, signed: Forest.*

In America, Jack cleared passport control and customs. Heading up to the international gallery, he looked for his ride home. After twenty minutes of texting Carlos, the driver showed.

"Mr. Kendall?"

"Yes, that is me."

"Great, let's go," said Carlos.

Carlos loaded Jack's bags in the back of the vehicle. For the next two hours, Jack continued to try to get a hold of anyone back in Vietnam. Finally Tien texted back.

*Jack, things are bad here. Let me message you later; we are trying to help people get to safety.*

Jack completely understood and read his work emails instead.

*I was away from work too long; I need to get back into it.* Soon after 1 p.m., the car arrived at Jack's home. He thanked Carlos for the ride, tipped him well, and then gathered his bags and entered the house. Jack loved his house but he knew changes in his life needed to happen. He put his bags down and walked into his office.

Silvia had placed all his mail on his desk. *I see you have opened everything. Great.* After a quick shower, Jack called William to check in with his oldest son.

"William, Dad here. I just arrived back from Vietnam. How are you?"

"Good day, glad you are home. I watched on the news that Vietnam got hit with a tremendous storm. I am glad you are safe. What are the plans now that you're home?"

Jack took a deep breath. "Working on being a wonderful father. Can we meet next week?"

"Sure, Dad. You and Mom are always welcome."

Jack told his son about the water company and cycling tours.

"Dad, that sounds exciting. I am glad you had a great time. I need to go. Let's catch up soon."

Jack said goodbye and called his daughter. The Coast Guard had stationed her in Maine. As the phone rang, he received a text from Linh.

*My love, we are safe. Did you make it home?* Jack smiled, knowing she and her child were all right.

"Regina, how are you, young lady?"

"Dad, I missed you—glad you are home from Vietnam. Have you seen Mom yet?"

"Mom isn't here. On a girls' weekend. She will be home on Sunday."

"Figures! Dad, we are heading out. Can I call when we return?"

"Love you, Reg."

"Love you, Dad."

After checking his work emails and his regular mail, Jack read the secured message from Forest:

*Moving your water company to Annex Seventeen for safety.*

After reading this message, Jack began to cry.


*Message: US_GOV_Consulate_Saigon: Encryption: Jack Kendall: Forest Adams: Thank you, Marine, I knew the storm would cause so much damage. Thank you for looking after my team. Signed: Jack.*


After finishing the rest of his messages, Jack headed to his room to sleep. Still significantly jetlagged, he conked out almost immediately. After sleeping for nearly thirteen hours, Jack woke up to an empty house. *Way of the future, I assume.* He walked outside to collect the mail along with the garbage cans. He loved his home so much. He'd worked so hard for this, including all the upgrades to the backyard. The house sat on top of a hill with a view of the Pacific Ocean. *Linh, I know you are over there, and I hope you are safe, my love.* Jack reflected on the life difference between America and Vietnam, especially now, after the storm, which created so much suffering in that now-far-away country. After fixing some dinner, he went upstairs to his TV room to watch his favorite movies. After a few movies, Jack decided to fall asleep on the couch.

Jetlagged still, Jack was asleep when Silvia arrived home.

"Jack, Jack, wake up!" called Silvia.

"Oh, hi, hun. When did you get home?"

"An hour ago."

Jack sat up for a moment.

"I want you to tell me what happened in Vietnam," said Silvia.

Jack, realizing he would need to have this conversation with Silvia at some point, told her about the water company and the cycling shop.

She held her temper until the very end. "You spent our money and just threw it all away?"

After several messages from Chau, he'd found out that the factory was completely destroyed by the storm. Jack realized that his whole investment into the water business was gone, with no hope of recovering any of the funds. Jack knew that at the end of the day, Silvia was correct.

She got up from the couch. "Jack, I can't believe you did this to me. I am retired, and I trusted you with my wellbeing."

Looking at it from her perspective, he did initially agree with Silvia's assessment. "Well, Silvia, I went to Vietnam for so many reasons. Among others, the water company and the cycling shop. Both of those were a part of my plan."

"I don't care, Jack. Those are dumb reasons to waste our money!"

"Silvia, first off, yes, that is true. Yet, you haven't worked, thanks to me, for eight years now. The money you are talking about, I earned it. Yes, you are entitled to half of my assets in case of a divorce. We aren't divorced yet, so I can spend the funds as I see fit."

As Silvia stomped off and back to her room, Jack sat back on the couch. *Round One.*

The next day, he woke and found Silvia on the phone with William.

"He took my money and spent it in Vietnam; now, the money is all gone!"

She continued to put Jack down while on the phone with their son. After fifteen minutes, Silvia hung up, noticing Jack sitting up behind her.

After taking a brief nap, Jack received a Skype call from Linh. Still wanting to keep their relationship a secret, Jack typed back to her:

*My love, stick is here, no video at the moment.*

Linh replied:


*No worries, my love. I am at the shipping company dealing with the mess. Let's chat later.*


Jack sent messages to Chau to check on her. She informed him that the water flow system was in pieces, and the building had collapsed that morning because of the rain. The business was completely gone. Jack felt sorry for her.

Jack also counted the money he lent to Tuan, the donation to the nuns, and all the money he spent on the water plant.

He couldn't believe that he'd spent that much money in the course of two weeks.

"Silvia, here is the total amount I spent over the last two weeks."

Silvia couldn't believe her eyes. "Jack, I really hate you—you ruined my life!"

"I guess I screwed up badly."

"Oh, don't tell me you slept with someone over there!"

Jack remembered Father Flanagan's words: *Unless you are prepared to stop, you can't seek forgiveness.*

He picked his words carefully. "Yes, I did."

Silvia stomped out of the room, screaming, "Wait until you hear from my lawyer!"

# Chapter 30
# Deterioration

Over the next few weeks, Jack thought about his decision. *I am not going back, and the chances of having a life with Linh are less than zero.*

Being home for a month now, he watched his life falling apart. However, he also knew this was the right time for rebuilding and refocusing on what he wanted out of life. *Okay—now you know where you stand regarding Vietnam and your marriage. What else?*

"Dad, William, got a minute?"

"Son, what is it?"

"Dad, Mom called three times this week. Did you spend $100,000 in Vietnam, and now all of the investment is gone?"

Jack never believed in dragging the children into their problems, especially money issues.

"Son, the brief answer is no. I didn't spend $100,000 in Vietnam. I know this may sound harsh, but please, be selective with what your mother is telling you."

For years, William had always sided with Silvia, even when his mother was wrong. Jack considered for a moment how to fix this, but the boy's mind had been made up.

Jack also needed to consider a new source of employment. His current company had lost most of their investors and clients. Jack still had several client connections and relationships with business partners. However, his company did not have any capital funds to continue operating.

After spending the last few days researching new companies, Jack found a global technology firm based in Pasadena. A recruiter reached out to Jack, asking him to consider joining their company. While researching, Jack found several good reasons for him to join this new firm.

Jack received an email from the Techline CEO, Thomas Wilson, requesting a meeting time. Over the next few hours, Jack called a few people he knew over at Techline and asked what they felt about the company. Mostly, everyone was very excited about the company and the direction they were taking. After spending the day researching the company, Jack replied to the email and set up an interview for Friday morning.

After reviewing some last-minute data, Jack joined the WebEx by Cisco Systems for a remote meeting via video.

"Good morning, sir. My name is Jack Kendall. Very nice to meet you."

The CEO replied, "Yes, it is very nice to meet you, Jack. Thank you for making time for this meeting. You come highly regarded, Jack—you are what we are looking for. We need someone who has sold in Asia Pacific and understands the culture, the people, and the technology limitations. I understand you have some experience in this space."

"Yes, I have sold technology in Japan, China, Taiwan, Singapore, and Vietnam."

"Splendid! Let's discuss some logistics. We understand your salary and commission requirements, but we will need you to relocate. Is that going to be an issue?"

Relocation had always been a problem for Jack. He wanted his children to grow up and attend kindergarten through college in the same city. In the past, he'd turned down jobs because they required relocation. Another major factor was Silvia. Her entire family lived within thirty miles of each other, including her father, who was terminally ill with diabetes. To maintain peace, Jack traveled to see clients instead of moving the entire family.

"Mr. Wilson, where are you considering me to move to?"

"Jack, we will give you a few choices, here are the locations: Pasadena, California, Dallas Texas, Northern Virginia, or Seattle Washington."

"Thank you, I will review these with my wife and let you know. When should I start?"

"Yesterday, we were having issues with a client in Japan that knows you, Jack, and we'd love to have you on board and heading over to Tokyo to help make things better."

Jack was curious to know who the client was. "Ah, who might that be?" Jack asked.

"Bank of Tokyo ring a bell?" asked Thomas.

Jack looked away for a moment. "Oh yeah, I know them all too well."

*More travel.* "Mr. Wilson, I have held a global position before, and I understand there is a lot of travel involved. Are there any domestic projects I can also focus on?"

"Jack, if you can solve this issue overseas, I will promise you we will have you take over some domestic workloads."

"Okay, let's talk again, Mr. Wilson. Are you open on Tuesday?"

"Jack, call me on my cell on Tuesday, and let's discuss this further."

"Thank you, Mr. Wilson."

After the call, Jack felt overwhelmed with so many decisions in front of him. Coping with now three powerful life-changing events, Jack took Saturday off and went cycling.

For many years, he had found peace and balance in life, including taking time to cycle. *Today, let's do fifty miles, and stop at your favorite coffee and lunch place.* He unloaded his bike and pedaled toward the Pacific Coast Highway. Cycling in southern California always brought him happiness. With thousands of fellow cyclists on the road, he felt like he belonged to a group of passionate people, all out enjoying the open road. After nearly three hours of cycling, Jack stopped at Coffee Grind to order a triple espresso. Noticing an empty table, he removed his helmet and gloves. *Sitting here seeing the ocean now this is heaven.* Jack, long remembering the spirited cycling in Vietnam just sat back and enjoyed the moment of peace.

After finishing his second espresso coffee, he jumped back on his Cervélo S5 cycle and began the journey back home. Soon after 5 p.m., Jack arrived home and parked his bike inside of the garage.

"Jack, I need to see you," Silvia called. "I have spoken to a lawyer today. He told me you can't sell any more assets unless you have my agreement. Going forward with any financial decisions, you will need me to approve."

Jack already knew the domestic laws in California. "Silvia, that isn't true unless you are under a divorce-freeze period."

He smiled and headed to his office. *I have more significant issues ahead at the moment.* While taking a much-needed shower, Jack drafted an email to his son, William.

*Dear Son, I am sorry that our phone call didn't end well today. Your mother and I always have had issues. We try to resolve them without impacting you or your sister. I hope you can understand that. Someday, when you are a parent, you will understand more.*

*Love, Dad.*

*It's Tuesday, Jack. What are you going to do?* Jack realized that he would need to give Mr. Wilson an answer. Somehow, these three issues could merge into one solution. How would he earn back the loss, develop a better business career, and help Silvia move on? These things had one commonality: money. *Will the new company allow me to make more money? Will I get to live a good life without being married to Silvia? And how much will I have to pay to be free?* He also felt the desire to think about Linh in his life again. *I miss you, my love.* Jack knew he needed to fix the mess he caused in his life first.

"Mr. Wilson, I will accept a role in Pasadena. My relocation place should be close to the airport and near to my current home. If that is possible."

Thomas was ecstatic. "Very well, Jack. When can you start?"

"Let's try for the first of the month?"

The Chief Executive Officer agreed.

*New job, new life, and a new place to live.* Jack knew this was the transformation he was seeking. He knew that all roads led to his divorce from Silvia. He also knew he wouldn't become healthy again and happy unless he moved away. He needed to put himself as a priority. *My children are grownups now and have their own lives.* Jack went to see his doctor; he needed to check his blood sugar and blood pressure.

"Well, Jack. I can see you lost some weight—must be the cycling," Dr. Chen said.

"Yes, Doctor, I just got back from Vietnam a few months ago and had a great time cycling there. My diet is also better. I took a new job in Pasadena, which should help with stress levels."

"Good, Jack, but your sugar is still too high, your blood pressure is getting worse, and I am afraid I need to place you on insulin."

Jack knew that insulin would mean his diabetes was getting worse. "Doctor, I want to continue to get better. I know I need to change my life around."

"Okay, let's recheck your blood in six months."

"Thank you, Doctor."

At home, he confronted his wife. "Silvia, I need to regroup on our finances. Please let me see the monthly expense sheets."

Silvia hadn't done the home finances for many months. Her job was to take Jack's paychecks, pay the bills, and save money for home repairs and other expenses. Silvia decided that the money would always come in and chose not to stay up on the budget. So, she stopped keeping track of the money and never recorded any of her spending.

"I stopped doing those, Jack, months ago."

"Silvia, can we start again and use those? How much do you have in your savings account?"

She had been taking a portion of Jack's salary and commissions, hiding them into another bank account in case someday she needed it.

"Ah, we have very little. With all the bills, we have $1,000 in savings."

"What? I made $300,000 last year, and we have less than $1,000 in your savings?"

"Well, Jack, you spent most of that on me and the children!"

Jack had heard this same line from Silvia for years. He worked tirelessly, and somehow, they seemed to have very little to show for it.

"Okay, Silvia, starting today, please document all expenses, and let's review it each month."

Silvia laughed; she had no intention of following through with Jack's request to keep track of the finances.

Jack understood that he could be the creator of these issues more than Silvia. *Empowering the bad only makes them worse.* Jack took a moment to explain to Silvia about the new position.

"I am considering changing companies."

"Oh, we aren't moving, right?"

"Well, for this new role, we will need to move to Pasadena."

"What!? That won't happen. I guess you will need to drive more."

Jack knew Silvia would act this way. Deciding to continue another day, he retreated to his office. Needing a break from his married life, Jack opened Skype and noticed Linh was online.

*My love, it's me. I know it has been a long time since we chatted. I hope you are well.*

After a moment, Linh typed back:

*My Jack, glad you are safe. We are still digging out of the storm here. What are you going to do about the factory?*

*I don't know. I believe the storm destroyed everything.*

*You can still save some equipment and sell it for scraps.*

Jack hadn't thought about that.
*I didn't know that, my love. Thank you.*

Linh thought about how to help him. *Jack, let me discuss it with Chau and see what we can do.*

She dropped off the line.

Silvia asked, "Jack, who are you chatting with?"

"Someone back in Vietnam—they think we can recover some money if we sell off the plant for scrap metal."

"Good, I want to see everything coming back, Jack—everything!"

"Just like I see everything here, Silvia. Every month, right?"

Silvia stared at Jack and stomped off back downstairs. After finishing his dinner, Jack checked his sugar per his doctor's request. After a small prick on his finger, he dropped the blood into the test strip. *175! It has to be the food!* Jack headed downstairs to ask Silvia what she had been cooking.

"Silvia, you know I am a diabetic. How much sugar are you putting on the food?"

"Geez, Jack. I always cook with sugar."

Jack realized the heavy sugar meals, the beers, and sodas were causing his health to worsen even with all the cycling he had done.

"Silvia, could you stop using oil and sugar in the food you cook?"

"I will try, but if you don't like my food, cook something for yourself." Jack knew that Silvia did not care for him or his health. He realized that she was a non-loving person and only wanted the material things from him.

"I don't want to be in this anymore," Jack whispered to himself.

He nodded and walked back upstairs. *Okay, Jack, let's go shopping tomorrow.* In the afternoon after work, Jack went shopping to pick up some healthier food items. While out, he received a message from *Linh.*

*My Jack, Chau found a scrapyard willing to take all the equipment to their plant. He will fix the gear and restart the water plant and hire the workers.*

*Wow!* he typed back to Linh, *Thank you, my love. How much is he offering for everything, including the license, truck, and scooters?*

*$8,000,* she replied. *Jack, sorry, that is the best we can do.*

Jack took a moment to steady himself. *Linh, that is perfect! Thank you, my love.*

He continued to shop for his new meal diet. As he was picking items, a lady walked up behind him.

"Excuse me, if you are trying to lose weight, that won't help," she informed.

Jack was caught completely off guard. "Excuse me?"

"Look, you are an older guy and way overweight. Those food items will make you sicker."

"Thank you. What do you suggest then?"

"Follow me."

She pointed. "Here. Three nights a week, eat only veggies, nothing else." Then the lady took Jack over to the meat section. "Eat meat only once a week." Then, she took him to the seafood section. "Eat fish twice a week."

"Thank you, I appreciate this. My name is Jack."

"Nella Liu Fiero—nice to meet you. Get well; you'd be handsome if you could lose weight," she said as she walked away.

Listening to her advice, Jack got rid of all the food and only purchased what she recommended. *What a strange woman! I don't know who she was, but thank you, Lord.* Jack arrived home and made room in his refrigerator for his new meals. He placed his name on each item and asked Silvia to not touch his food.

"Silvia, I am trying a new diet to see if my sugar can get under control."

Silvia laughed under her breath. "Okay, sweetie, you get better!"

Jack knew Silvia didn't wish the best for him anymore, but he chose not to let those negative emotions get to him.

"Silvia, I have decided not to drink anymore. No more beers, wines, etc. I am done."

Silvia laughed again. "Well, I don't have a problem with it—good luck!"

Jack knew that would be her response. He retreated back to the office. Once he settled into his office, he reviewed the messages from Chau and Linh. The scrap owner would transfer $8,000 to Linh's Canadian company first. The Canadian company would wire the funds out of Vietnam to Canada and Jack's American account. He realized that he'd made a promise to Chau to send money to help the workers. Jack typed a message back:

*Chau, please keep $1,000 US dollars. Distribute the funds among the workers.*

Chau replied, *Mr. Jack, we can't take your money. You have done so much for us. Please keep this for yourself.*

Jack, realizing his own financial fate and current situation with Silvia, typed back to Chau: *Then please take $100 and give it to the nuns.*

Chau agreed.

Jack also sent a message to Linh.

*My love, before the transfer, please keep $1,500 for yourself. Please use it to help with any storm damages or anything that you need.*

Linh cried after reading the message.

*Jack, you don't have to; we are fine.*

Jack just thanked Linh for everything she had done for him.

Jack opened up Excel and created a meal menu for himself. Each day, he would eat only one fruit, three veggies at lunch, and a simple salad for dinner. One day a week, he would eat meat, and two days a week, he would be eating fish. He'd also check his sugar three times a day to see which meal caused him the most significant issues. *I can do this.* After finishing his meal plan, Jack drafted an email to his current manager, Steve.

*Please accept this email as my two-week notice. I have moved on to a new company to focus more on international sales.*

The next day, Jack received a reply from Steve, wishing him good luck.

Jack spent the better part of the next two weeks closing out deals and saying goodbye to coworkers and clients. He was never a fan of long goodbyes.

After the last day of happy hour, Jack drank water and tea while his teammates drank beer and scotch.

"Jack, no beers tonight?" asked Steve.

"No, I am giving it up. I want to live longer."

Steve and Jack both laughed and gave each other a high-five. Jack was sad to see his old company go out of business, but he knew he was heading to a better place.

# Chapter 31
## Ascending

On his first day at Techline, Jack drove up to Pasadena to meet with Thomas. He was already familiar with the commute from San Diego to Pasadena. He booked a hotel off Colorado Boulevard for a few days while getting used to the office and new team members. Jack needed a fresh start, both personally and professionally. "This is another first day in your new life, Jack—take it all in."

While he sat in his car, he couldn't get the vision of Linh out of his mind. It had already been a few months, and Jack remembered her distance at the airport the day he left. Jack allowed himself a brief moment of reflection—he also knew the path forward in life required him to take the first step. That leap started with him getting out of the car and starting his new job.

"So, Jack, I understand you know the client already?" asked Ryan, his new team member.

"Yes, I know the Bank of Tokyo. What seems to be the issue we are trying to resolve?"

Overhearing the conversation, Thomas interrupted Ryan. "We haven't shared that data with Jack, yet."

"Oh, sorry," Ryan said.

"Well, Jack, now that you are here in the company, we need you to fix the Bank of Tokyo's global cash management system. They believe they are getting hacked by the Chinese Triads out of Taiwan."

"Ah, what?"

"Yes, Jack. I see you have heard of them."

"Yes, sir, I know the Triads from my military days. We need contacts in Taiwan to help get close to them."

"Well, Jack, I guess you will go on and recruit one."

Jack's heart just sank. He knew anyone associated with the Triads tended to end up dead. "Thomas, the Japanese Police should be handling his case, not us. I know someone on that police force. I can reach out to them. I suspect the client has already reported this?"

Thomas looked away from Jack. "Well, not yet. The bank handles the funds transfer for businesses connected with the Triads."

Jack became lightheaded for a moment. "So, we need to unhack the hackers' bank without upsetting the Triads?"

Thomas smiled. "Welcome aboard, Son."

*Wow! I didn't see that one coming.* "I need to get an espresso; I will be back."

Everyone smiled while Jack departed for the coffee shop next door. *This is a mess.* Jack sat in the coffee shop to reflect on his first day at his new job. *Recruit a Taiwan contact to help fix a Japanese bank with connections to the Chinese Triads. Outstanding!* Jack took his mind off things and decided to message Linh.

*My love, I hope you are well. I started my new job today in Pasadena, and well, it will be a challenge for sure.*

Jack checked his time and realized it was 3 a.m. in Vietnam. He finished his coffee and returned to his new office.

"Mr. Wilson, may I have a moment?"

Thomas already had a busy day. "Jack, what do you need?"

"Well, sir. Where do I begin?"

Thomas's smile returned to his face. "Jack, here is the crypto-key; the files are in the cloud storage. Read them over."

Jack thanked his new boss and went to his new office to begin the research. After a few hours of reading, Jack messaged William, letting him know about the new job, who wished him good luck.

Then, Jack texted Silvia.

*Hun, I am here in my office. I will stay a few days up here.*

Silvia didn't reply back for a few hours.

*Okay, Jack, see you whenever,* she finally wrote.

Having finished his first day, Jack said goodbye to everyone and headed off to the hotel for some dinner and rest. He loved Pasadena so much. Jack loved cycling around the city. He loved walking around The Rose Bowl, eating at his favorite restaurants, and touring the museums, including the world-famous Norton Simon Museum. Even at night, Pasadena was a wonderful town to walk around. He always made a point of stopping in at Sushi Roku in Miller's alley for some blue-fin tuna. Sushi Roku also served the famous 'popcorn shrimp tempura,' another one of Jack's favorite foods.

People from all over the world came to cycle here. *I can't wait to move up and bring my bike*, Jack told himself enthusiastically.

# Chapter 32
# Forward

Getting settled into his new job, Jack spent his days working in the Pasadena office and taking the train back to his San Diego home. Each day at home, Jack's only thought was how to move beyond his marriage and gain a sense of peace within himself. He knew the divorce will be a devastation to Silvia and the children. *But somehow, this step back in life could lead to three steps forward for everyone.* He started creating a list of places to move to in Pasadena. *Expensive for sure, but manageable.* Once he determined the ideal condo to purchase, he began creating several financial models, pre and post-divorce. The post-divorce economic outlook seemed on the surface very complicated and challenging to live with, but Jack knew it was time he made this move.

"Silvia, we need to have a conversation."

"Okay, Jack. Let's have it out."

"Silvia, I will move up to Pasadena. My new job is challenging, and I can expect to travel a lot."

"Jack, are you planning to move back here when you are done working?"

"No, that will become my new home."

Silvia held back the tears. "Okay, does that mean you will pay rent in two places?"

Jack weighed his words. "No, I only plan to have one house."

"Okay, Jack. If you are planning to run around up there, I want papers."

Jack took a deep breath as he realized the time he had been waiting for fifteen years had come. "Okay, I will hire the lawyer and get started. Thank you, Silvia."

"Well, Jack, I will move up there if it means it will save our marriage."

"Silvia, you won't be happy."

Silvia could only nod and agree with him. He knew this was a very painful decision to make. However, Jack believed Silvia would be happier in the end.

Jack went back into his office and put on some music to just take the moment in. Finally, he could be happy. Jack knew divorce was never a good thing, but in his case, this breakup would most likely end up with both parties better off. He sent a series of emails to his lawyer and asked about starting the process of divorce. In secret, Silvia had already had a lawyer briefed several months before, who was prepared for this if Jack ever asked for one.

Silvia started deleting all her social media pictures so Jack couldn't use them in court. She received a message from her lawyer.

*Okay, I am contacting his lawyer. What do you want out of this?*

*Everything,* replied Silvia.

Jack in turn got a message from his lawyer, Walter. *Jack, are you still in the same house as Silvia?*

*Yes,* he replied. *Jack, just prepare yourself for a long fight; she wants everything. Granted, if this goes to court, which could take a year just for your case to be heard, she could drain you financially, and you will have nothing.*

Jack had already considered this possibility. *Walter, at some point, where it does, the law kicks in and emotional stuff drops off?*

*Jack, she could drag this out for years,* replied Walter.

*Yes, so can I,* Jack typed back. *Okay, let's start with where we are and go from there, Walter. I will send you over a proposal to give to her lawyer.*

Walter was already profoundly impressed with Jack's proactive attitude. *Okay, send it to me, and I will review it.*

Jack went downstairs to see Silvia, who was already telling the world her version of the events.

"Silvia, I ask please that you dial down the noise to other people. This is our issue, and we need to work together so we both can move forward."

"Sure, Jack, whatever."

"I sent over a proposal to my lawyer. Your lawyer should get it soon."

Silvia could only laugh back at Jack. "Oh, you have a proposal? I have one too. I want everything, Jack—now get out of my face!"

Jack could only smile back at his soon-to-be ex-wife and retreated to his office. He compiled a series of a post-marriage budget for him to manage his money. *Okay, with a new mortgage, utilities, car payment, and now alimony, money would be tight.*

While Jack was typing away, he continued to hear Silvia calling her friends and family. She was sharing with them the divorce decision.

Jack headed downstairs to get something to eat, only to find someone had thrown his food out.

"Where is my food?"

"I threw it out. You don't live here anymore!"

"Silvia, okay, don't open my mail anymore, and don't throw out any of my things, including my food!"

"I don't have to listen to you anymore, Jack!"

Jack realized living with Silvia while going through the divorce would be a nightmare. He grabbed his keys and headed out to have dinner. While waiting to be served, Jack began to message Linh.

*My love, my divorce process has started. Finally. This will be a long road*

After finishing his meal, he noticed that Linh hadn't answered yet. Jack knew that she had a lot going on at home and at work. He also messaged Chau and asked her how she was doing.

*Mr. Jack, we are fine. We have settled at the new plant, and the workers are happy.*

*Thank you, Chau,* he wrote back. *I am glad you are well.*

Over the next weeks, Jack continued to deal with Silvia and her lawyer. They were requesting information about financial support and asset allocations. He had to deal with the fact that his legal bills were piling up. Each letter or phone call between lawyers cost him close to $1,200.

"Walter, you cost me more than what I can afford. Between her, her lawyer, and you, I am losing more!"

"Jack, this is how it is in California. They rejected your proposal, and they have sent over one for you."

"Okay, send that to me."

Jack noticed the email from the lawyer and headed back to his office to read it. When Jack arrived back at the house, he saw several cars parked in front. Many of Silvia's family and friends had come over for a party. *This will be fun.* As Jack walked into the house, he could hear Silvia yelling and carrying on. "Oh, there he is. My husband, who loves me!" Jack could only smile at the family members while heading to his office.

"Dad!" yelled William.

"Oh, son. I didn't see you. How are you? When did you get in?"

"Dad, let's talk."

They headed up to his office for a conversation.

"Okay, Dad. Let me get this straight—you spent $100,000 in Vietnam, and now you are divorcing Mom?"

"William, as I told you before, please don't get in the middle of your mother and me! This isn't what you see at the moment."

"Son, this is the same claim your mother is making over social media."

William stared at his father. "So it may be true then."

Jack realized his son wouldn't listen. "Okay. Why don't you get back to the party?"

"Still telling me what to do!"

Jack could only smile back. William, sensing the conversation was over, left the office to rejoin the party. Jack started reviewing the draft proposal from Silvia's lawyer. *Basically, she wants all the assets and wants me to take on all the debt, lovely!* He became upset and felt his blood pressure was getting worse. *Let me sleep on this.* While the party continued to be loud downstairs, Jack slept on the floor in his office.

He woke at 6:30 in the morning and ventured downstairs. He wasn't surprised to see many family members asleep on the couch and on the floor. The house looked like a complete mess, but Jack understood the need to blow off some steam. Quietly, he headed out to get some coffee. He had to continue reviewing the legal documents.

While sipping his favorite triple espresso, Jack thought about Silvia's proposal and checked his emails, hoping to see a response from Linh. Jack knew that the day he departed from Vietnam could be the last time he'd ever see her again. He loved Linh so much, but Jack knew there was more than a river between them now. His journey to Vietnam only served as a temporary bridge for them to meet. Listening to Adams's advice, since he returned home, he had focused on getting things 'squared away.' *Should I email her or let it go?*

After a few hours of reading and coffee, he headed back to the house. The good news for Jack, most of the family had already left, and only a few friends remained. He walked into the house and noticed that people had done a marvelous job cleaning up after the party.

"Jack?" called Rose. "Thank you for everything you did for my family and me."

Jack reached down and gave Rose an enormous hug. "Thanks, Rose. I needed that."

He turned to his wife. "Silvia, I got your proposal."

"Jack, talk to my lawyer!"

Jack knew that was the best thing to do.

"Oh Jack, I am heading to Fuji for two weeks. Remember what I said—no selling anything, including stocks without my permission."

Jack knew his limitation because of the pending divorce filing. "Yes, Silvia. How do you plan to pay for Fuji?"

"Jack, I have money."

Jack stared at her. "I bet you do." Quietly, Jack knew Silvia had taken large portions of his paychecks and stashed the money in secret bank accounts.

Over the next few days, he said very little to her. William continued to not speak to Jack for several days. Finally, on Sunday, Jack received a phone call from Regina.

"Dad, I heard Mom's version of what is going on. How are you holding up?"

Jack felt a sense of pride and happiness for his daughter. "Reg, not well, to be honest. But I will manage."

"Dad, you aren't the bad person; please remember that." Over time, she had grown to appreciate her father even more. Especially due to his backing her decision to go into the Coast Guard, Regina loved her father very much.

Jack cried listening to his daughter.

"Dad, whatever you do and wherever you end up, I am here for you."

Jack could only cry harder, hearing those loving words from his daughter. "How is the Coast Guard treating you?"

"Doing great! Catching bad people and saving the world, like you did, Dad."

"When are you coming home?"

"Soon. Maybe you come this way?"

"Absolutely, Reg. I miss you, dear."

"Miss you too."

Jack couldn't stop smiling after the phone call. He turned his attention back to the legal documents and noticed he'd missed a critical paragraph that Silvia added. "Silvia also wants temporary spousal support of $5,000.00 US dollars per month until an agreement between all parties is reached." Jack, closing his eyes in disgust, couldn't believe Silvia's demands. After completing the document, he went to the kitchen to get some more green tea. This time, he avoided saying anything to Silvia. *Be cool, Jack. There is a light at the end of the tunnel upon us.*

After spending nearly five hours crunching numbers, Jack created a viable solution.

Jack knew Silvia was leaving for Fuji soon, and she wasn't going by herself. Jack felt that Silvia would continue to live her 'single life' while taking no responsibility for their collective debts or bills. Not only did Silvia want $5,000 per month but she also wanted to pay zero toward their joint debts. *I have to pay for her and pay all the bills? I don't think so.*

On Tuesday, Walter sent Option Two over to Aston to review. After a few back-and-forth calls, Aston declined the offer and told Walter they would see each other in court.

"Walter, I expect Jack to start paying Silvia $5,000 per month, and let's see if she wants to change her mind," said Aston.

Walter called Jack. "They turned down the offer. They want the support to start now. What do you want to do?"

Jack knew the law already. "I believe they need a hearing in front of a judge, correct? Awarded temporary support?"

Walter respected Jack's knowledge. "Correct."

"Well, let's get a hearing in six months and then delay it for another six more."

# Chapter 33
# Liberation

After spending nearly two weeks in Fuji, Silvia received a message from her lawyer.

"Silvia, I sent over Option Two. Please review it," said Aston.

Silvia had no interest in this option. "Aston, when is he starting to send me money? I am in no rush to settle."

"Oh, that. Well, we need a hearing before a judge, Silvia. That will take six months."

Silvia, a bit hung over, yelled back at her lawyer, "What do you mean six months?! Jack has to pay me now, right?"

"Well, not until there's a hearing. Jack could delay the hearing for another six months. Until then, he doesn't have to pay you anything."

"Aston, I have no money left!"

"Silvia, look at Option Two. We have ten days before that deal is off the table."

Silvia slammed her phone, almost breaking it.

"Silvia?" asked Ramon, her vacation date. "What is wrong?"

Silvia began to cry. "Go away, Ramon."

A few days later, she arrived back in the US and called her lawyer. "I won't take this deal. Let's go to court. I want everything!"

Aston realized his client had become delusional. "Silvia, in California courts, Jack will get fifty percent just like you, even after he spent money on a water plant. To save your legal fees, we need to consider a settlement."

"No!"

"Okay, call me when you want to settle."

After arriving back from Fuji, Silvia spent the next few days talking to her family about the options. Each family member couldn't believe how generous Jack was.

"Son, do you think I should settle?"

William felt very confused by what was happening. "Mom, Dad is taking care of you for life—what is the problem?"

Silvia couldn't stand other people's opinions. She grabbed her wine, heading outside to be alone. William decided not to follow her and instead called his sister Regina.

"Girl, what do you know about Mom and Dad's divorce?"

Regina, always the clear-minded thinker, said, "William, stay out of it. Let them work it out."

"Hey, don't tell me what to do! I care about Mom; Dad screwed her."

"Are you kidding me? Mom parties way too much. How many times did I have to help Mom to the bathroom when she was drunk? Dad has been there for her since even before we were born. Dad owes her nothing!"

"Dad isn't giving any money to Mom until she takes a deal."

"I am sure he's being plenty generous."

Silvia, still living in the same home as Jack, continued to open his mail. While she was stilling at the kitchen table with William one day, the doorbell rang. William got up to see who it was. The delivery man had a special envelope marked 'confidential' for Jack Kendall.

William looked at the envelope. "My dad isn't here. Can I sign for it?"

"Yes, sign here."

William thanked the delivery man and headed back inside.

"William," asked Silvia, "what was that?"

"A special letter from Vietnam for Dad."

Silvia leaped up from her seat and snapped the letter from William's hand. "Give that to me. Vietnam. I bet this is from some lady!"

William was completely shocked by his mother's behavior. "Mom, this says 'confidential.' Shouldn't we wait for Dad to open it?"

"Absolutely not!" Grabbing a pair of scissors, she proceeded to open the secured envelope.

*From the office of Ambassador David Orwell, US representative, Saigon Vietnam.*

*Dear Mr. Kendall,*

*I regret to inform you that your water plant within District Thirteen due to the recent typhoon storm has been completely destroyed. All of your equipment is deemed unsalvageable. The building owner has condemned the property. I wanted to personally thank you for your investment in Vietnam and all the work you accomplished.*

*I have received several correspondences from several people within Saigon including Father Flanagan of the Norte Dame Church, Sister Florence and Sister Nguyen of the children's orphanage, and Ms. Bui Liu of the Renaissance Hotel. All these people praised you deeply for your commitment to the community, your donations of water and money to help the orphans, and helping raise awareness for the continued struggle against human trafficking in Vietnam. As a fellow American, I am very proud to have a citizen like you in Vietnam making a difference and supporting our very important strategy. I recognize that your entire investment is in jeopardy as a result of the storm. If you do decide to return to Vietnam and consider rebuilding your water business, the embassy here will be at your service to assist.*

*You are a great American.*
*Thank you,*

*The honorable David Orwell,*
*Ambassador – United States to Vietnam*
*CC: Forest Adams – Undersecretary of Trade*

William looked at his mother while she read the letter. "Mom, what does the letter say?" But Silvia just dropped it and walked away.

William, picking up the letter, began to read. After a few minutes, he said, "Oh my God," and placed it back in the envelope.

"Mom, you should be proud of Dad—regardless of the money he lost, he really made a difference in other people's lives."

Silvia started to laugh. William shook his head. "Mom, Dad is giving you what you want—get real!"

He walked upstairs to his father's office, removed the document, and scanned the letter to an electronic format file. William then emailed the letter to his sister. *Sis, you have got to read this.*

Regina, on her end, opened the attachment. After a few minutes, she started to cry. "Dad, you are the man!"

After sending the email, William left the letter on his father's desk.

Jack, returning home after shopping, walked into the house and went straight up to his office. "William," called Jack. "Son, did you do anything today that I can help you with?"

William looked at his father with newfound respect. "I am good, Dad." Jack nodded and entered his office, immediately seeing the opened letter on his desk.

After a few minutes, he put the letter down and began to stare out his window. "Everything gone."

# Chapter 34
# Settlement

Over several weeks, both Jack and Walter maintained complete radio silence with Aston and Silvia. After repeated communication tries and threats of lawsuits, Jack continued not to speak to her unless it had something to do with the kids. Finally, after thirty-five days, Aston pressed Silvia one more time.

"Silvia, it's the time! You need to accept the deal. I have an extension in place with the other lawyer."

"Fine, take Option Two; I will sign off on Friday."

Jack had already been living away from Silvia in an Airbnb in Pasadena, close to his work. Over the last several weeks, he had finally made some progress with the Bank of Tokyo account.

"Mr. Thomas, we have a lead into the bank now."

Thomas, deeply impressed with Jack, celebrated the good news. "Let's have it, Jack!"

Jack told him the story of the water company in Vietnam. "Long story short, the Vice President of Technology for the Bank of Tokyo's outsourcer that handles their application development is connected to an old client of mine in the water business. The IT company will help to make an introduction for me to this gentleman."

"You mean, someone you sold water to in Vietnam knows the person we have been trying to get in front of?"

"Yes, sir, that is correct."

"Okay, Jack, keep me in the loop and let me know where this is going."

Jack nodded and went back into his office. After work, he met up with a real estate agent to look at a beautiful two-bedroom condo overlooking Colorado boulevard.

"Mr. Kendall, the unit goes for $550,000. With your credit, I will need only $1,500 down."

Jack used a Veterans Home Purchase benefit for the purchase. "Okay, I will try to wire the $1,500 as soon as I can."

*This place is perfect! All I need now is $1,500 US dollars as a down payment to open escrow.* Jack was short of funds because of the pending divorce. He needed to find the money soon. So, Jack sold his wedding ring and his university class ring to collect money. He also had money coming from Vietnam via Linh's Canada company. He knew at some point Silvia would ask for that. He checked his messages and found one from Walter:

*Silvia will accept Option Two and plans to sign this Friday. Well done, son.* Jack felt overwhelmed knowing that Silvia had finally agreed to sign.

Friday came quickly. At one, Jack received a phone call from Walter.

"Jack, she doesn't want to sign now."

Jack knew that nothing was certain with the woman. "Walter, offer her $8,000 wired to her in the next forty-eight hours if she signs the agreement."

Walter was surprised by Jack's offer. "Where will you get the money?" Jack let Walter know about the water company in Vietnam being sold for scraps.

"Get her to sign both documents today, and I will get her funds in the next two days."

After a few phone calls between the lawyers, Silvia agreed to sign both agreements. And at 5:45 p.m. that evening of April 17, 2017, she signed the divorce papers.

Jack opened his laptop and messaged Linh.

*My darling, she has signed the financial agreement. Could you request the Canada company to wire the funds to the bank of shores? Account number 6673838381. Thank you.*

Linh received the message and sent back a reply.

*I am so happy for you, Jack. You finally got what you've been looking for all your life.*

Her tone felt off.

*My love, is there something wrong?*

Linh didn't want to discuss matters of the heart with him. *Jack, I will get the wire done today.*

*Thank you, my love.* Jack didn't receive any further reply.

After too many years of Silvia, Jack finally had the peace he sought.

Soon after the papers were filed with the court, Jack started moving into his new place in Pasadena. Silvia moved in with Rose until she figured out her next move. Capitalizing on the divorce, Silvia walked away with $250,000 and no debts.

Once Jack moved into the new condo, William reached out to his father.

"Hey, Dad. How are you?"

"Fine, son. How are you?"

William and Jack hadn't spoken much, with William having moved away to another state and planning to get married to Tricia soon. He missed his father. Similar to Regina, William had grown to appreciate his father more. In time, William had realized how much his father cared for him and his sister while tolerating his mother's alcoholic addiction.

"Dad, I just wanted you to know I am sorry for not supporting you. Mom had no one here for support; I needed to be with her."

"Yes, son. I put you in a terrible place. By being the only son, you needed to look after her."

"Thank you for acknowledging that, Dad. So, when can I come up to see your new place?"

"Anytime."

Jack, troubled by the last communication with Linh, reached out to her. *My love, I'd love to chat with you again.*

*My Jack, I know it has been a while—we haven't seen each other in three years. I miss you too.* Linh took a moment before continuing typing. *Jack, I love you, and I wish you well in your new life.* She cried deeply. While she loved to hear from Jack again, Linh knew she had no future with him. Her life with Jack wouldn't turn out the way she hoped for. She needed to continue to take care of Ngoc and plan for her next move.

Jack, reading Linh's last message, knew the distance between them was more significant than the ability to build a long enough bridge to see her again.

Over the next several months, Jack spent most of his time traveling. He went to Japan and Taiwan to meet with clients and helped to move the new project forward. Jack hoped that one day, Linh and he could meet in Singapore, free from any restrictions.

*One day, we will walk in the park, my Linh. We will be able to walk, hold hands, and kiss each other.* Jack, now a single man for the first time in thirty years, felt a warm sense of freedom. He'd hidden in the shame of having an affair. Yet, he knew at some point, he would have an open relationship with someone he could love and wake up to each day. Jack sent a message to Linh again, asking her to meet him in Singapore. He didn't get a response from her.

Jack continued to excel at his new company. New projects were on the rise in Asia, thanks to his efforts. Clients in Taiwan, Japan, and now China were discussing longer-term deals with his company. Thomas couldn't have been more thrilled with Jack's progress. He also thought about expanding his options in Vietnam and Singapore. *Maybe, if we develop in Southeast Asia, I could see Linh more.* Before getting ahead of himself, Jack mapped out what businesses he could go after in Vietnam.

The contacts in the Vietnam company helped to open a small door with the bank. Jack needed something else to make the contact list grow bigger. He revised his water company client list, which could prove valuable to his expansion efforts. After reviewing the list, Jack came up with several targets he could focus on. Over the next several weeks, he started reaching out to those clients, seeking the first meeting. Initially, Jack had minor success, until noticing that most of those clients had offices in the United States. After researching a few, he found one client in Pasadena, twenty minutes away from his office.

Jack dug into the company's background and reached out to the Chief Executive Officer for lunch. Mr. Nguyen Vu, president of ITE software, welcomed the lunch invitation with him. Having successfully booked his first meeting with a Vietnamese company, Jack couldn't wait to share the information with Linh. Jack opened his messaging application to send a message. Before he could type a single word, he saw that Linh had already sent a text to him.

*Dearest Jack, when you receive this message, please don't be upset with me. I have several challenges here in Vietnam, and I will need to make some decisions that will affect my life and Ngoc's life. I ask you, please, don't message me for a while. I will always love you, my Jack.*

Jack couldn't contain his emotions. The message from Linh was so painful that he couldn't stand anymore. He loved Linh so much and wanted to be in Vietnam with her. Sitting quietly for almost fifteen minutes, he couldn't muster the words to type back to her. Jack and Linh had known each other for nearly nine years. But Jack wiped away the tears, knowing it was best to send a message now and move on.

*My loving Linh, I am sorry to read your last message. If there is any way I could help you, I will. I miss you, my love, so much. I will respect your wish. I am not going to message you for a while. Please keep me updated as things get better for you. All my love, Jack.*

After sending the message, Jack needed time to reflect on things. Having to say goodbye to Linh drained him emotionally. He felt depressed, so he walked over to Thomas's office.

"Hey, Mr. Wilson, I need a few days off. Do you mind if I take an extended weekend?"

"Jack, is everything all right? I know you have been hitting the work heavily with all your trips. Anything I can do for you?"

"No, sir, I just need a few days to cycle and rest."

Thomas smiled. "Enjoy, Jack. See you next week."

Jack packed up his things and headed to the train station to go back to Carlsbad for a long weekend. While walking with an espresso in his hand, he suddenly realized that he wasn't even sure why he wanted to go back to his old city. *I have no one there anymore; Silvia, William, and Regina have their own lives now.* Sitting on the park bench near Colorado Boulevard, Jack realized that work was the only thing he had in his life. *No real friends and no love. Okay, Jack, what is next for you?* He sat on the bench for almost an hour. Undecided on what to do with himself, he checked the plane schedules to visit someone. *Let's check flights to Vietnam.* After a few minutes, he realized that thinking like that would only cause his depression to come back worse. Jack, after taking a few breaths, began a silent prayer.

After a few moments of peace, Jack got up from the bench and headed off to the train station. After much consideration, he decided a weekend in Carlsbad would be pleasant and relaxing.

After boarding the train, he noticed he forgot his bike, so he decided to rent one when he arrived. On the two-hour train ride to Carlsbad, Jack used the time to communicate with several key clients in Taiwan and Japan. He needed to plan for the next series of meetings. While the Asia projects continued with outstanding success, he thought about doing something else. Not seeing Linh or even communicating with her anymore took the life out of him. The projects in Asia didn't seem important anymore. Traveling all the time wasn't something Jack really had any interest in doing any longer. *I need a life.* He reflected on his 'path to happiness.' He expected to enjoy a better experience in life after divorcing Silvia, including the chance of falling in love with someone else. He loved Linh, but their love would be nothing more than an affair. Jack knew that being a couple was impossible for them, mainly if they wanted to be together in Vietnam. This reality was painful for him, and he could imagine the same for Linh. She loved Jack so much and wanted to spend the rest of her life with him. Yet, she also followed the same trail of reality.

When Linh read Jack's last message, she also felt heartbroken. "Jack, love, I will miss you. This is for the best," she whispered.

Linh had to cope with work, stress, and problems at home with Vo. Her husband continued to live up in Hue with another woman, but he spent a great deal of time with Ngoc. Ngoc was ten years old now and loved her father very much. Not only did Linh have to be a good mother and an excellent wife but she also needed to consider her future. Her calendar at work was full, and she appreciated that Vo was spending more time with their daughter. This time allowed Linh to think about other places where she could go to build up her career. Her Chief Executive Officer, Royce Miller, was deeply fond of Linh. He appreciated her hard work and problem-solving skills. He also felt a deep love for her, though he chose not to tell her that.

"Linh, Royce here. Do you have a moment?" asked the CEO.

"Yes, sir."

"Linh, have you considered coming here to Canada? I'd love for you to manage the whole shipping operation, not just the Vietnam project."

"Sir, I can't believe it. How, when?"

"Well, how about within six months, after we figure out the immigration issues."

Linh couldn't contain her joy. *I wish I could share this with you, Jack.*

"Sir, I accept. Please let me know what I need to do."

"Just keep doing what you are doing; our people will handle it from here."

Linh couldn't stop thinking about the call from her boss. *Who do I tell? And how do I tell them?* She knew her parents on the coffee farm would be sad to see her and Ngoc go. Linh also had to think about her relationship with Vo. *What will he do? Should I finally divorce him and be free?* Linh had a million thoughts going through her mind. She decided to call her sister.

"Sis, I got an offer to move to Canada."

"What? Are you leaving us here in Vietnam?"

"Yes, my company wants me to move to Canada and focus on all the global shipping."

"What about Ngoc, Vo, Mom, and Dad?"

Linh knew how painful a transition could be. "I am taking Ngoc with me. I am not sure about Vo."

"Why aren't you sure?"

Linh knew that she needed to decide about her life with her husband.

"Linh, does this have anything to do with Jack?"

"No, Jack and I aren't talking for a while. This has nothing to do with him."

Linh would have liked nothing more than to be in Jack's arms again. "I wanted you to know, sis. Let's meet next week for lunch."

Chau agreed and hung up. Linh headed home after a long day at work. While in the taxi, she checked her messages to see if Jack had sent anything to her. As Linh arrived at her mother-in-law's house, she noticed Ngoc sitting outside, playing.

"Baby, come to Mom!" yelled Linh. Ngoc, always excited to see her mother, got up and jumped into Linh's arms. "Mommy, Daddy is here!"

Linh was surprised to hear he was here and not in Hue. "Vo, why are you here?"

Vo, still tired from the travel, said, "I came to see you and my daughter. Is that okay?"

"I am glad, Vo. I will make some dinner."

Vo smiled at his wife and sat down. Over dinner, Linh discussed the move to Canada with him.

"So, I will leave, and I want Ngoc with me," said Linh.

Vo paused. "Do you want me to come as well?"

Linh knew she had reached an essential vortex in her life. "Yes, I'd love for you to come with me. But if you aren't coming as my husband, I will ask you not to come."

"What do you mean? I am your husband."

"You need to stop seeing that lady in Hue, move home, and start being my husband again, and a full-time father. Anything less, I will file for divorce."

Vo also loved Ngoc with all his heart. He knew he needed to make a choice. While Linh continued to discuss the upcoming move to Canada with Vo, Ngoc came over and gave her father a hug.

"Daddy, I love you. Come with us, please."

Vo, already shocked by the news from Linh, couldn't resist his daughter's love. "Okay, my angel. Daddy will come to Canada with you and Mommy."

While the news was joyful, Linh's heart still yearned deeply for Jack.

# Chapter 35
# Unplanned

Jack arrived in Carlsbad after a few hours on the train. He used the time to answer any remaining emails and messages before starting his brief vacation. He checked into the Weston Resort in Carlsbad, unpacked, and showered. After a powernap, he headed downtown for dinner. Carlsbad was known for its excellent restaurants. Jack grabbed a table at his favorite Italian spot, Cicciotti's, on Grand Avenue, always famous for their delicious veal. He settled on a small table near the sidewalk.

While Jack enjoyed his salad, someone spoke to him.

"You won't lose any weight eating like that, Jack!" said Nella.

Jack recognized the voice. "Nella, what a shock!"

The woman was coming from her yoga class. "May I join you?"

"Ah, sure, please do."

Nella sat down and motioned to the waitress. "Ice water with lime, please."

She turned back to him. "So, what brings you here, Jack? Do you have a date?"

"You are a direct one, aren't you?"

Nella smiled. "You have no idea, pal." She ordered a salad with salmon while Jack enjoyed his veal.

"So, Jack, do you live around here? I don't see you much around."

"I used to; I moved to Pasadena eight months ago."

"For work, or because of someone special?"

"Work, mostly—I love to cycle up there too."

"So, are you married, not married, want to marry, sleeping with a married woman?"

Jack tried to get used to Nella's directness. "All of the above."

"Sinner."

"And you, Mother Teresa, what is your story?"

"Ha! You will never know, pal! Not after one meal. You will have to get me drunk to tell you!" Nella continued, "Jack, are you here for the weekend? Where are you staying?"

"Weston. I will be staying there through to Monday."

Nella was happy to hear she could see Jack again. "Are you open for a cycling ride tomorrow?"

Jack was always up for cycling down the 101 to Del Mar. "Yes, let's meet here at 10 a.m. for coffee."

"Sounds like a plan."

As they finished dessert, Nella wanted to ask Jack one more question. "Who was she, Jack?"

Jack didn't understand. "Who?"

"The woman who stole your heart."

"Not today, Nella—some other time."

After they finished their dinner, they gave each other a hug and parted ways. He decided he wanted to head off to the beach for a pleasant evening walk while Nella headed home to clean up after yoga.

The next morning, Jack rented a cycle to take on his date with Nella. He pedaled back up the restaurant and went in for a quick espresso.

"Jack, get me one, a triple. Please!" yelled Nella.

Jack appreciated anyone open for a triple espresso. "Got you."

After a few minutes, he brought out the drinks. "Okay, Nella. Where are we going today?"

Nella was an expert in road biking. "Well, old man. How about Del Mar, up Torrey Pines, down to UCSD, and back?"

Jack was always up for a challenge. "Okay, let's roll, lady."

After a few adjustments, Nella and Jack took out their road bikes. Jack, remembering the years while he was cycling on the 101, thought about where his life was heading to now. *Silvia is single, happy, and running around like a twenty-five-year-old in a sports car. She never had to work a day in her life, thanks to my monthly donations. William is finally marrying Tricia, and they are living well in Virginia. Regina, my pride, is saving the world, one bad guy at a time.* He reflected on the years of turmoil leading up to the divorce; while painful memories, each of them had found their peace within their lives. *I guess the timing was right to make the change.* Jack felt happy to see his loved one find what they were looking for in life.

"Jack, focus!" screamed Nella.

"All right, lady. See if you can catch up with this old man!"

He hit his top gear on his bike and flew past Nella.

"Hey, you may get a heart attack, fatso! Slow down!"

Jack knew his weight was still a problem. However, he had committed himself to eat better, take his medicine, and exercise every day. *I want to live for a long time, God.* After passing Del Mar, Jack and Nella pulled over next to the Torrey Pines Beach.

"Well, old man, you have heart and legs—impressive!"

"You do too, lady. You have guts for sure."

Jack and Nella shared some snacks she'd packed for the ride.

"Jack, allow me to be straight. Where are you at in life, in love, retiring?"

"Nella, I am working because I have to, alimony, and my retirement."

"Alimony? How much alimony does she get per month?"

Jack felt a bit pressured to disclose this to Nella. "That is private, sorry." He was still adjusting to paying Silvia alimony each month. The financial toll was a challenge for him.

"Yes, I know. I was married before. I didn't need alimony. I didn't want to see him again or to have anything connecting me back to that person."

Nella nodded in appreciation for Jack's openness. "Let's continue."

They cycled up to the Torrey Pines as the day grew sweltering. The hill had several curves with a few small plateaus. Nella reached the top a few minutes before Jack. Already short of breath, Jack pulled over and collapsed on the road. Seeing Jack falling, Nella jumped off her bike and ran back to help him.

"Jack, holy shit! Are you okay?"

Jack felt dizzy and threw up on the side of the road. Nella grabbed his water bottle and started pouring water behind his neck. After a few moments, she picked Jack up and placed him carefully off the road. After checking his pulse and breathing, Nella moved Jack's bike to safety. Still trying to focus on what happened, Jack cried from the pain after the fall.

"Jack, it's Nella. You will be fine."

He was starting to feel better. "Thanks, Nella, I am."

Nella helped Jack to get on his feet. "No, pal, you are not."

Jack and Nella walked their bikes up to the top of the hill. She took Jack to the Scripps Urgent Care Clinic.

"Jack, I am taking you to the ER. I will leave your bike here."

She walked Jack in and asked a nurse to come.

"Mr. Kendall, are you are all right?" asked the nurse. She checked Jack's vital signs. "Mr. Kendall, are you on any medications?"

"Yes, I am a diabetic."

The nurse moved Jack and Nella into a treatment room and began a series of tests, including drawing blood.

"We will keep you here for a few hours in observation."

Nella waited outside. After the nurse came out of the room, she went in to check on Jack.

"Hey, pal, are you all right?"

"Yes, thanks, Nella."

"Look, Jack. You will be here for a while. I will ride back with your bike, return it, and bring my car back to take you home."

Jack already felt so much appreciation for her, and this took it over the top. "Thanks, Nel."

Nella smiled and headed out to return Jack's bike.

The nurse, while making her rounds, asked, "Mr. Kendall, is there anyone we can call for you?"

Jack, holding back the tears, said, "No one, but thanks."

The nurse nodded and walked out of the room. Jack closed his eyes to take a rest. After a few hours and one IV bag completed, Jack felt much better. The doctor came in to see how he was doing. "You took a nice fall, Mr. Kendall. Nothing was broken, but your sugar is still high. I would suggest you drop fifty pounds."

Jack knew all of that already from his own doctor. He sat up and began checking out.

"Thank you all for your help," he said to the doctors and nurses.

He walked outside and sat down on a bench, waiting for Nella to return. Jack noticed he didn't have his phone. *It must have fallen out. I don't even have her number.*

Within a few minutes, Nella pulled up in her white SUV. "Climb in, Jack!" she yelled.

Jack, smiling, jumped into the passenger side while Nella loaded her bike on the rack. "Well, what did they say? Are you going to live?" asked Nella.

Jack, looking away from her, replied, "I need to lose weight, control my sugar, and eat better."

"Oh, where we have heard this one before!" Nella drove back to Carlsbad. "Jack, I will take you to my place. I will cook you a proper meal—no hotel food tonight for you, pal."

# Chapter 36
# Equivalent

Linh continued to focus most of her attention on the upcoming move to Canada. The decision to stay married to Vo weighed on her. She knew she could never trust Vo again after his affair with Niu. Linh also had to live with the guilt of her cheating with Jack. One evening, Vo and Linh had dinner together at the same table, something they hadn't done for several years.

"Linh, do you remember when your parents rejected our wedding party?" he asked.

Linh remembered, even though that was twelve years back. "Yes, why?"

"Why did you stay with me?"

"Because I loved you."

Vo felt deeply ashamed. "I loved you too."

Linh didn't want to show her feelings to him. "So, how is Niu?"

Vo cleared his throat. "She is gone. I will move back here to be with you and Ngoc."

While Linh welcomed this news, her heart still belonged to Jack. "I like that. It will thrill Ngoc to see you every day."

"How about you? Are you happy I am back?"

Linh wanted to tell Vo the truth about Jack but saved that moment for another time. "Yes, I am glad you want to be back here with us again."

As Linh's departure date for Canada grew closer, they began to spend nights together in the same bed.

"Linh, may I touch you again?"

She closed her eyes. "Yes."

For the first time in several years, Linh and Vo made love to each other. Linh tried desperately to keep the vision of Jack out of her mind. He needed to focus on Vo now. Vo also deeply struggled with trying to keep Niu out of his mind, knowing he needed to be in the moment with Linh. Linh rose up to kiss her husband for the first time in several years and felt a dry, cold feeling from Vo. As he attempted to kiss his wife, Vo found her kisses overly passionate and himself unable to reply to her. As he entered her, he slowly moved his hips and climaxed within minutes. Linh held her husband's ear. "I missed you, Vo."

The next morning, Vo got up early to make breakfast for his wife and daughter. "Good morning!" he said to Linh.

She smiled. "And to you, my husband."

Vo smiled back. He left for work after serving breakfast, while Linh finished her food and cleaned up.

Chau arrived to see her sister. "Sis, are you leaving?"

"Yes, I leave tomorrow."

"And Ngoc and Vo?"

Linh took a deep breath. "Ngoc will join me in six months, after I get settled."

Chau nodded with approval. "Sis, you must know what you are doing. Will you see Jack again?"

Linh gazed back. "I don't believe so. Jack has a new life now, and so do I."

Chau didn't want to press the issue. "Okay, I've got to work—see you later for dinner, sis!" Linh gave her a hug as she departed.

Having a few minutes to herself, Linh opened her message application to see if Jack had sent her a message. Seeing nothing, Linh sent him a poke to see if he would answer. She wanted to see Jack again, to be held in his arms and make love.

She also knew Jack wasn't married anymore and that he'd moved to a new city. *I wish you well, my love.*

Meanwhile, Jack was finishing a wonderful dinner made by Nella. "Thanks, Nel. I feel much better now."

Nella smiled in appreciation. "Jack, I am worried about you, the way you collapsed today."

Jack knew it could have been much worse if Nella wasn't there. "Yes, I want to live better. To be honest, I've been through a lot in the last six years, and I think my health issues are now catching up to me."

"Look, I don't know you well enough, but I believe that in life, we bring more problems on ourselves by our own actions than someone doing harm to us." She continued as he looked up. "Jack, during your marriage, I suspect you probably had an affair or two. You are good at what you do in life, but overall, you are carrying a lot of pain and guilt, and it shows on your stomach."

Jack took a moment to process Nella's comments. "You are very direct."

Nella nodded with a small smile.

He added, "Nella, yes to all the above."

"Yes, I can see that. So, this lady in your past, where is she and what is she doing now?"

Jack was surprised that Nella didn't ask about his marriage. "Her name is Linh, and she lives in Vietnam. We had a beautiful relationship, but life, distance, and age prevented us from having more."

"So, you would have a long-term relationship with her if it was possible?"

"No," Jack replied. "At one point on my first trip to Vietnam, I hoped that could have that. However, like with all things, reality set in."

"How old was she, Jack?"

"Thirty-four—twenty-two years younger than me."

Nella jumped back in her seat in mock surprise. "Impressive for an old man!"

Jack didn't want the conversation to continue, so he asked Nella, "And you, mother superior, what is your story?"

"Well, I am from Portugal, and I'm in real estate development and investment. I moved here when I was twenty-four. My father is Portuguese, and my mother is Chinese. I was married for five years. My ex-husband stole money from me and had several affairs with way younger women."

"I am sorry."

Nella waved off his comment. "In the past. Anyway, I am happy here. I love to cycle here in California."

Jack began cleaning the plates, but she stopped him. "Jack, no need. You're my guest."

Still, he insisted on helping where he could. After finishing the cleaning, Jack asked Nella for a ride back to the hotel.

She smiled at him. "Hey, pal. Why don't you crash here? I will set you up in my spare bedroom."

"Thank you, but too soon?" said Jack.

Nella looked a bit annoyed at him. "Give me a break, pal. How old are you?"

He could only smile back and accept her offer. The next morning, Jack woke up before Nella and made her breakfast. Smelling something delicious she said, "Oh Jack, thank you. That is so sweet."

As they headed out for a walk on the beach near Nella's house, she walked up to Jack and gave him a big hug. Jack was surprised and didn't know what to do. He gave a tender hug back to her. "Jack, I am beginning to like you. hope you feel the same?"

Still torn from saying goodbye to Linh, Jack wasn't ready to commit his heart to another woman yet. "Nella, I do like you very much, and I enjoy our time together. I have no one else in my life but you. However, I am not ready for a full commitment yet, but I hope I will come around soon." Nella felt a bit hurt by Jack's words. Still, she wanted to love him with all her heart.

Over the next few weeks, Jack spent most of his weekends away from Pasadena and back in Carlsbad with Nella. He realized each time he woke up in Nella's arms that he believed one day he could find love and happiness again.

They spent each morning together, enjoying each other's conversation and a few triple espressos. After a brief cleanup, they headed off to the beach to walk.

One day, while walking, Nella reached over to hold Jack's hand. Jack wanted to pull back but he didn't. A bit farther on, they sat along the Carlsbad seawall and enjoyed the morning sun.

"Jack, can I be frank with you?"

"You are asking me if you can be direct? Please do!"

"Look, I want you to know I like you. I believe someday I could love you. But if you aren't able to have one genuine love in your life, please tell me now."

Jack smiled while looking down at the sand. He spoke to himself remembering Father Flanagan's words in Vietnam—*do not confess and ask for forgiveness if you are not prepared to stop doing the same sin over again.*

"Nella, I promise you. If I am with you, I will only be with you."

Nella smiled at Jack and reached over to give him a soft kiss. In a short time, Jack saw a better life in front of him. They had been dating for just a few weeks, but thanks to Nella, he had lost fifteen pounds, and his sugar level had stabilized.

She was very proud of him. "Darling, look at you—you are so sexy for an old guy!"

"You aren't too bad for a young lady either."

Nella reached over, playfully slapping Jack on the back.

"Plans for today, my love?" he asked.

"Jack, we will need to go to Portugal."

Jack was always open to global travel. "Business or pleasure?"

Nella took a serious tone for a moment. "Jack, I'd like you to meet my family."

Jack knew what that meant. Nella wanting him to meet her family could only mean she desired to get married someday. He considered the best way to reply to Nella without offending her.

"Yes, I would love to meet your family." Nella jumped up and kissed him gently on his lips. "I love you, Jack."

Jack didn't know if he was ready for love again—but he did start to love Nella. He still felt a distant connection with Linh. Within moments of those feelings, Jack began to feel emptier and emptier. Staring at the ocean as the sun set, Jack turned to Nella. "Nella, with all my heart, I love you."

Nella welled with tears and then walked up to Jack and kissed him deeply on the lips. "Jack, with all my soul, I will forever love you."

A few weeks later, Jack contacted his daughter, Regina. "Reg, how are you, young lady?"

Regina was already out of the Coast Guard and now attending law school in Boston. "Dad, things are great. How are you holding up? How is Nella?"

Jack had introduced Nella to the kids a few weeks ago. Regina took to her well. Both women had influential personalities and were very successful in their line of work. William and Tricia were glad to meet Nella, but William remained a bit distant.

"Regina, I am heading to Portugal to meet Nella's family. Last night, she told me she loved me. She loves me, and I love her too. Are you okay with this, Reg?"

Jack knew that his children thought it may be too soon for him to be in love with another woman, but Regina seemed more open to it than William.

"Dad, I am so happy for you," she said. "Go get a life!"

Jack was overwhelmed listening to the words of support coming from his daughter and had to wipe away the tears. They talked for almost an hour. After they finished their conversation, he noticed a poke on his phone from Linh.

They hadn't exchanged texts for two years. *Should I respond…? No, I should not. I promised Nella.* He deleted the poke, hoping not to receive another one again.

# Chapter 37
# Unite

After arriving in Windsor Canada, Linh settled into her new house and began her life away from Vietnam and the memory of Jack. During two months into her time in Canada, Linh experienced her very first snowstorm and cold weather. *I moved here for this!* While settling in, Linh understood why Royce had asked her to move here. The global operations were a complete mess. Many of the ocean containers were getting lost at sea or ending up at the wrong port. Linh developed a new international shipping workflow, designed to interface directly into the ship systems instead of using brokers. In a matter of weeks, the company's containers started arriving on time and in the correct place.

"Linh, well done," said Royce.

Linh smiled. "Thank you, sir." She finished her work and planned to head off for dinner.

"Linh, you free for dinner?" her boss asked.

"Yes, I am."

They headed out in the cold Canada winter to a local steakhouse.

"Getting used to the cold yet?" he asked.

"No, Vietnam was never this cold!"

After arriving at the restaurant, Linh felt sick to her stomach. "Ah, sir, I need to use the restroom."

She scrambled off to find the bathroom. After throwing up for nearly ten minutes, Linh thought about what could have made her sick.

After returning to the table, Linh apologized to Royce. "I am sorry, sir."

"Are you all right? Still want to eat?"

Linh took a deep breath. "Yes, let's enjoy."

Royce took a moment and then ordered dinner for both of them. While chatting about work, he asked about Linh's decision to move to Canada.

"So, is your husband coming here at some point?"

Linh felt that her boss was getting a little too personal. "Yes, he will bring my daughter here next month. He plans to immigrate here as well, in the next year."

"That is great to hear. If your husband needs help to come here, please let me know."

Linh nodded and thanked her boss. Soon after the waiter delivered the main course, Royce received a phone call.

"Yes, love, I am here having dinner with Linh."

Linh, overhearing Royce's wife questioning her husband's motives for dinner, finished her meal sooner than expected.

"Sir, thank you for dinner. I need to call my daughter."

"Thank you for your splendid work. I am glad you are here!" replied the CEO.

Linh got up and bowed to him. Afterward, she rushed home to video call with her daughter.

"Mommy!" screamed Ngoc in the video camera.

"My baby, it's me!"

Ngoc always loved seeing her mother in the nightly video calls. "Mommy, when are you coming back? I miss you!"

"Ngoc, I am working hard to get you and Daddy to come here!"

"Mommy, do we have a home to live in?"

"Yes, we do. Baby, where is Daddy? I need to speak to him, please."

Within a few moments, he appeared. "Yes, Linh, I am here," said Vo.

Linh gave Vo the details about the house she'd purchased and background on the city of Windsor.

"There is an auto plant here in town that is hiring. I will send you all the details."

Vo appreciated his wife helping him to find work in a new country. "So, how cold is it in Canada?"

"Beyond words!"

Both Vo and Linh smiled at each other and sent virtual kisses before hanging up.

Linh started to think about why she got sick early. 'I haven't had my period yet. No! No, not now!' Linh cried. She thought about what would happen if she was pregnant and how she could work in Canada while expecting a child. She was alone in a foreign country. Linh cried, not knowing what the future might hold for her. She tried not to think about Jack but wondered what he was doing at that given moment. Linh decided to 'poke' Jack one more time to see if he would reply.

Taking a moment to finish up some last-minute work, Jack noticed a buzz on his phone. While he was checking his messages, Nella came over to give him a kiss on his cheek. Jack already knew that it could be from Linh, so he closed up his phone to answer later. Once Nella went back to the kitchen, he opened his phone and replied.

*My dear, glad you are well. How is Vietnam?*

*I moved to Canada, Jack. My company moved me to Windsor.*

Jack was taken off guard. *Canada? Oh my, that must be so cold in the dead of winter!*

Linh took a moment to cherish the conversation with Jack. *Yes, how are you, my dear Jack?*

Jack knew this wasn't the best time to chat with her. *I will ping you later for a chat.* He closed his phone and joined Nella in the kitchen.

A few days later, Jack took a moment to write to her again. *I am so happy for you and your new life in Canada. I am very proud of you, and I hope Ngoc is safe and enjoying her unfamiliar country.*

Linh was tied up in meetings and just answered, *Yes.*

Linh decided it was better not to contact Jack anymore. 'Life moves forward. The river will always be there, as Jack would say.'

Jack never got the chance to reply fully to Linh either. Realizing his past faults in life, he decided to be true to his word with Nella. He didn't respond to Linh anymore.

His heart hurt all the time, knowing she was in Canada, in the cold winter. He also realized if he contacted Linh again, he would lose Nella and all the trust she had in him.

Listening to his heart, Jack knew his adulterous behavior hurt more people than he'd ever realized. He couldn't do this anymore; he needed to stay faithful to one person.

Choosing to focus on his work, Jack received an email from Thomas.

"Jack, when you have a moment, could you come up to Pasadena for a power meeting?"

Jack, realizing the sense of urgency, booked his train ticket for the next morning.

"Nel, I need to go to the office tomorrow for a power meeting with our leadership."

She was already fixing dinner. "Okay, be safe."

They enjoyed a traditional Portuguese dinner, including fish, rice, and Spanish spices. Nella, a lover of excellent wine from Lisbon, opened a fresh bottle for them to share.

"Jack, I know you don't drink anymore. Would you mind if I have a glass?"

Jack appreciated her respect for his choices. "Nel, pour me one, please. will join you."

She reached over and kissed Jack passionately. "I love you, Jack."

Jack felt confident in his feelings. "I love you, Nel."

She poured a small glass for Jack while they enjoyed dinner. "Jack, I mean to ask you—when can we go to Portugal to meet my family?"

"Nel, we can go after I get this issue with the Japanese client resolved. promise I will put in for a vacation."

Nella couldn't contain herself. She reached over and kissed him while moving him away from the dinner table, undoing his shirt buttons. They didn't wait until they came to the bedroom. They made love on the couch overlooking the Pacific Ocean. Feeling a deep, warm passion for Nella, Jack's mind was clear and absent of any thoughts of Linh. The love in his heart, he knew, was for Nella. By touching her hair and seeing her smile, Jack felt a new sense of passion, completely different than what he'd felt with Linh. Nella deeply loved Jack; only his heart and the past held him back from loving her more. He tried to shed the emotional connection from Linh and knew Nella felt the conflict within him.

Nella always loved to hear the ocean at night. The sound of the waves crashing gave her a sense of peace and reminded her of her home in Portugal. She always left the windows open every night just to smell the salt in the area.

yearning to be home again. They realized how loud their lovemaking was, and Nella tried to get up, but Jack playfully pulled her down to the couch.

"Let's try to be louder," Jack commented with a smile. Nella pressed herself on top of Jack and kissed him deeply and passionately. She wanted Jack to know that she wanted to give everything to him and wanted nothing more in life than to be with him. Jack felt the driving passions from Nella with every touch of her lips and her strong fingers running across his back. He desperately wanted to be with Nella as well. Listening to her powerful moans, Jack became excited and started to climax loudly. "Oh, Jack, release please," said Nella. Jack felt his release inside of Nella. Breathing strongly, Nella climaxed wholly along with him. As she gazed into Jack's eyes, she could see how much he wanted her. "Take me please, Jack," pleaded Nella.

Jack knew the time had come to move on from Linh and live his life. "I am yours, Nella, as long as you want me."

Jack and Nella fell deeply into sleep, never wanting to let go of each other.

"Jack, thank you for wanting to go to Portugal. This means the world to me."

Jack felt thrilled and loved by her. "I feel the same, my loving Nel."

He was awoken by his morning alarm and remembered he needed to catch a train to Pasadena.

Kissing Nella goodbye, he said, "Love, I will be home around seven."

"Be safe, my dear."

Jack headed off to the train station. While he was boarding the train, he noticed several emails from Thomas Wilson. *Must be some serious drama.* As Jack read the messages, he saw that the issues revolved around the client's project in Vietnam. The bank in Japan and the World Bank were threatening to pull their investment if the problems didn't get worked out. After reading further, he saw the client also referred to a consulting firm in Detroit. The firm had suddenly become involved in the deal. *Where did they come from?* As the train pulled into the Pasadena station, Jack jumped off and headed to the office. Just as he felt the need to stop for a coffee, Jack received a text from Thomas.

"I see you, pal. No espresso for you. Come to the office!" the man yelled.

Jack didn't know if Thomas was kidding or if he was really in a jam. Wasting no time, he headed into the office.

"Oh, your grace," barked Thomas. "Here is your espresso, Son."

Jack nodded to him. "So, where is the fire, Chief?"

"Okay, here we go, Jack. The project in Vietnam is in jeopardy. In Japan, the bank is pulling the investor because some junior pencil neck in Detroit told them and the World Bank we overpriced the project. They could do the same work better and cheaper."

"Some pencil neck claims his company is better than us for the Vietnam forest project?"

"Yes!" Thomas shouted.

"Okay, Chief. Let me dive into it."

Thomas smiled and padded Jack on the back. "How is Nel?"

"She's great. Oh, Chief, I need a vacation soon. I need to go to meet her parents in Portugal."

Thomas was always happy to do good things for Jack. "Okay, sport. Make the wicked man go away, and I will flip for the airfare!"

"Deal!"

"Detroit company trying to take over our Vietnam project—something doesn't sound right," whispered Jack.

He started digging into this consulting firm in Detroit, Transworld Global Transformations, LLC. After reading about the firm for several hours, Jack realized there was more here than he thought. He started to whiteboard out the connections between Transworld Global, the Chinese Triads, and the Vietnam project, mumbling to himself, "Why would a group of lawyers need to access the bank of Tokyo and jump into bed with Chinese Triads for a project in Vietnam?"

Jack started looking at some of the notes he'd received from his contact at the Bank of Tokyo. The notes included several loans and wire transfers to a bank in Canada to an unknown corporation for the sum of one million dollars. "Okay, that is truly strange." Jack then looked into the various business associates and partners within. He noticed several members of the board were either from China, Taiwan, or Vietnam. Some were in even from Russia. Something was deeply wrong here. Jack realized that he needed to get ahead of this problem, so he decided to fly out that evening to meet with this shadow company.

"Nel, love. I need to save the world from terrible people; I need to fly to Detroit tonight."

"Save the world? Just remember, Jack, I love you. Go get them!"

258

He walked back into Thomas's office. "Chief, I am heading to Detroit tonight. I am trying to get a meeting with pencil neck himself."

Thomas got up and gave him a hug. "Thank you, son!"

Jack smiled and headed off to the airport. In the taxi, he decided to message Adams to see if he knew anything on the Vietnam side.

*Forest, John here. I hope you and Ms. Bui are well. Our project is getting crushed because of a new player called Transworld Global Transformations. Any Intel would be most helpful.* He hoped that Adams wasn't tired of answering his question. He also checked his messaging app to see if he'd received any more pokes from Linh. There was nothing.

*Jack, leave the past behind to make room for the future.* He still felt a deep love for Linh, but he knew he would only hurt Nella if he contacted her.

# Chapter 38
# New Life

After a few days of feeling morning sickness, Linh confirmed she was pregnant. While having a second child was never in her plans, she openly accepted the opportunity to have a new baby to play with Ngoc. After some consideration, she decided to message Vo and share the news with him.

She uneasily waited for his reply. After fifteen minutes, Vo sent, *Linh, I can't wait to be a father again!* She cried, overjoyed—Vo was thrilled about being a father again.

"My love, please come to Canada. Let's make our family whole again." Vo knew that bringing Ngoc and his mother wouldn't be easy. "Yes, let me get the arrangements started."

Linh was excited, knowing they would be a family again. Soon, they would welcome their new baby.

After finishing with Vo, she walked into Royce's office. "Sir, I will be a mother again!"

"Oh my gosh, girl, I am so happy for you! What is the plan, and how can I help?"

"My husband will come here with my daughter and my mother-in-law. If you could help him find work, that would be wonderful."

Royce, feeling like a father figure to Linh, said, "Let me take care of that one for you."

Linh gave a warm hug to her boss and headed back to her office. She reflected on how much her life had changed, but she still had time to think about Jack. She sent him a message sharing the glorious news.

*Dearest Jack, our lives have evolved and changed. I'll miss you forever, my love, but I also would like you to know that I need to move on and open my heart to Vo. I will be a mother again. My husband, Ngoc, and my mother-in-law will move here soon. I hoped someday to see you again and make love as we promised. But life comes at you. Our paths have changed forever. I will never forget you or the love you have for me. I'll love you forever, my Jack.*

Jack heard the beep on his phone as he was about to board the plane. He read the message from Linh and felt pleased to know that she would finally get to have her family whole again after twelve years.

*My Linh, my joy in hearing this makes me so happy. I bless your new baby and hope your family arrives and settles in Canada well. I also will miss you and remember our love together. I am heading to Detroit tonight. I love you, my Linh, always.* He started to cry quietly as he boarded the plane.

Linh couldn't believe he was coming to Detroit, just across the river. She messaged Jack back.

*Detroit is across the river from Windsor. Any chance we can meet?*

Jack saw the question but waited until he landed before answering. He wanted to answer with back to Linh his heart. He also knew the promise he'd made to Father Flanagan in Vietnam. *I need to prove to God and myself I can be loyal and loving to one true person.* Jack realized the spiritual and emotional recovery he had been on for the last few years would be for nothing if he communicated with Linh again.

The plane ride to Detroit lasted about three hours before Jack connected to the Wi-Fi to catch up on any last-minute messages. He needed to save this deal for this company, and he needed to put his thoughts of Linh behind and think of his future. This sudden impact to the project in Vietnam by a shadow company—Jack knew this was why Thomas Wilson had hired him to begin with.

To his surprise, the pencil neck, Travis Jones, accepted meeting him. Jack spent a good hour reading about Jones on LinkedIn.

*Harvard graduate, internships in Japan, China, and Russia. He speaks seven languages and served time in the United Nations Peacekeepers. This guy will be a piece of work for sure.*

While scanning other messages, Jack saw a response from Forest Adams.

*Jack, Christ, I am retired. Bui and I finally moved out of Vietnam. Her mother passed away, so we moved to Singapore. To answer your question Marine, the firm you are talking about is a slimly underhanded group of lawyers and bankers taking down deals all over the world. They have deep connections with the Chinese Triads and the Japanese Yakuza, so watch your back, Jack. Good luck!*

Jack always loved reading emails from Adams. He replied:

*Give my love to Ms. Bui. I hope your life in Singapore brings you happiness forever.*

Adam responded:

*Too mushy, Marine!*

Jack could only laugh at the response from his friend.

He typed a message to Thomas Wilson.

*Based on the latest Intel from Vietnam, the firm is a bunch of slimy lawyers and global money men. This shouldn't be a problem.*

Jack arrived shortly after midnight and checked into the hotel. From his room on the fifteenth floor, he could see the Detroit River and lights coming from the Canadian side. He opened his phone to reread Linh's message, asking if they could meet. Thinking about his next move, Jack adjusted the couch to face the river view from his window, just like he had years ago in Vietnam. Slowly, sitting on the couch, he fell asleep.

After six hours, Jack woke up to the morning sunrise over the Detroit River. While the sun shined brightly, there was still snow on the ground and an icy chill in the air. He looked at his watch and realized his meeting was in five hours. Rising from the couch, he grabbed a quick shower and shave. After cleaning up, he headed downstairs, looking for breakfast. While in the elevator, Jack noticed a young couple holding hands and kissing each other.

*Only in America.* When Jack reached the lobby floor, he stepped to enjoy his breakfast. As he ate, he read more about this mystery firm. The more he read, the better he understood why the World Bank and the bank of Tokyo were considering giving Transworld Transformation the project. Most of the leadership in this firm worked in China and Russia for several years. Some even served in the military. What surprised Jack was that the firm was based in Canada, not in the United States. *I need to be smart here.* His phone kept buzzing every few minutes from Thomas, asking for an update.

*Jack, I know you are on the ground. What is the latest?*

*The meeting isn't until four hours. I will update you then.*

After breakfast, Jack went up to his room, sitting on the couch facing the river. The view of Canada stirred some deep emotions within him, knowing Linh was within four miles, just across the river. He decided not to answer her, but that decision began to eat away at him.

Jack knew this trip symbolized a turning point in his life. After reading over his notes, he took a power nap. When he woke, he put his favorite business suit on. Heading down to the lobby, Jack jumped into a taxi and headed over to meet 'pencil neck.' Upon arriving at the office building for World Transformation, several security guards greeted Jack personally, all looking like they just came out of the military.

After entering the lobby, Travis Jones came down to greet Jack. "Travis Jones, CEO, nice to meet you." Jack shook the man's hand.

"So, Mr. Kendall, you are here to save the day. Come on up." Both men remained silent while heading up in the elevator. After departing on the fifteenth floor, Travis and his security guards escorted Jack to the main conference room.

"Come in, Jack, and have a seat. Coffee?"

"No thanks. I am full of espresso at the moment."

Travis laughed and sat down across from him. "So, why are you here exactly, Mr. Kendall?"

Jack noted the three other gentlemen in the room. "Jack, please. Mr. Kendall is my father."

The security guards all laughed.

"Okay, Jack, why are you here?"

"I am here to save you and your firm from a mistake."

Travis was caught entirely off guard. "What? What mistake?" asked Jones.

Jack let his initial message sink in before replying, "The World Bank will pull our investment off the table because of your deal." He knew Travis to be a real global player, one with strong criminal connections. Yet, he also knew his company did not need exposure to the various law enforcement organizations like the FBI, Interpol, and RCMP.

Travis smiled at Jack's opening comment. "So, business is business."

"Yes, and the business isn't yours. Your firm is trying to buy something that will only get you into deeper mud with the World Bank and IMF."

"What the hell do the World Bank and IMF have to do with this?"

Jack explained how the core funding for the Vietnam project came from the World Bank and the Bank of Tokyo.

Jack realized his adversary hadn't done their homework. "The project itself is a phased reconstruction project to resolve years of jungle destruction caused by the Vietnam War and failed commercial projects. The World Bank and IMF are contributing to the project, along with the Japanese."

"Again, so what? Their money, my money."

Jack sensed Travis didn't get the problem. "The IMF and the World Bank will require your firm to disclose your investment. They also need your corporate officers and your global license trade compliance document. They need to validate that you can do business with them." He waited a minute before continuing. "By not having those documents, you can't bid on this proposal, regardless of your bullshit pricing model."

"Who told you we don't have those documents?"

Jack considered bluffing Travis. "The Central Intelligence Agency."

Travis and the other three gentlemen froze after Jack's statement.

"The CIA?" Travis asked.

"Yes. They informed me of your background and past failed projects. Your intent is to win the contract and sell it off for additional cash flow funds. The IMF and the World Bank will be screwed, and you will be hiding in some third-world country collecting twenty percent interest."

Travis rose from his chair. "Kendall, you're over your head here, pal. My associates need this project in Vietnam. Your company is getting in their way.

I would suggest we come to an arrangement now, or the path forward for you and your firm will not be a pleasant one."

Jack knew Travis had just threatened him. Considering the man's connections, Jack also knew he needed to think about the best way to save his deal while not creating an enemy with Travis. "Look, this is our deal to begin with—I am open to discussing a joint venture with you if this means that much to you."

Travis sat back down. "Kendall, I don't think you understand me. I have my partners already."

Jack knew that without this project, Techline would lose millions of dollars in new business in Asia, and possibly their most important client—the bank of Tokyo. "Jones, I hear you loud and clear. Let's compete, and let's see who wins."

Travis stared back at him. "We have already won, Kendall—you just don't know it yet."

Jack stood up and reached over to shake Travis's hand. "So be it then. Nice to meet you." Travis refused to shake Jack's hand.

Jack took a moment to gather his things. He was led away by the three gentlemen. While moving toward the elevator, he could hear screaming and window glass breaking. *I bet he will have a bad day tomorrow.* He took the elevator and headed to the lobby. After they entered the hall, the security officer took Jack's badge away without even a smile. He headed out the door and texted Thomas with the details.

*Back on schedule, pencil neck is pulling out of the deal. All is well.*

While savoring the immediate victory, Jack also knew that he would see Travis Jones again. Having never been to Detroit before, Jack decided to take a walk around the city. As he looked up, to his amazement, he saw the famous Ford Motor Company's headquarters. Then he spotted a small glimmer of the river and decided to walk in that direction.

While the sun set upon the city of Detroit, Jack took a walk to the river. With each step, he realized that he was moving closer to seeing Linh again. Still feeling the passion from within, Jack fought the conflict in his heart between honoring his commitment to Nella and remembering the love and passion he shared with Linh. Within a few minutes, Jack reached the Riverwalk and started up toward the international crossing bridge. The view from the bridge brought Jack to a place of deep reality. Linh and Jack had always known there would be a river between them. They'd both tried in their own way to find bridges to connect them together again. Yet, each bridge, emotional and physical, seemed to dissolve within moments of appearance. Linh had moved on to her new life in Canada with her husband. As an expecting mother, she needed to close off the love in her heart for Jack. Similarly, Jack wanted to give his heart to Nella and never look back, only forward.

He noticed how beautiful the sun was as it set over Canada, hitting the maple leaves with a beautiful glow. Reaching for his phone, Jack thought about messaging Linh and letting her know he was close. He typed the words. But before he hit 'send,' Jack closed his app and deleted Linh's profile. "Goodbye, my Linh," he whispered softly as he stared across the river.

Jack opened his phone again and decided to call Nella. "Nella, the meeting went great. I am coming home, my love, tonight. Let's leave for Portugal—I would love to meet your family."

## The End

# Reviews

"Patrick Greenwood's debut novel, *Sunrise in Saigon*, sheds light on an important question we all ask ourselves in one way or another—What makes one's journey worthwhile? The author eloquently marries the question with one's pursuit of the truth surrounding the Vietnam war, inviting the reader to ponder upon the question both in personal and historical contexts. With Greenwood's talent in tapping into the deepest human emotions, *Sunrise in Saigon* offers the pleasure of seeing ourselves in the stories of others and reflecting upon our own lives." — Yujin Kim, author of *A Place To Take Root*

"Introducing his characters, Jack Kendall and Linh Ngo, Greenwood carefully paints their family's lives in enough detail the readers immediately empathize with them. The desperation of two people stuck in failed relationships, enduring the pain of finding their soul mates while married to someone else at the same time. The consequences of toxic relationships are on full display and he describes in detail the effects on all four.

He captures the taste of life in Vietnam during the period of the war and after. His demonstration of how the country being occupied over and over affects the people of Vietnam. How the wars have left scars on every aspect of life in Southeast Asia, even now, almost fifty years later.

Americans do not know how different other societies function, what is acceptable and what is not, more importantly, why. Greenwood is excellent at navigating the minefields of the differences in social morays.

Greenwood does an outstanding job of transitioning between Vietnam and the U.S. and chapters are seamless. A bit of steam between lovers, heavy charged emotionally and helps readers stay engaged in an amazing trip back into history. The story of Jack and Linh is a microcosm of how painful the war was for everyone on all sides is coupled with a satisfying resolution. Highly Recommended. Five Stars." —Isabella Steel, author of *Revenge is Reason Enough*

"A classic love story, Beautifully written by Patrick Greenwood. Despite all odds, their love never dies. The memory of Jack and Linh gives the reader hope and strength to live with. *Sunrise in Saigon* in my opinion is better than *The Notebook* written by Nicholas Sparks. The story has a number of simila and tasteful plot lines like the classic *Casablanca*. In *Sunrise*, Jack and Linh never got together in the end but they love each shared never went away. Their desire to be together never wavered like *The Old Man and The Sea* by Hemingway. Even to the very last moments of this beautiful novel, the hope of Jack and Linh finally 'crossing the bridge' kept me at the edge of my seat. The author, Patrick Greenwood has a bright future as an author, it's really a well written love story. —Susu Smitzh, author of *Don't Do It, She Likes It.*

"I must say I was captivated by the story of Jack and Linh. I think as much as it was compulsive to read, and well-crafted at that. I specifically liked th ending and how Jack overcame his infatuation with Linh to channel hi energies into a new life with Nella." —JR Rogers, author of *The Italian Couple*

Ingram Content Group UK Ltd.
Milton Keynes UK
UKHW021811140423
420194UK00008B/599